I0736133

Chapter 1

Danny Lupan stood in the lobby of the movie theater. He was happy to be back with his partner, Connor McGriffin, but he wasn't thrilled to be back in Los Angeles. The month he spent in the pack compound had been nice in a way, but he'd been so lonely without his Cat. Skyping every night wasn't the same as curling up listening to Connor's gentle purrs. Of course, he'd never admit to Connor that he missed that 'irritating sound'.

Helping Kyle Jameson come to terms with his new status as a werewolf had not been easy. The teen missed his mother and little brother. The emotional turmoil of first being kidnapped and forced to endure the bite of a wolf, then being cast out by his father while dealing with both being a werewolf and entering puberty, was hard on the boy, but he had a good support network around him in New Mexico.

Danny's mother, Doralee's soothing ways had helped calm the teen through the many changes his body was experiencing. With Danny, Doralee, and even

Cortez, their pack alpha, beside him and Connor on Skype, Kyle had made it through his first shift without any problems.

The alpha's involvement in helping Kyle had been a surprise. Cortez didn't like being around 'turned' wolves. However, Cortez wanted to be sure his newest wolf had the help he needed to keep him from going rogue.

The tantalizing aroma of movie popcorn assailed Danny's nostrils as he waited for Connor to pick up their tickets from the will-call kiosk. He'd read great reviews of this movie and was looking forward to an evening of relaxation with Connor. Critics had acclaimed the performance of the young female lead, Maria Lopez, as Oscar-worthy. Danny liked movies with a strong heroine. In the trailers, the young actress reminded him of the third member of the Shifter Force, Lisa Collins, or as he and Connor called her, Lady Bird. A kestrel shifter, she was small, but mighty, and had saved their hides on more than one occasion by providing air support.

With his sensitive hearing, he picked up a whisper to his right. As casually as possible, he turned slightly to look. There was a stress level in the voice that raised his hackles.

"I don't want to do this." The speaker was a young woman wearing a short skirted red dress with a plunging lacy neckline that revealed a little more cleavage than necessary. A blue-tooth earpiece rested over her right ear. Her bright-blue eyes and fawn-colored hair didn't really go with the slight oriental slant in the corners of her eyes. She chewed on her lower lip and looked around nervously.

Visions of Stars

Shifter Force:

Book 3

by

A. M. Burns

and

A. T. Weaver

All rights reserved. No part of this book may be used or reproduced by any means, graphic, electronic or mechanical, including photocopying, recording, taping or by any information storage retrieval system without the written permission of the publisher except in the case of brief quotations embodied in critical articles and reviews.

Except where actual places are being described for the storyline of this novel, all situations in this publication are fictitious; any resemblance to living persons or places is purely coincidental.

See what A.M. Burns is up to.
Visit his website www.amburns.com
And sign up for his newsletter

Copyright 2019 © MysticHawker Press
http://www.mystichawker.com/

ISBN: 13: 978-1-945632-60-0

Edited by Robert Brownson
Cover design by Silver Circle Images

Shifter Force Books:

1: Visions of Rage

2: Visions of Shadows

3: Visions of Stars

Other Books by A.M. Burns and A.T. Weaver:

The Black Fin Case

Other Books by A.T. Weaver:

Catriona's Curse

Earthquakes

Touching Yesterday

Other Books by A.M. Burns:

Blood Moon Yellow Sky

Dark Stars of Dallas

Coyote's Pup

Familiar Path

Familiar Spirit

Glancing up at one of the movie posters before she caught him studying her, Danny thought she looked familiar, but couldn't quite place her. He could barely pick up a garbled sound as someone answered her. As fear hormones washed off her, along with the scent of cat, she walked toward a well-dressed man a few feet away. Her lithe, cat-like movements reminded him of Connor.

With an easy thought, Danny sent a mental message to Connor. *"Hey, Cat. I think we may have stumbled onto something."*

Connor walked over with the tickets in his hand. "What's up?"

"See the girl in the red dress?"

With a questioning eyebrow, Connor fell into rapport. *"Yeah. Why the telepathy?"*

"She's afraid of something." Sometimes Connor could be rather dense, particularly for a psychic mountain lion shifter. *"I don't think she wants to go with that man, but someone on her phone is forcing her. And she smells like some kind of cat. I don't want her to overhear and bolt."*

The girl slipped her arm through the arm of the man, smiled up at him, and they turned and walked toward the exit door. Her steps weren't completely fluid and easy, like some part of her was resisting the rest as she walked at the man's side.

Unable to just let her walk out when he could be doing something, Danny started after them.

"What are you doing, Dawg?" Connor touched his shoulder.

"She's some kind of shifter, and she's in trouble." Not understanding Connor's hesitation, or denseness

with the situation, Danny gave him a quick glare over his shoulder, then continued toward the door. *"Isn't that what Shifter Force is for?"*

"You're right. Let's roll." In two steps Connor was ahead of him and out the door.

Shaking his head, Danny followed. They'd been together for several months and just when he thought he understood Connor, he did something dense, or unexpected. If he didn't fill some part of Danny he hadn't even realized had been empty before they met, he might not deal with it very well. Connor was his cat, and he knew that, but like any cat, he could be irritating as hell at times.

As Connor led the way out of the theater, he tried to pick up on the girl's thoughts. If she was a shifter, he should be able to communicate telepathically with her. He was normally the one leading them into a situation, not Danny. As far as his psychic visions were concerned, there was nothing special about the girl, although there was the scent of a house cat heavy in the air. He trusted Danny's instincts. His wolf had been a deputy sheriff long enough to spot things other people might miss.

He brushed his thoughts against her mind. *"Are you in trouble?"*

The girl looked wildly around. *"Who are you?"* Her thoughts were frantic. *"Go away. He'll hear."* There was the feeling that she was about to bolt. What could have her so terrified? Even with the public feelings toward shifters swinging toward the violent, she shouldn't be freaking out so much without another cause. She was looking for an escape route. Fear rolled through her emotions and left a stink about her any other shifter would detect.

"Who? The man with you? He's not a shifter so he can't hear me." Connor lengthened his stride, knowing Danny would be behind him if things got out of hand.

"No. Go away." She stopped and shook as the man at her side stared at her.

Connor caught up with the couple and stepped to the girl's side between her and the man. "Hey, little sister. What are you doing down here? Does Mom know you're out?" He did his best to sound like a concerned brother so the human with her wouldn't suspect anything.

"I don't know who you are, or how I'm able to communicate with you." "I told you to leave me alone!" She let loose of the man's arm and ran toward the alley a few feet away.

"Hey!" the man shouted. "Come back here. I've already paid for you."

Ignoring the human, Connor gave chase. As he entered the alley, he nearly tripped over a pile of clothes as a sleek, fawn-colored form darted under a fence at the end of the alley.

"Sir, are you saying that the young woman with you is a prostitute?" Danny asked as Connor turned back toward the street.

"What?" the man sputtered. "Are you some kind of police?"

"You said you had already paid for her." Danny pressed him. "That implies you bought her services."

"Ah." The man looked down at the sidewalk. "It wasn't anything, not really. I'll just go to my hotel."

Connor walked over to Danny's side. "Do you have the number you called to pay for her?"

The man shook his head. "No number. Dating app. John's List. They have all sorts of entertainment for traveling men like me." The way his lower lip quivered, he looked like he was about to start crying. "I always use them when I'm away from home. My wife doesn't know. Please. Don't arrest me. I can't go to jail. My wife, she's not well. This would kill her."

He'd gone from slightly defiant to pathetic. Connor hated it when people, particularly humans, went pathetic. "John's List, you say?"

"Yes." The man nodded frantically. "That's it. They have an app and a website."

"Good. You can-"

"Can we get your phone number?" Danny cut Connor off. He had his ever-present pen and pad out.

"My phone number?" The man looked worried, his gaze darting around.

"Yes." Danny reached into his pants pocket and pulled out his badge case. He flashed it quickly at the man. "We're working a case and we might need to talk to you about this again. We'll be careful to make sure your wife doesn't find out."

"Oh. Thanks, Officer." The man quickly gave Danny a phone number and name. "If that's all, I don't want to miss Fox News tonight. They're doing a shifter exposé."

"That'll be all." Danny closed his notebook.

The human didn't need any other encouragement. He took off, all but running, the opposite way down the sidewalk.

"Let's see what she left us." Danny walked into the alley. He took a deep breath. "Don't smell any nearby cats."

"She was running pretty fast when she slipped under that fence." Connor pointed to the spot where he'd lost the cat shifter. "But she did leave behind a few things." If Danny hadn't been interrogating the human, he'd have already gathered her things up for a closer look.

Danny knelt down and picked up a small piece of plastic, the girl's earpiece. "Wonder if you can 'see' anything on this."

Connor took the Bluetooth earpiece and closed his eyes. Luckily, it was fairly new and didn't have lots of residual psychic residue. Pushing his senses into it, he tried to see if there was anything that stood out. Knowing Danny would get things down, Connor rattled off what he picked up. None of it was visual, but earpieces were a verbal form of communication. "Dark guttural voice. Sounds male. Fear. Siamese cat. That's all." He opened his eyes and looked at Danny.

"Not much to go on. Let's try the clothes she left." Danny walked over to the pile of cloth and leather and picked things up.

Connor opened the small evening purse first. He frowned. "A few condoms, a pack of Kleenex, breath mints. No wallet or cellphone."

Danny cocked his head. "No cellphone? She was talking into the Bluetooth. Those things don't have a huge range. How is that possible?"

"Maybe her phone was dropped on the sidewalk?" Connor shrugged, thinking back to their following the girl out of the theater. She'd only been out of sight for a minute or so. "But I think we'd have seen that."

"They also work with radios." Danny looked around them. "There's apartments all over this area. Also been a lot of car traffic. The person on the other end could've been close and we didn't even know it."

Connor frowned. He hated it when his psychic senses missed things like people in trouble nearby. The girl needed help, but he'd missed it completely. There should've been something more he could've done. He slowly checked the clothes and shoes for any kind of psychic imprint that might be a lead for them, but they were all too new to have anything. It was like either the cat, or the person who set up her John had gotten the clothes just for the encounter.

Shaking his head, Connor pursed his lips. "There's nothing here. Everything's too new."

"Then there's nothing more we can do here. We need to see if we can get a lead through John's List." Danny took the clothes and rolled them up into a small red bundle.

"Sounds like a fun way to spend the evening." Connor hated dead ends.

Danny slipped his arm around Connor's waist as they walked out of the alley. "Can we go to the movie now?"

Connor pulled the tickets out of his pocket and looked at them. "These are for the showing that started twenty minutes ago. Even allowing for a dozen previews, they're no good now. Let's grab a bite to eat before we go back to the hotel. We'll try another night."

Chapter 2

Still half asleep, Connor sprawled on the rumpled bed. The hotel room bed wasn't nearly as comfortable as his big feather bed back in Santa Fe, and he was getting tired of sleeping on it. Although he hadn't said anything to Danny, he was about ready to give up waiting for his falling stars vision to come to fruition and head back to the New Mexico mountains they both called home. He flipped on the TV news. After a couple of minutes, a story caught his attention, and he turned up the volume, so he didn't miss anything. "Hey, Danny."

"What?" Danny came out of the bathroom wiping a hand-towel across his face from brushing his teeth. His smooth, firm chest was still glistening from the shower he'd just gotten out of.

Although Connor could watch Danny walk naked around the hotel room all day, and had spent hours doing so since they'd been staying there, his gut told him there were more important things to do.

"This news bulletin. They found the body of a shifter this morning. Say it's a suicide. Unusual for a shifter to commit suicide." It was one of the more unusual things he'd heard recently. Most shifters had a tight family group and would go to them with problems before they resorted to suicide.

His phone rang with the ring tone he'd assigned to Mark Moreau, a ring-tailed cat who was the fourth member of their team. Although he'd officially been let go from the FBI when he was outed as a shifter during their takedown of the gang dealing in child sex trafficking, he was still their go-between with the Bureau. "Hey, Moreau, what's up?" He pushed the 'speaker' button so Danny could hear everything without having to strain his sensitive ears.

Danny sat on the edge of the bed beside Connor. His scent filled Connor and stirred his body into more awareness than the news had. Connor put his arm around Danny's waist and resisted the urge to play with things.

Moreau continued, "The cops have a body they want our help with. Looks like a shifter suicide."

"Whoa! I just saw that on the news." Connor frowned. He should've gotten a psychic vision, not seen it on the news if it was something he was supposed to be involved in. He wondered if his brain was on the fritz and he just didn't realize it. "I don't know if I've ever heard of a shifter committing suicide. Why'd they call you in?"

"The guy has a record of smuggling drugs in from Mexico. Since he's a known shifter, Captain Lawrence called me. Reed and I worked with him on a case a couple of years ago. He's one of the few people who called me and offered sympathy when Reed was killed and my shifter status was outed. As far as he knows, I'm no longer with the FBI." Moreau sounded tired. "Can you guys meet me at the city morgue in an hour?"

"Oh, we may have stumbled on something else involving local shifters. We'll talk to you then." Connor closed the connection. "Looks like it's time to roll, Dawg."

"At least we're going to do more today than walk on the beach and see the stars on Hollywood Boulevard." Danny gave Connor a long kiss, then rolled off the bed.

"Where are you going?" Connor grabbed for him.

"We've got a case to work." Danny opened one of the dresser drawers, pulled out a pair of underwear and socks, and threw them at Connor. "We need to have clothes on to do that. Moreau will be uncomfortable, and I'm sure the coroner will be too, if we show up like this." Danny gestured down his firm, naked body.

"And we can't take our time?" Connor arched his hips as he pulled on his boxer briefs.

"Nope. Official business. That also means drive-thru food." Danny hopped slightly as he put his leg through his pants.

"Official," Connor mumbled as he got his socks on. "Life is better when it isn't so official." Inwardly he cheered at something happening, even if it wasn't connected with their case.

They were halfway across the hotel parking lot when Danny froze at the sight of a muscular man with slicked-back black hair leaning against the hood of the Jeep.

"Buenos dias, Wolf. I assume this is your cougar." He gestured to Connor who was bristling next to Danny.

Putting a hand on Connor's arm, Danny did his best to not sound put out with the intrusion. "Hello, Jaguar. Connor, this is the jaguar who patrols the border for Montezuma."

"Not today. Today, I come with a message from Montezuma." He looked directly at Connor. "You, Seer, you've seen something?"

"I saw stars falling from the sky into the water." Connor stared back. His voice was smooth and even, a sign to Danny that he was pissed at the cat on his car. "Diego, I'm not sure what it means yet."

Danny stared at Connor, for a moment it didn't register as to how he'd known the Jaguar's name, then it clicked. Connor must've either mentally asked, or just looked into the other cat's mind and pulled out the information.

Seeming not to notice, or just not caring, Diego continued, "Montezuma is worried about his granddaughter. Something is troubling her. He wants you to find out what."

Danny put his hands in his pockets. The move helped him at least look more casual. "Who's his granddaughter?"

"She's a popular actress," Diego explained. "Her name is Maria Lopez. She's starring in that new action movie that just came out, *Amazon Warrior Princess*."

Still staring unblinkingly, Connor said, "We know who she is. We were supposed to see her movie last night, but something happened."

"We know. You chased a cat shifter out of the theater. Don't worry about her." He waved his hand in dismissal. "She's nothing."

Connor pulled his lips back in a snarl. "She's a shifter, and she was in trouble. Probably still in trouble. That makes her our business."

Danny touched Connor's arm. It was normally a soothing gesture that didn't do anything to help his mood. "Easy, Cat." He turned to the jaguar. "Our job is to help *all* shifters. Tell Montezuma we'll see what's up with his granddaughter, but we will also see what's going on with the cat shifter too and the body they found this morning."

Diego straightened and pulled away from the Jeep. "See that you do. I'll be watching. Remember, you owe Montezuma." He turned and strolled away. The way his hips were swinging, if he'd been in cat form, his tail would've been lashing back and forth.

Danny forced the anger that had been building up in him out. He shouldn't have let the jaguar get to him. He was used to dealing with Cortez. Pack was everything to the wolf alpha. If he expected the jaguar lord of Central and South America to feel any different, he was wrong, very wrong. "Looks like the Shifter Force is definitely back in action, Cat."

"Good thing. I was getting a bit bored waiting for something to happen." Connor closed the rest of the distance to the Jeep and opened his door. "Let's roll, Dawg."

Danny waited until Connor was pulling out of the parking lot before he voiced a concern that gnawed at him, almost as much as Diego's casual dismissal that other shifters mattered as much as Jaguars. "You pulled his name out of his mind didn't you?"

"Who's mind?" Connor stopped at the first light beyond the parking lot.

"Diego's."

"Oh. Yeah. I like knowing who I'm talking to." Connor turned the corner as they got to it.

"But he's a messenger, and possibly a member of Montezuma's court." There were a lot of things Connor didn't understand, and being part of a species that wasn't into group politics, he wasn't used to having someone to answer to.

"Are you trying to say he doesn't matter?" Connor spread his hands from the wheel to give a who-cares motion.

"Not exactly. But as a messenger, particularly one between two major groups, he expects to be all but invisible. Sure he drops off warning, invites, and such, but he is basically speaking with Montezuma's voice. You invaded his mind to pull out his name. If he tells Montezuma, that could come back to bite us." Danny rubbed the bridge of his nose.

"And if that happens, we'll talk our way out of it." Connor pulled onto the freeway. "Dawg, you know I don't care about group politics. Cougars are solo creatures. I had thought Jaguars were too."

"In the wild, they are, but when the Spanish invaded Central America, Montezuma realized that if he was going to keep his people safe, they needed to band together. Sometimes shifters do act different than our animals."

"Right. Look, if it's such a big deal, I'll just think of the next messenger by their species, unless they offer me their name. What did you want him to do spread his arms and dramatically declare his name in the middle of delivering his message? That would've been funny."

Danny chuckled, trying to envision the muscular man waving his arms around like an extravagant drag queen on TV while he announced who he was. He just hoped Connor's break of protocol didn't come back to bite them in the ass. At some point, Connor's attitude was going to rub a powerful shifter the wrong way, and they'd be in a fight for their lives.

Danny picked up the movie magazine that lay on the console between their seats. Being stuck in traffic was one of the things he liked the least about being in a big city like LA. He'd had time to finish his coffee a few minutes earlier and was rapidly getting bored on the parking lot the locals called a freeway. The magazine was one they'd picked up the previous day when trying to plan their aborted movie night. There were reviews and write-ups on most of the upcoming movies and even a bit on a couple of local plays that were currently performing. Halfway through, he stopped and stared at a picture. It was a fairly familiar-looking Asian face with tawny hair. He turned the magazine toward Connor. "Isn't this the girl from last night? It says her name is Lindy Lui, and she has a small part in that movie we were supposed to see last night."

Before Connor could answer, Danny's phone rang. Caller ID said it was Jime. "Boy! Things are busy this morning." Danny laid the magazine on the table and swiped to answer the call. "Good morning, Jime. What's on your mind?"

"Hey, Fuz-Cuz, what's going on?" Jime sounded fairly upbeat, but then he'd probably had time for a relaxed breakfast, might even still be eating, although he should be at work, since he took Danny's place as the deputy in Jemez Springs.

"Traffic."

"Traffic?"

Danny huffed. Jime had been dense for years, but sometimes dealing with both Connor and Jime was a little too much. "You asked what's going on. We're stuck in traffic."

"Cortez wants to know if your cat's been seeing anything." Like normal, he didn't seem to notice Danny's frustration.

When Danny glanced at Connor, he shook his head. "Like what?"

"Remember Cousin Trina?"

"The one who went to Hollywood to be a *big* movie star?" Most of the family hadn't been real keen on her going, particularly since she was a wolf, and everyone knew wolves didn't do well in the big city. Danny'd faced the same opposition when he went away to college. "Yeah, I remember. She certainly has the looks if not the talent."

Jime laughed. "Don't let Aunt Agatha hear you say that. According to her, Trina ranks right up there with Meryl Streep. Anyway, Trina came home a couple of weeks ago. She says the shifter community in Hollywood operates pretty much on the DL because the studios don't want the general public to know their stars are shifters. In fact, most of the studios won't even hire you if they know you're a shifter. Kind of like back in the 40s and 50s when the fans weren't supposed to know their favorite leading man was gay. It's gotten worse since that idiot in Phoenix got everyone up in arms about shifters when your last case went down. But, anyway, Trina's worried. She hasn't heard from her boyfriend since she left L.A. He isn't answering his phone, and no one seems to know where he is. Someone was sending texts and messages on social media threatening to expose him as a shifter."

Connor set his cup in the cup holder between them and leaned closer to the phone. "What kind of shifter is he, and what do they want from him to keep it quiet?"

"Good morning, Cat. He's an Alaskan Malamute. Name's Reggie Winters. He's starring in that new movie with Maria Lopez." Jime whistled. "Now there's a woman. I want to go to Santa Fe to see her new movie. I understand it's great."

Danny chuckled, sometimes the world really was a small place with Jime mentioning their failed movie night without knowing about it. He put the phone on speaker so Connor didn't have to lean toward it. If the traffic started moving it would be safer. "We almost saw it last night."

Jime gasped. "Almost? What happened? The Cat see something?"

"Later." Connor straightened and managed to move the Jeep forward by one car length. "Don't want to speculate at this point, but it might be related to what Trina said. Back to Reggie. What do they want from him?"

"Apparently they want him to carry a package across the border," Jime said.

"In or out?" Danny asked. He leaned awkwardly in his seat so he could pull his pad out of his back pocket and take notes.

"In. He's supposed to go to Acapulco, stay at a certain hotel, and pick up some souvenirs. They told him to bring them back to San Diego, and he'll be contacted."

Connor hissed. "Sounds like drug smuggling." He took another sip of coffee.

"That's what Cortez thought. He wanted you two to look into things. I tried to get him to let me come out there and help, but he said no." On the other end of the phone, Jime sighed. "Something about me staying and being a good deputy."

"Tell him we'll see what we can find out. It may be related to something else we're looking into." Danny stared out the windshield. It didn't make sense that all this was happening and Connor hadn't gotten anything more than a vague flash.

"Will do. Better not take too long looking into things. You know Cortez likes to get answers quickly."

Danny nodded to himself. "He'll know as soon as we find out anything. Don't let any speeders get past you, Cuz." With a soft chuckle, and not waiting for a response, Danny tapped the phone off.

"That may be what Lindy Lui was afraid of." Danny picked the magazine back up, wishing he could get some kind of vision like Connor could, when looking at a picture. "She may have been forced into sex work to hide the fact she's a shifter."

"You could be right." Connor sighed as traffic finally started moving. "Let's see what Moreau has for us at the morgue. If we don't hit another backup before we get there. I hate this traffic."

Danny couldn't disagree. He'd missed Connor the month he was back in New Mexico, but not the traffic. Even though Santa Fe and Albuquerque could get backups, they weren't anywhere near as severe as the ones they encountered in LA. The only plus to the traffic, was that it gave him time to research on his phone. Not as smooth and easy as on a computer, but he could make it work. They had cases piling up and the only link he could see was the people involved all wanted to be stars. If he was lucky, he could find more connections.

Danny sighed and turned off his phone as they drew close to their destination. He hadn't been able to find any major links between the three shifters beyond being in the movie *Amazon Warrior Princess*. But trying to look up things on the phone while bouncing around in the Jeep was an exercise in futility. He kept fat-fingering things with every bump or stop. Hopefully, he'd find more when they got back to the hotel and he could get on the laptop.

Connor wove his way through heavy traffic on the side streets. At least it wasn't as bad as the highway had been. "God, I hate driving in this town. Too many cars, and the air is so heavy I can hardly breathe." He pulled the Jeep into a parking garage next to the address Moreau had given them.

"I know what you mean." Danny rubbed the back of his neck as Connor found a parking spot. "I ache for some open space and clear mountain air."

"As soon as we're done with this case, we're out of here. I've never liked the west coast." Connor undid his seat belt and slipped out of the Jeep.

Danny hurried to follow. The parking garage was dark and crowded, but everything in LA was crowded. The place had such a heavy oil and gas scent it made him cough.

With his usual air of superiority, Connor pushed his way into the building.

A burly cop held up his hand just outside the door. "Hold on. I need to see some ID."

Moreau stepped up behind the guard. "It's okay. They're with me."

"They still need to go through the scanner."

Connor glared at the officer. He looked like he was about to say something rude.

In an attempt to smooth over the situation, even though he hated the shifter scanners that had recently appeared, Danny took Connor's arm. "Come on, Cat. We have to play by their rules."

Connor hissed. "That doesn't mean I have to like it."

An alarm sounded as Danny walked through the gate ahead of Connor.

"Halt right there." The policeman turned to Moreau, his hand quivering close to the gun on his hip. "This guy's a shifter. After the scare we had, they aren't allowed in the building. Captain's orders. They can't be trusted."

"Call Lawrence if you have a question." Moreau handed him a slip of paper. "They've already been cleared by the FBI. We're here about the dead shifter the police found this morning."

The guard read the paper, turned his back to them, and dialed his phone. "This is Jefferson on the main door. There're a couple of shifters here who say they've been cleared…Yes, sir. I'll let them in."

Danny nodded to Connor, wandering if their job was going to continue to grow more difficult as shifterphobia spread like wildfire across the country. He hoped things would calm down, but with the president and prominent members of congress speaking out against them, it was unlikely. It made him wonder if the shifter they were about to see was a victim, rather than a suicide.

Trying to ignore the reek of formaldehyde and ammonia that made his nose wrinkle, Connor looked down at the body of the young man on the mortician's table. "What do we know about him?"

As the police officer, who had accompanied them to the morgue, opened a file, he sneezed. "Name: David Wallace. Age: twenty-nine. Job: waiter at a restaurant in Marina Del Rey/aspiring actor. He lived in Venice Beach." He looked up from the file and snorted. "Isn't everyone in Hollywood an aspiring actor?" He looked back to the paper. "From: Des Moines, IA. Cause of death: apparent self-inflicted bullet wound to the right temple." He sneezed again.

"Are you okay, Officer?" Moreau handed him a box of tissues from the desk near the table.

The officer pulled a tissue from the box and blew his nose. "Something seems to be triggering my allergies."

Moreau set the box down. "What are you allergic to?"

"Cats."

Connor ducked his head and smirked as he placed his hand on the dead man's arm. "Did they recover a bullet? When did he die? Who found the body?"

"They just brought him in this morning and haven't done an autopsy yet. The coroner established time of death sometime between nine and ten p.m." The officer sneezed as he thumbed through the file. "Police received an anonymous phone call at 5:46 a.m. this morning. Our tech department is tracking the call. Wallace is apparently known to the police having been picked up several times for suspected drug dealing. The last time, he was carrying several ounces of cocaine. He was set for a hearing next Monday. Since it's a Federal case, Captain called in the FBI, and you guys showed up." He took another tissue and wiped his eyes and nose before sneezing again.

"Glad they haven't messed with him yet. That may help." Closing his eyes, Connor concentrated on the young man. His powers kicked in. *The man was laughing with another man, taller, darker, human. They were sitting on a couch watching television. The other man got up and went out of the room. Wallace walked over to the sliding door and stepped out onto the patio. He took his clothes off, stacked them neatly on the plastic chair there and shifted into a raccoon. He scurried up the side of the building. On the roof he stopped and sat for a while, enjoying the moonlight. He thought about a pretty red-haired girl and a working farm. A cellphone rang. David jumped from the roof back to the patio. He answered the phone. Everything darkened. "Hey, I told you already. I'm not doing this anymore. I don't care. Just leave me alone." In the distance another phone rang. The vison got fuzzy. Connor tried to dig deeper, see more, but a haze of red filled his mind.*

He blinked and stared at Danny, Moreau, and Officer Allergy. "He was getting phone calls and trying to stop whatever." Sighing he closed his eyes again, trying to distance himself from what he'd seen.

Conner opened his eyes again. "I'd like to see where he lived."

The officer was belligerent. "Our officers already went over it." After sneezing again, he wiped his eyes repeatedly.

Danny leaned slightly, as if reading the name on the officer's badge. "Perkins, it's just how we work." He stared into the man's watering eyes. "Besides, you might want to not stand so close to Agent McGriffin. He's a cat. A big one, but still a cat.

"Okay. I'll see if I can get permission for you to check it out." He sniffled.

Danny took the file from him. "It says they brought in a laptop computer, a cell phone, a bank book, and a passport. Moreau, see if we can get access to them and the apartment."

Moreau pulled out his cell phone, quickly tapping before putting it up to his ear. "This is Agent Moreau. I have a couple members of the Shifter Force here who would like to see Wallace's apartment and his personal items."

"Shifter Force?" the man on the other end of the call sounded like Moreau had made a joke.

"That's right, Shifter Force. It's a new agency set up to deal directly with the shifter community." Moreau rolled his eyes and looked like he was doing his best not to sigh.

"Oh, I think I got a memo on them a couple of weeks ago. Had really been hoping not to deal with them. Tell Perkins to go with them. He knows where the scene is and will make sure they don't disturb it much. I'll see about getting the evidence to them, once our guys are done with it."

"I'll tell them." He ended the connection and turned to Connor.

"That may be too late." Connor said before Moreau could relay what he'd been told. "See if your FBI friends can pull strings to get it. I'd also like to see the gun."

Perkins consulted his paperwork. "It doesn't say anything about a gun being brought in."

Connor opened his mouth and stared at Perkins. "You mean to say, they didn't find a gun, and yet they're calling it a suicide? What happened to the gun?" He couldn't believe such an oversight had been made. Even with the public opinion of shifters getting worse, such an error was grievous.

Perkins turned red and stammered, "Ah, ah, I don't know."

Squinting in anger, Connor brushed past Perkins abruptly. "Let's roll, Dawg." He wanted to get to the scene and get things resolved as quickly as possible.

The longer he stayed in LA and dealt with the fools there, the less he liked it.

Connor paced in front of the police tape enclosing the door to Wallace's apartment as they waited for Perkins and Moreau to arrive. The traffic had gotten bad again and they'd managed to get ahead of Perkins. Luckily Danny was able to get Moreau to relay the address so they didn't have to pull over and wait for Perkins to drive past so they could get behind him again. Connor wasn't dealing well with the waiting. Every minute that went by, the more chance the psychic images would be too faint for him to get a good reading on them. It didn't help that the officer on the scene had told them they had to wait for Perkins. People were slowing him down and getting on his nerves.

A uniformed office stood behind the tape. The look on his face was one of boredom.

"Calm down, Cat." Danny laid his hand on Connor's shoulder. "You know how humans operate. We have to work on their time."

Connor snarled. "Like I said, that doesn't mean I have to like it." He wasn't sure why he was so on edge. It might've been that he still hadn't gotten a spontaneous vision. Sure, he could still get readings off of things, and people, but his spontaneous visions were often what helped him make headway in a case, and he hadn't had one since the stars. There had to be more to this thing than just falling stars. The shifters involved weren't even big names. It didn't make sense.

Moreau parked a few spaces down from the Jeep and walked back to them. "Director Mills will get us what we need. He'll meet us at the Bureau headquarters this afternoon."

Perkins pulled up in front of the apartment and angled the squad car into a 'no parking' spot. He stepped over the police tape and asked the officer there to unlock the door. "Sorry it took so long." He sniffled as he looked over at Connor. "When I lost you guys, I decided to stop for some antihistamine."

Connor grinned. "Hope it helps." The fact that Perkins was allergic to him helped his mood a little.

A tall, dark young man wearing sunglasses approached Perkins. "Officer, when can I get into my apartment? When I got home, this officer said no one can enter. Something about a suicide."

Danny sniffed. *"Non-shifter. Human."*

"He was in my vision from the morgue. We'll need to talk to him." Connor stepped closer to Perkins. "Have you questioned this young man?"

"No. We didn't know anyone else lived here." He turned to the man. "I'll need to see your ID and prove you live here before I can let you in."

The young man pulled out his wallet and driver's license and handed it to Perkins.

Perkins looked at the license and opened his phone. "Wait here while I check with my captain." He took a couple of steps away from the young man.

"I thought the other guy already did that, but he never heard anything back." The young man crossed his arms and glared at Perkins. "Really. I live here. On the second floor. Are you stopping everyone else in the building too?"

Not willing to wait any longer, since the door was unlocked, Connor briskly brushed past Perkins and entered the small apartment. His cat-like aversion to a mess made him feel the need to clean the place. It was a sty, but then it was also the residence of two young straight guys.

Perkins tried to grab his arm, missed, sneezed, and stumbled in, still on his phone. "Yes, Sir. I'll tell him." He shoved the phone in his pocket.

A sparsely furnished living room covered most of the front of the place with a kitchen off to the right. Beer bottles, glasses, and a pizza box littered the coffee table. Slices of pizza were scattered on the floor. Halfway along the back wall, a doorway led to a hall. A bathroom flanked by two bedrooms occupied the back half of the apartment.

"Tell me something, Perkins." Connor turned and glared at Perkins. "You said your guys went through this apartment, and yet you didn't know two people lived here? Sounds like you didn't look very good." He was beginning to get the feeling the cops weren't taking the death of a shifter seriously. First, no gun, and yet they called it a suicide. They didn't even realize two people lived there. Where was the roommate when Wallace was shot? Where was the gun? These were questions he shouldn't have to ask; they should already have been answered.

Perkins stared at him with clenched teeth and didn't answer.

Sniffing which bedroom belonged to the dead raccoon, Connor ignored the living room and wandered around the bedroom, touching different items, hoping to get something that would be helpful.

Danny stood inside the door watching him. He didn't look happy either, but the way he had his arms across his chest, he was providing a good shield between Connor and any of the humans who might cause a problem.

A taped outline of a body enclosed a pool of blood that had soaked into the carpet where Wallace's body had lain.

Connor knelt and touched the carpet, careful not to get in any of the blood. Almost instantly his powers kicked in… *Wallace faced the other man. He had a soft voice, almost caring, with a slight Midwest accent. "I can't hide what I am anymore. I'm a raccoon shifter. Also, I can't afford to keep letting you have stuff free. Things are too tight. I need help. If you can't help, I'll have to find another roommate who can." He turned his back on the second figure and reached for something on the dresser. A shot rang out, and Wallace fell to the floor. The second figure picked up the item from the dresser and left."*

Danny's thoughts brushed his *"You saw something, Cat. What was it?"*

"We'll talk later." Picking up a hairbrush from the dresser, Connor smelled it. "He wasn't taking any drugs."

Perkins slipped past Danny, frowning. "How can you tell?"

Not willing to answer questions for a cop who didn't care, Connor ignored him and went into the bathroom.

Two sets of toiletries were scattered haphazardly on the countertop, one on each side of the sink. One of them wore Axe, the other Old Spice. Definitely straight boys. Dirty towels lay on the floor. The toilet paper roll was nearly empty, and like the rest of the apartment, the toilet needed cleaning. Connor wrinkled his nose and moved on.

Again he wondered how the police missed the fact that two people lived there. He opened the medicine cabinet. Aspirin, condoms, cough syrup, Band-Aids, and several generic items. No prescription bottles or any suspicious-looking items.

Two clothes hampers stood against the wall of the bathroom.

Danny walked over to one and pulled out a white shirt with the logo of a nearby pizza parlor and a pair of black pants. Both items had pizza sauce on them. He held the garments closer to his nose, breathed in the scent, and rolled them into a ball. "Perkins, you need to have your forensics department test these. I smell blood."

Perkins partially unrolled the shirt. "Looks like pizza sauce to me."

"The blood is in there." Danny was being more patient than Connor felt. "Trust me; I'm a wolf. I smell things humans can't."

"Dawg, if he doesn't want to do it, Moreau can get the FBI to run it through their lab. It's probably a better lab anyway."

Going into the kitchen, Connor opened the refrigerator door. "No alcohol, no meat. He didn't smell like a vegetarian to me. How about you, Dawg?" Taking a covered container out of the fridge, he opened it, smelled the contents, it was so rank it crossed his eyes. He quickly put it back.

"I didn't think so either." Danny glanced over Connor's shoulder into the fridge. "I've tried to identify scents, but there have been too many people in here to separate them."

Connor straightened and closed the fridge. "I know what you mean. Probably a lot of the scents are the police and medical examiners."

Again, Perkins asked, "How do you know?"

Danny grinned. "Again, we aren't human. We have an enhanced sense of smell. Most humans can't smell the difference, but vegetarians have a different body odor from carnivores."

Positive they were not going to get anything else, Connor headed for the door. "There's nothing here. Let's talk to the roommate, then we'll see what Wallace's computer and phone say." He was thankful Danny was there to run interference between the police and him. Having been a deputy, Danny knew how to deal with them in ways that were foreign to Connor, even though Connor had been working with various forces across the country for years.

He walked to the young man who was sitting on a concrete wall that formed a barrier between the sidewalk and the small front yard. "What can you tell us about Wallace?"

The young man removed his glasses, and his gaze flickered nervously between Connor and Perkins. "You a cop? You don't have a uniform on."

He pulled out his Shifter Force badge. It was good for getting civilians to take him more seriously than when he'd just been a special consultant. "You might say I'm shifter cop. My partners and I help the police when shifters are involved." Connor sat on the wall beside him. "My name's Connor McGriffin." He remembered what Danny kept telling him about his attitude and tried to tone down his usual arrogance.

"Jack Johnson. Are you telling me Dave was a shifter? If I'd known that, I'd never have roomed with him. I don't like shifters, especially after that deal with the shifters kidnapping young boys and turning them into shifters." He tilted his head and looked at Connor. "You're one, aren't you? That's why you have that badge." Fear clouded his glassy eyes as he looked at Danny and Moreau. He got off the wall and walked over near Perkins, like the police officer could protect him from the shifters.

Connor forced himself to remain outwardly calm. "Where you from, Jack?" *"Got your notepad, Danny?"* "How long have you been in Los Angeles?"

"Always." Danny held up the small pad.

"I think he's lying. Be sure you get everything."

Jack looked at Perkins. "Do I have to answer him?"

Perkins tightened his fist like he wanted to hit something, then relaxed very slightly. "I'm not fond of shifters myself, Johnson, but he's in charge." He sniffled, took a tissue from his pocket, and blew his nose.

"I'm from Kansas City, Missouri." Jack picked at a blade of grass out of the crumbly wall. "Been out here about six years."

Connor continued, "How long have you known Wallace, and do you have any idea why he'd want to kill himself?" He slipped a hand into his pocket and turned on the video on his phone. It wouldn't capture a picture but should record Jack's voice.

Danny stood next to Perkins, a little closer to Jack than Connor was.

"We've been rooming together about six months. I saw his advertisement for a roommate after my girlfriend caught me cheating and kicked me out. Didn't want to get involved with another woman right now. I'm hoping we get back together. If I'd known he was a shifter, I'd never have moved in with him. Seems like shifters are taking over this country more and more and ain't nobody doing nothin' about it." He paused. "As for why he'd want to kill himself, no idea. He seemed okay. I wondered if he had a girl down in Acapulco since he traveled down there about once a month. Maybe he got her pregnant and didn't know what to do and killed himself."

"Where were you last night?" Danny asked.

"I had a date with my ex. We went to a movie after I got off work and ended up at her place for the night."

Danny wrote something on his pad. "Does your ex have a name? Will she verify your story?"

Jack again allowed his gaze to shift between Connor and Perkins. "Do you have to contact her? I'd rather not. Like I said, I'm hoping to get back together with her. Don't want to upset her. She'll be upset when she finds out Dave is dead. You call her and she'll totally freak. She's not really emotionally stable. I don't want to be responsible for her having an episode."

"We'll only call her if it becomes necessary." Connor could tell the man was hiding something. But what? Connor wasn't getting anything off him and figured if he walked up and touched the man, he'd totally freak out, probably before Connor could get anything from the contact.

"Mary Nelson." Jack gave Danny her address and phone number. According to Google Maps, the address was about half an hour away; farther inland from the beach. Beads of sweat broke out on his forehead, and he squirmed on the wall.

Moreau asked, "Did Wallace seem to have any money problems?"

Johnson snorted. "Just the opposite. He always had money. Flowed through his fingers like water. This place ain't cheap. He couldn't afford to live here if he had money problems."

"Any idea where he got it?" Moreau asked, coming over from his car and leaning against the wall. "Did he have a job?"

"He said it was family money. No job. Actually, he just kind of laid around if he wasn't on the beach." Jack twisted his mouth. "For an actor, he didn't go on many auditions."

Raising his eyebrows questioningly, Connor studied Jack. "What do you do for a living, Jack?"

He chuckled. "Same as everyone in Hollywood. I do a little acting. Between parts, I work at a pizza place. Which is why I need to get into the apartment. My clean uniforms are in there, and I need to get to work."

Connor motioned to Perkins. "I don't see any reason Jack can't get into his apartment, do you? Just stay out of Wallace's room until we clean it."

Perkins held up his phone. "I just talked to the captain. He says it's okay if you're finished here."

Connor placed a hand on Jack's shoulder and reached out with his gifts.

Jack was washing his hands while a woman shouted incoherently at him.

"Dude, don't touch me. I don't like shifters, hear." Jack jerked away from Connor's hand.

"Sorry." Connor pulled the hand back. He reached into his pocket and handed Jack a business card with the Shifter Force logo of a wolf head and cougar head on either side of the words. "If you think of anything else, here's how you can contact me."

"What about his stuff? What should I do with it? I'll need to get another roommate since I can't pay the rent by myself. And who's going to pay for cleaning up the blood out of the carpet?"

Connor stared at him. Did he realize how stupid he was to acknowledge the blood when he claimed to have not been in the apartment? It was almost a confession, but they needed hard evidence to convict him.

"Cat, how does he know there's blood?" Danny's thoughts rang in his head. *"He hasn't been in the apartment."*

"I caught that, Dawg."

Danny pulled out his wallet and handed him $200. "That should hold you for a week or so. If you'll pack things up, we'll have someone come by and get them. We'll probably ship them back to his folks. Once the police have everything they need, they'll handle the cleanup."

"You got it." Jack looked from Danny to Connor to Moreau. "I guess you guys aren't so bad for shifters. Let me know if you need anything else." He stood, slipped his glasses back on, and walked toward the door. Before entering the apartment, he turned to Perkins. "Can I have that key you have to the place? If you need back in, I'll let you in."

"You'll get it back when we're done with everything." Perkins replied.

Connor walked to the sidewalk. "Let's head back to the station. I want to talk to that friend of yours, Moreau. There are a couple of unanswered questions."

He wanted to know why the police were being so sloppy with the case. If it had been a human instead of a shifter, they never would've missed things like the bloody shirt Danny found, or the missing gun. He wanted to see what he could do to get them to do their jobs and make everyone's life easier.

The same officer who'd been there earlier let them into the precinct building. He didn't react when the shifter alarm went off the second time.

"We need to see Captain Lawrence," Connor said as he glanced around the squad room that was just off the entrance hall.

"I'll see if he's available." Moreau hurried off.

"He'd better be available. I want to know who searched Wallace's apartment." Connor was getting madder by the second, and the traffic on the way back across LA hadn't helped his mood in the least.

Danny placed a hand on his arm. "Calm down, Cat. You've been on edge since we left the apartment."

He jerked his arm away. "I can't stay calm when it looks like the cops are glossing over an obvious murder and calling it a suicide."

A tall older man came out of an office. "Who says we're glossing over a murder. Moreau, who is this man?"

"This is Connor McGriffin." Moreau gestured to Connor. "He's in charge of the Shifter Force. Connor, this is Captain Lawrence."

Perkins approached them from another hall and started sneezing again.

Connor gritted his teeth. He tried to keep his tone softer than he really wanted to, but it kept creeping up, getting louder and louder. "Good. Tell me how you can call this a suicide when there isn't a gun, or any other means of killing oneself? Did the gun fly away after Wallace shot himself, or did someone pick it up and lose it? Also, how did your officers overlook the fact that two people lived in that apartment? It seems they just wanted to ignore the facts since a shifter was involved. After all, shifters are no good."

"Connor, back down," Danny snapped through their link. *"You don't know Captain Lawrence well enough to treat him like this. What's gotten into you?"*

Connor didn't have time to respond to Danny.

"Look, McGriffin, you've raised some good points." Lawrence got up in Connor's face. "I hadn't read the reports yet when I called Moreau. You're right about the gun, but I don't appreciate your attitude. I don't know about you, but we're overworked in this office and we do occasionally miss things. That doesn't mean we're not doing our jobs right." Lawrence turned to Moreau. "Get this man out of here before I find some reason to lock him up."

"I'm leaving, but I'll be back." Connor spun around toward the door. "This isn't a suicide, it's murder, and I'll find the killer. That roommate knows something he isn't telling. How did he know there was blood on the carpet in Wallace's bedroom if he hadn't been inside the apartment?"

The captain roared, "Perkins, you stay with them. Don't let them out of your sight."

Connor looked back with a snarl.

"Yes, Sir." Perkins sneezed as he hurried after them.

"Are you sick or something, Perkins?" Lawrence asked.

"I'm allergic to McGriffin, sir. He's a cat." He pulled a tissue from his pocket and blew his reddening nose.

"Well, take something for it," Lawrence said as Connor pushed open the squad room door and headed down the hall toward the street. He didn't have time to stand around and be yelled at by some idiot human who didn't know how to tell when his men weren't doing their job.

Hoping they could make better time if they split up, Connor opened the door of the Jeep and looked at Danny still standing on the sidewalk. "Dawg, you and Moreau head over to the FBI lab and see what you can find out." He tossed his phone to Danny. "Trade phones with me. See if they can pull a 'voice recognition' for Johnson off of here. Also check into John's List, see if we can track anything from there on our cat."

"What are you going to be doing?" Danny slipped Connor's phone into his pocket before throwing his phone at Connor.

Easily catching the phone that seemed to have a bit more anger behind it than Connor expected, he put it in his jeans. "I want to find Trina's boyfriend, and see if I can talk to Wallace's agent, once you get me his name."

"Cat, are you going to be okay going off on your own? You seem a bit on edge."

Connor didn't bother responding. Danny knew better than to question him when they were on a case.

Perkins held up his hand. "Wait a minute. I need to stay with you. I'll have to call in someone else if you split up."

"We work alone." Connor glared at him. The locals were proving to be completely incompetent and he didn't need them slowing him down. There were shifter lives at stake and they obviously didn't care. "Tell your superiors to stay out of Shifter Force business. We have the backing of the FBI." He turned abruptly, got into the Jeep, and started the engine.

"Connor!" Danny mentally shouted at him. *"I thought you were beyond treating the locals like trash. You keep this up and we'll lose everything we just gained."*

"We'll talk about it if it becomes an issue. These LA people are just pissing me off. I need space." Connor shut down the link between them. He didn't need to have a fight with Danny. He'd been hoping that Danny shared his frustrations, but he might've been wrong.

Biting back his anger at Connor's cavalier dismissal, Danny stood in the middle of the sidewalk and watched the Jeep squeal away, narrowly missing a car that was coming up the ramp into the parking garage. "Come on Moreau, the great man has spoken." He led the way to Moreau's Explorer, climbed into the passenger seat, and fastened his seat belt. Danny was determined to not lose it in front of Perkins, and he really wanted the police officer to go away. There wasn't much he'd be able to say to make up for the way Connor had treated him, or the captain.

"What am I supposed to tell Captain Lawrence?" Perkins asked.

Moreau leaned out of the SUV window. "Tell Lawrence the FBI and Shifter Force will handle things from here. He can send all the files over to my desk. If humans end up involved, we'll call you in." He backed out of the parking space.

"Hold on." Danny scribbled something on his notepad, tore the page out, and handed it to Perkins. "Tell Lawrence to call this number and ask for Chief Kennedy. He'll tell you about Connor's abilities, attitude, and the way he works. It might not help, but maybe. I am sorry about his attitude. He's worried about too many people right now, and he needs a break in at least one of the cases we're working."

Perkins took the paper with his mouth hanging open. "One of the cases? You mean there's more than one suicide?"

Danny shook his head. "No. Not yet at least. But there are several missing shifters we're looking for." He didn't elaborate.

"Okay. Thanks." Perkins walked away. "FBI can deal with you guys. Good luck."

When they reached the exit, the bar was down blocking them from leaving. Danny took a deep breath as Moreau rolled down his window and approached the guard shack.

"What up? Are we on lock down? I haven't heard anything." Moreau gestured to the police band radio under his dash.

"The captain said he wanted to speak with Connor McGriffin." The officer leaned slightly like he was trying to see into the back seat of the Explorer. "Is he with you?"

Moreau shook his head. "Sorry. He was in the Jeep that left a few minutes ago."

"Captain isn't going to be happy about that. When you talk to him, let him know. If he takes too long, depending on what it's about, Captain might have to issue an APB."

"I'll handle this when I get back to the FBI," Moreau glanced at Danny and rolled his eyes.

Danny groaned as things just seemed to be getting worse and worse. Connor was going to have to learn to control his natural arrogance or they were going to lose the respect they had gained with the FBI. The way the humans were feeling about shifters, it wasn't going to take much.

As the officer at the gate stepped back in and hit a button, the red and white board barrier rose slowly. Moreau pulled forward, stopping to wait for traffic to get past so he could pull onto the street.

"I know Connor's got everyone's best interest at heart, but sometimes I wonder how other agencies have put up with him." Moreau sighed as they stopped for a red light half a block from the garage exit.

"He's got a big heart for the victims," Danny said. "But sometimes I think the fact that he can see the future, and or sense things the rest of us can't sets him up to think he's…" he struggled to find the words that wouldn't put Connor in a really bad light.

"Better than the rest of us." Moreau started forward from the light. "Yeah, I've seen that all too well. I believe that we need a group of shifters working for the good of shifters who are having to deal with authorities, and sometimes saving us from ourselves. If I didn't, I wouldn't hang out with you guys. Not sure what I'd be doing, since the FBI doesn't believe in letting shifters be on the force, but I'd find something."

"There are lots of other agencies that aren't so limited in their employment practices." Danny said, thinking how if it wasn't for Connor he'd still be back in Jimenez Springs writing traffic tickets, and that if anything ever happened and Shifter Force flew apart, Rusty would give him his old job back. The thing was, he didn't want his old job back. After just two cases, taking down a shifter serial killer and saving a bunch of kids from sex traffickers, he was hooked. He wanted to stay on the move helping people.

Chapter 3

After finding parking nearly a mile away, Connor wove his way between the people crowding Ocean Front Walk fronting Muscle Beach. The parking and the overpopulation of the beach, even though it was a weekday, didn't do anything for his mood. He wanted to stop and sit at the beach and watch the waves for a little while. Realization hit him. Water. Salt water. Lots of it. Maybe being so close to the water, and not having intense emotional connections to the victims was impacting his visions.

Connor dodged a hunky rollerblader, walked over to a bench, and sat in the shade of a palm tree. He didn't look over his shoulder at the ocean but stared at the souvenir shop. The ocean hadn't blocked his visions of the kids they'd saved, but they'd picked up their trail back in Arizona. The vision he'd had of the stars falling into the ocean had happened on a pier, but what if the ocean was having an impact on what he could and couldn't see? He'd proven he could still pick things up from items, and places, but a general vision, something to help him find the next step on the path, maybe the water was blocking him from that. It could explain the vague vision of the stars.

Visions of Stars

"I need to talk to Grandmother." For several minutes, Connor sat there watching the people come and go out of the souvenir shop, but he couldn't bring himself to call her and ask for help. His grandmother lived in Florida. She was nearly surrounded by salt water, and she still had visions. Or at least, she did of her family; of people she had an emotional attachment to.

"I've got to stay on the case. I'll check with her later." He forced himself to stand and checked his phone for the address Jime had given Danny. It wasn't much farther. Two blocks down and one in. Once again, he wished parking wasn't such an issue in the city. He was used to pulling up to a place, getting out and walking up to the door. Not parking and walking forever before getting to the place he was looking for.

It was a stucco apartment building and the unit he was looking for was up some concrete stairs and down a walkway that looked like it was ready to crumble into the street below. The other buildings in the area were close enough that it would be easy to watch what was going on in the complex. The way Lindy Lui had been acting, she'd been under observation from someone. If Reggie Winters was being threatened by the same people, it was logical they might be watching him too. Finding the right unit, he rapped on the door.

An average-looking bearded man who appeared to be in his mid-twenties answered. Thick dark hair and a muscular build accompanied the smell of 'dog'.

Even though he'd been warned the boyfriend was a Malamute, the hair on Connor's neck still bristled. Maybe it would've been better if he'd let Danny come see Winters. He still wasn't used to having Danny around. For too long he'd done things on his own, but somehow, he expected Danny to be there, watching his back.

The man growled, forcing Connor to stop thinking about Danny and focus on the task at hand. "Whatever you're selling, I don't want."

"Reggie Winters?" Holding his badge case close to his body so others couldn't see it, he flipped it open. "I'm a friend of Trina's cousin, Danny Lupan." *"Cortez sent me. Trina's worried about you."*

"You're that cat Danny hooked up with who almost got him killed by a werebear." *"How can I mind speak with you? You aren't my species."*

Connor looked around nervously. *"I'll explain later. Don't say anything you don't want overheard. Your place may be bugged by the people who are threatening you."* When he stopped and thought about it, if the people threatening could use a Bluetooth headset to talk to Lindy when she didn't have a phone on her, it made sense to Connor that they might actually bug someone's home to keep track of them. He wanted to go back to Wallace's place and see if there were bugs there. "Trina knew Danny and I were going to be in town and said you might show us around. How about we grab something to eat on the Boardwalk, and you can tell me some places to go?"

"Where's Danny?"

"He had some business to take care of." Although it made sense that Winters would have questions like that, and might even be a bit jumpy with people threatening him, Connor really hated it when people didn't instantly do what he wanted them to do. Danny kept telling him he needed to stop that, but it still grated on his nerved.

"Sounds like Danny," Grabbing his keys off a table next to the door, Reggie stepped out of the apartment, closed and locked the door, and led the way down the stairs. "You like tacos?"

"Love them." As Connor stepped up beside him, he wondered how Reggie would know what sounds like Danny, but he didn't voice his doubt. He kept his tone low so as not to carry to any of the people walking, skating, and boarding past them. "I have an ability to mind speak with almost any shifter regardless of species. It comes in handy when I don't want to be overheard. Trina said you're being harassed because you're a shifter."

"Right. I've been getting emails threatening to expose me to the studio. The head of the studio is a complete shifterphobe. Won't have a known one around. I've heard of others who have been threatened since that problem with the kidnappers. People are afraid more than ever. But why are you checking on things?" Reggie walked up to the window of a taco stand. "Give me three beef tacos and a cola." He received his order and walked toward a nearby table.

Connor placed his order for the same items and followed Reggie. There were enough people coming and going for Connor to feel comfortable talking. None of the people around them stayed for very long, but their meals were small and quick to eat. It was a bright, sunny day that urged people to go down on the beach as opposed to lingering near the walk. He sat across the table from Reggie. "Danny and I are members of a new agency that's being authorized to investigate shifter crimes. We work with, and are sanctioned by, the FBI. We're investigating the apparent suicide of a Raccoon shifter named David Wallace."

"David Wallace?" Reggie nearly chocked on a drink of soda. "Dave killed himself? I didn't think it was possible for a shifter to commit suicide."

"Depends on how badly you want to die. We think he was smuggling drugs into the country from Mexico. We aren't sure what, only that he made trips to Acapulco about once a month and seemed to have a lot of spending money." He took a bite of taco before continuing. Compared to the road-side tamales they'd gotten in Arizona on the last case, it was easily some of the best Mexican food Connor had eaten in a long time. He just hoped it didn't come back to bite him. "There seems to be some discrepancy as to whether it's suicide or murder. That's why we're looking into it."

Three men carried trays to the table next to them, sat, and began to eat silently.

The short hairs on the back of Connor's neck bristled. Something wasn't right. Like the past few days, he didn't get anything concrete. Normally such a feeling would be accompanied by a vision, but that wasn't happening.

"Hummm." Reggie looked thoughtful. "I think that's what they want me to do. They're talking about me going to Acapulco, picking up something, and dropping it off in San Diego. They threatened to out my shifter status if don't do what they want." He scratched his beard. "Like I said, the studios won't have anything to do with actors if it comes out they're shifters. Kind of like back in the middle of the last century if they found out you were gay.

"Do you have those emails? Can you send them to me? I'll have our experts check them out." It might be a long shot, but maybe the person sending them wasn't smart enough to hide who he was, or where he was sending them from.

"Yeah." Reggie nodded as he chewed a bite of taco.

Pulling out Danny's phone, Connor fumbled a bit. It felt strange using Danny's phone and not his own. The background wasn't the same, and the apps were scattered in places he wouldn't have put them. It took him a minute to check for the message Jime had sent and then find Reggie's number before Connor could message him with Danny's number…would Danny be mad about giving Reggie his number?

Reggie jerked with surprise when his phone message tone sounded. He pulled out his phone and looked at it. "Hey, is this you? Where'd you get my number?"

"It's actually Danny's phone. He got your number from Trina. Like I said, she's worried. You might give her a call. That is unless you've decided not to continue your relationship." Again Connor felt like Danny should've been there. It was Danny's family business, even if it did tie into the case. Cortez might be accepting of him and Danny, on a species level, but he might feel Connor was overstepping his bounds by being the one handling pack business. Maybe he should've brought Danny along, but they needed Danny and Moreau to do research.

"I'll call. I'm not sure about the relationship. I know Cortez doesn't approve of me or the fact that Trina wants to be an actress."

"Do you think Cortez would've sent me if he disapproved of you?" Connor took another bite, chewed, and swallowed. Technically Cortez sent Danny, but he didn't go there, and he hoped there wouldn't be any fallout from him coming. Pushing that thought out of his head, Connor decided to change the subject. Maybe he could find out something about the other cases. "Can you tell me anything about Maria Lopez or Lindy Lui?"

"I know they are both some kind of cat shifter." Reggie grinned. "Trina got a little jealous of Lindy. She thought I was interested in her. I told her, Lindy's just a kid; reminds me of my little sister. Besides that, she's a cat, and I prefer to stay with a canine partner. Are they in some kind of trouble?"

"I don't know about Maria, but I think the people who are after you are forcing Lindy to participate in prostitution." He knew he was jumping to conclusions, but it felt logical. If someone was trying to blackmail one shifter, it made sense they might be blackmailing others. "Danny and I intercepted a trick last night. She ran off scared."

"Like I said, she's a sweet kid." Reggie patted his lips with a napkin before wiping his beard, knocking shell crumbs to the table. "I'd hate to think she's being forced into sex."

"I would too. It's not a good life for anyone." Connor stood. "Thanks for the information. You have my number to send those emails to. We'll be in touch. Let us know if they contact you again."

Reggie stood and held out his hand. "You're not bad for a cat. If Cortez sent you, I'll go along with it." He walked away.

Visions of Stars

Strolling away from the taco shop, Connor went over what information he'd gathered. Was this what his vision of falling stars meant? Why would Montezuma be concerned with a raccoon, a Malamute, and a Siamese cat? There had to be something he was missing. Maybe he needed to talk to Maria Lopez. And he still wanted to talk to Wallace's agent; he'd forgotten to ask Reggie about that. He had Reggie's number and could call him later about it. He glanced back toward the taco shop. Reggie was still in sight, walking down what had previously been the boardwalk.

The three men at the next table stood and hurried off in the direction Reggie had gone. They were moving just fast enough to make it seem like they were trying to follow him.

Connor squinted as something fluttered across his mind. Something he couldn't quite put a finger on. He glanced at the ocean and cursed its closeness and the interference it was having on his senses.

Turning, he followed the three men at a discreet distance. He wasn't about to let something happen to another shifter if there was something he could do about it.

Chapter 4

An uneasy itch worked down Danny's spine as he walked into the FBI headquarters behind Moreau. The last time he was here with Connor, things hadn't been comfortable. But Connor's ability to rub people the wrong way had been on display the whole time. Things were even more uncomfortable since Phoenix Police Chief Nelson's announcement about the condors forcing their captive shifters to turn human kids into werecreatures had turned the public more against shifters than they had been. He was amazed at the amount of hate people were capable of. Thankfully, Cortez had been able to help the kids who'd been changed find similar shifters in or near their homes to help them adapt to their new reality. It was going to be a lot harder on them than if they had been born shifters. A couple of them had been abandoned by their parents, which made what had been done to them all the more horrible.

Seconds after the shifter detector near the elevator went off, Director Mills approached them. "Where's McGriffin? Not out causing more trouble, I hope. I just got off the phone with Captain Lawrence. Y'all didn't make a good impression with him."

"Connor's working another angle of the case," Moreau replied. "Sorry about Lawrence. Their team is being really sloppy in a case and Connor was mad about it. He came across a bit strong."

Danny bit back a smile. A bit strong didn't exactly cover it. He hated the fact that he and Connor were going to have to have another talk about how to handle the local authorities. The need to frequently remind Connor about proper ways to interact with the locals was getting old. If Connor didn't hit so many good buttons for him, he wouldn't be trying to be so tactful about trying to explain it to him. Maybe he needed to bite the bullet and get a little more forceful with his Cat

Mills' frown deepened, extending from the corner of his mouth to the deepening crow's feet around his tired eyes. "Well, tell him to watch himself. I backed you guys and this Shifter Force thing, as did Kennedy in Santa Fe. If you guys screw up too badly, or piss off too many people, we're going to have egg on our faces, and that's not a good thing. Do I make my point, Moreau?"

"Yes, Sir." Moreau nodded slightly. "We'll talk to McGriffin."

"Good. I know you know how to handle inter-agency work, and I've heard good things about Lupan and Collins. Even though you're shifters, you understand how to do your job. Don't let McGriffin's attitude color what other people think of you. I've seen his talents in action. He's impressive, but nobody likes his attitude. Rein him in." Mills turned and retreated to his office.

"That could've been worse," Moreau muttered.

"I really don't think Connor's used to dealing with bigger city forces." Danny followed as Moreau headed toward the FBI lab area. "But I'll talk to him again. Somehow, I'll make him understand." Danny realized he was also going to have to make Connor understand that to be effective, he was going to need to tone down the emotional response. Connor's emotions were running too high on this one, and there was something going on he wasn't telling Danny.

"Better you than me," Moreau said just loud enough for Danny to pick up as they went through the door to the lab. "What do you have for us, Timmons?"

A bespectacled blond man who didn't look much more than fifteen glanced up from his computer. "We've had trouble tracing things from the hard drive the Venice Beach PD sent over. The messages have come from several IP addresses: libraries, coffee shops, fast-food restaurants, etc. The sender – and we're sure it's one sender because of the terminology and grammar – has used about a dozen email accounts that have been disconnected. He – and I use 'he' generically, it could be a woman – has used a different name for each account."

As Moreau leaned against Timmons' desk, the thoughtful 'ik-ik' sound that came from him resembled the click of a typewriter. "Sounds like we're dealing with a computer expert."

"We were able to track a general area around a couple of studios." Timmons clicked his mouse, and a printer started. "Texts to both phones were sent from the same burner phones. There is one connection we were able to establish between Wallace and Lui.

They're both clients of Kelly and Associates Talent Agency."

Danny picked up copies of emails from the printer. He scanned over them but nothing really registered, other than it seemed the same words were used in the same order, so he would've assumed they were from the same person. Beyond that, they just looked like standard blackmail letters he'd seen in the police academy in Albuquerque. "Do you think this guy also works at the agency?"

Timmons tapped something on the computer and the printer started up again. "There's one guy who might be our man. Damon Lucas works as an assistant to Jerome Kelly, Wallace's and Lui's agent. Lucas has a record; been picked up a few times for possession. Small amounts. Served a couple of small sentences and paid some fines. Been clean for a couple of years now. He might have the connections to set up the drug running."

"Is he smart enough to be the mastermind?" Moreau asked.

"I don't think so. He appears computer savvy, but not too bright otherwise, at least according to the reports from his probation officer." Timmons handed Moreau the latest print out. "We've also tracked the purchase of the burners to a Fast Mart in Venice Beach not far from Wallace's apartment. They also sold the phone that was used to call in Wallace's body. In fact, it was sold about half an hour before the phone call."

Remembering why Connor had given him his phone, Danny pulled it out of his pocket. "Can you see if you can get a voice recognition match to any of the calls to what's on here?" He fiddled with things for a moment. Connor had his own way of arranging his apps, and his file option was a couple of screens to the right of where Danny kept his. It took him a couple of seconds to pull up the latest video file.

Timmons clicked the play button, and Johnson's voice came out for a second before Timmons turned it back off. "It's a little garbled, but I'll try. I'll get back with you later."

He stood and walked over to a computer across the room and plugged the phone into it. "Give me a second to download the file. We're not allowed to download strange files into a system connected to the network… security, you understand."

"Sure." Danny and Moreau both nodded and spoke at the same time.

With a shake of his head, Timmons tapped something on the phone. "Don't do that guys. Really. It's freaky. I know partners get to reading each other's minds and shit, but yeah, don't bring that into my lab." He unplugged the phone from the USB cable, and handed it back to Danny. "Voice recognition, particularly on a bad file like this can take a while. What, did you have it in your pocket or something? Lots of scratching."

"Yeah, that's it. If you get something, can you see if it matches anything at all? The least little bit will help." Danny put Connor's phone back in his pocket and pulled out his ever-present notepad. "Do you have an address for Lucas?"

Timmons went back to his computer and typed frantically. After a second, he sat back. "Yeah. He lives a couple of blocks from Wallace. That's not a cheap area of town. They both must be doing pretty good."

Visions of Stars

Danny looked over his shoulder and made a note of the address. "Can you get us a list of the agency's clients? Do you know if Reggie Winters or Trina Lupan are part of it? She might be listed as Katrina Lupan."

Pursing his lips, Timmons consulted his computer. He pulled up the website for the Kelly and Associates Talent Agency. "I see Reggie Winters, but no Katrina Lupan. I do see a Katrina Cortez."

In the picture that came up on the website, his cousin looked prettier than Danny had ever seen her. She also looked happy. "That's Trina." Danny pointed at the picture. "Can we get a printout of that list?"

"Sure." Timmons clicked on the print icon on his browser. "You guys do know you probably could've looked all this up on your phones, right?"

"But then what would there be for you to do?" Moreau asked with a chuckle.

"Oh, I don't know." Timmons leaned back in his chair. "Maybe try and pull a voice print off a crappy recording."

The printer spit out three more pages of paper. Danny pulled them out and glanced down the list. "Looks like Maria Lopez is on here also."

Moreau looked over his shoulder. "Might not be the same one. It's a fairly common name. Maybe we need to talk to these people."

Danny held up the page with Maria's picture. "Pretty sure this is her. Looks like the gal in all the movies."

"Right." Timmons agreed. "She's awesome in the Amazon movie. There's already Oscar buzz for her."

"Then why would anyone risk blackmailing her? This doesn't make much sense." Danny stacked the papers neatly, wishing he had something to put them in before they all went flying. He grabbed a large paperclip from the holder on Timmons' desk.

"Timmons." Director Mills rushed into the room. "Do you have those fingerprints processed yet? Interpol is waiting."

"Still waiting on the search to finish." Simons turned in his chair and looked at his boss. "These things take time."

"I know that. When that French guy calls me back, you get to talk to him." He paused and looked at Moreau and Danny. "I thought you guys were doing your own research."

"Mostly." Danny held up the printouts, trying to make it seem like they'd done their own searches. "We've got a good start."

"I think you Shifter Force guys might need to get your own lab resources and not eat up my budget with stuff that doesn't concern us." Mills started out the door and held it open as if waiting for Danny and Moreau to make an exit.

"Come on, Danny." Moreau headed for the door. "We can grab some grub on our way to catch up with Connor."

Danny followed, hoping the increase in quiet hostility from the FBI wasn't going to get more pronounced. They had a couple of people back in New Mexico who didn't mind doing research for them, but things like the recording would need local attention to be handled quickly. Not to mention the FBI had resources the Santa Fe Police department didn't.

The men Connor followed headed back the way he'd come with Reggie. From time to time, one or more of them would look back over his shoulder, as if checking for anyone following them. Connor listened to his gut and kept managing to sit on a bench or slip into a shop just as they looked.

When they walked past the road that they needed to take to get to Reggie's apartment, Connor relaxed a little, but continued stalking them. They were acting just suspicious enough to hold his attention, and his gut kept telling him they were somehow connected to everything. Even if they didn't go directly after Reggie, they might be able to shed some light on what was going on.

A few blocks from Reggie's apartment, the men paused. The biggest of the three pulled off his shirt and said something to the other two.

Connor sat on a bench, on the opposite end from an older woman who was throwing bread to the seagulls.

"It's such a lovely day, don't you think?" she asked.

Although he wanted to keep track of the three men, if he didn't answer the woman, Connor was afraid she might say or do something to draw their attention to him. "It is."

"You know you're a bit overdressed, don't you?" She pointed to Connor's jeans and polo shirt. "Not going to catch anyone's eye looking like that."

"Not what I had planned." Connor kept glancing at the three men, one of whom was suddenly on the phone.

"Oh, well, you looked like you were looking for someone." The woman finished feeding the gulls and wadded up the bread bag. "Good luck, young man." She heaved herself up with her cane and waddled down the walk, heading in the direction of the three men. The way she walked and her cane made him think of his grandmother and reminded him he wanted to call her.

The man on the phone slipped the phone in his pocket and said something to the other two. Shirtless guy tucked his shirt in the back of his shorts and headed out onto the beach. The other one who hadn't been on the phone, strolled back toward Connor, while the phone man turned down the road they'd stopped at the end of.

"Damn," Connor muttered to himself. He needed Danny, Moreau, or Lisa. In the urban environment, Lisa would've been the best. In her kestrel form, she could've followed one without drawing attention, and with her keen sight, depending on where they went, might've been able to watch two or all three. But he didn't have time to ponder what if, he needed to move.

Danny's phone rang. It was a recording of Connor's yowl. He hadn't known Danny had used the recording as his ring tone. It brought a smile to Connor, but he didn't answer the call. He needed to focus, and he could call Danny when he got back to the Jeep.

He took a deep breath, trying to make it sound like he was winded from walking, as the one went casually past him. The man smelled human. But that backed up Connor not spotting any other shifters at the taco stand.

Visions of Stars

Once the man walking his way had made it about a block down, Connor moved, heading toward the phone guy. He made it to the street but didn't spot him. There were people heading down the lane toward the beach, but no one going away at that point. Hoping neither of the other guys were following him, Connor risked running down the sidewalk, weaving in and out of the crowd. At the next intersection, he stopped and looked around. There wasn't anyone who looked like the phone guy. He took a deep breath, hoping to pick up something familiar, but he hadn't gotten a good scent from the man back at the taco stand, and there were too many people around.

When he tried to push out with his psychic senses, was suddenly flooded with too much input.

A woman shouts at her children as she tries to get ready to go to the beach.

A man sees Connor and is instantly attracted, feeling his cock get hard.

Someone yells at a person who took a parking place close to their beachside condo.

Shaking his head, Connor back off from the visions bombarding him. There wasn't anything helpful. He wasn't stupid enough to try to follow three men without back up. There was no doubt the other two would also be gone if he went back to try to find them. With luck, he was just being paranoid. Since his powers seemed to be on the fritz, he had no way of knowing for sure, if his gut was right and they meant Reggie harm or not. He needed to call Lisa and see how soon she could be out there. The team needed their eyes in the sky.

Danny stared at Connor's phone as Moreau headed toward Hollywood Boulevard and the offices of Kelly and Associates Talent Agency. "He sent me to voice mail."

Moreau shrugged as he stopped at the light at La Brea. "Maybe he's in the middle of interviewing a witness or something."

"Maybe." Danny twisted slightly so he could get the phone back in his pocket. "But normally when he doesn't answer the phone, there's something wrong." He really hoped Connor hadn't run into more than he could deal with on his own.

"He's been a bit more…ah Connor-like, than normal the past couple of days." Moreau pulled forward, then slowed as the traffic got heavier. "Maybe he opted to go take a walk on the beach and think about things."

Danny shook his head. "Doubtful. Connor's tired of our walks on the beach. They're nice and romantic and all, but he says he's tired of the water."

"That's right, the water interferes with his psychic abilities. Could that be at the root of his issue? Maybe all the water, you know, the oceans, rivers, lakes, swimming pools, around here are messing him up." Moreau pulled into a parking garage after his phone's GPS told him they had arrived at their destination. "Maybe not being able to be as sensitive as he's used to being has thrown him off in more than just his powers."

Danny undid his seat belt as Moreau slipped into a parking spot. "I might bounce that past him, right after I talk to him about being a bit mellower when dealing with Lawrence and the rest."

Moreau opened his door and got out of the car. "Tell you what, warn me before that discussion happens, and I'll see if I can be busy on the other side of town."

"I didn't realize ring-tailed cats were chicken shits." Danny grinned. "Maybe that can be your team nickname."

"No." Moreau shook his head as they headed out of the garage. "Not going to get a team nickname. Don't need one. I guess it's a good thing we decided to go ahead and check out this place, even though Connor said he was going to."

"After we got him the address," Danny chuckled. He figured if there was anything majorly wrong with Connor, he'd feel it through their telepathic link. "Yeah. After we check this out, I guess we should head back to the hotel and see if he's there. You know, I think it might be time to put one of those stalker apps on our phones, so I know where he is all the time. That is when I don't want to just ask him through our mental link."

"And that kind of dedication—" Moreau put a creepy intonation on the word "—is why I'm thankful I don't have a husband or a wife. Having you guys around to watch TV with is nice, but I'm so thankful nobody is tracking my every move."

"Pluses to being ace, I get it." Danny glanced down the sidewalk as they entered the bright sunlight. There were still too many people around for his taste. "But I tell you, I thought I was happy with just the occasional date, but having Connor around to keep me warm at night is nice."

"I don't know." Moreau stepped behind Danny to avoid a man walking down the sidewalk pulling a train of wagons with stuffed animals in it. "One of these days maybe I can find another ace guy and settle down to our own separate bedrooms and dinner and TV every night. That's my idea of a cozy relationship. But it would still take me a couple of years before I'd be ready for him to know my every move."

Danny stopped at the glass door that announced Kelly and Associates Talent Agency. He pulled on it and it barely moved. "It's past lunch time."

"But it looks like they're closed." Moreau pointed to the closed sign on the other side of the door. He sniffed. "Wow, is it just me, or do a lot of shifters come in and out of this place?"

Leaning closer to the bar on the door, Danny took a deep breath. The scents of wolf, cats, bears, otters, birds of prey, and others filled his nose. "I didn't realize there were this many shifters in Hollywood."

"It's not like we can't blend in." Moreau sighed. "Doesn't look like they have set hours. I wonder if we should try calling them."

Danny pulled up their website and frowned at the contact information there. "No phone number. It wants an email."

Moreau leaned against the door for a moment. "That leaves us with seeing what Timmons can dig up on a phone number."

"Or we could call Lisa and see if Larea in the Santa Fe Police Office can get us the data," Danny suggested. "To keep Mills from getting madder."

"That might be a good idea, but I've got another one." Moreau straightened from the door. "Let's try something." He walked into the record store next door.

Loud pop music surged out of the door as they walked in. It surprised Danny that they hadn't heard any of the music when they'd been on the sidewalk. The soundproofing in the walls must have been incredible, but then he remembered where he was and figured that along one of the most expensive streets in the country, the buildings were probably constructed to make sure tenants didn't bother each other.

Danny paused and stared. It was an old-fashioned record store. He hadn't been in one in years. As far as he knew, there weren't any more in either Santa Fe, or Albuquerque. Bins and displays of albums filled the place. Along one wall there were shelves of CDs. In the back were cassettes, and opposite the CDs were DVDs and blue rays. Posters and cutouts of singers, bands, actors and more adorned the place. "Wow."

"Yeah." Moreau agreed. "There are several shops like this scattered around the valley, but with streaming services taking over the world, they get fewer and fewer each year." Glancing around, he headed for the main counter where a brunette man in his mid to late forties sat on a stool looking bored. "But we're not here for that right now."

"Excuse me," Moreau said as they drew close enough to be heard over the music. "Can you help me out?"

"What are you looking for? We have at least one of everything." The clerk straightened, but still managed to look bored, or maybe he was just stoned. It made

Danny wonder if they would be able to get any useful information out of him.

"Can you tell me anything about the talent agency next door?" Moreau asked, leaning on the counter slightly.

"Dude, watch the counter. No leaning." The man jumped off the stool and pointed at the sign saying just that.

Moreau straightened. "Sorry."

"Man, that glass is expensive to replace." The man wiped his hands across the surface like he was trying to check for a crack.

"Okay." Moreau held out his hands as if to get the man to calm down. "Back to my question, do you know anything about the talent agency next door?"

"What do you need to know? Now ain't the time to find anyone there. They keep banker's hours." The clerk returned to his stool.

Danny glanced at Connor's phone, then shook his head. "It's only three."

"East Coast banker's hours." The clerk corrected. "They get in early and leave even earlier. But Kelly says he reps for people in New York as well as here."

"You don't happen to have a phone number for him?" Moreau gestured for Danny to get his pen and pad.

"I think I do. This something important?" The clerk began digging through an old-fashioned Rolodex.

"Just wanting to see about getting a rep here in town," Moreau said, trying to sound like he was an aspiring actor. "I've heard they're the best."

The clerk wrinkled his nose. "I don't know about that. He reps a lot of shifters. I don't know if that qualifies as the best." Pulling out a card from the Rolodex, he quickly read off the number, and Danny jotted it down. "Give him a call, if you don't mind getting fleas during the interview. But you know, he does rep Maria Lopez. There ain't no way a lady that pretty is no shifter."

Danny bit back a snicker. "You're right. We'll give them a call."

"Thanks." Moreau said. "Maybe after we get an interview, we'll stop by and pick something up. Something to celebrate by."

"I got lots of music that's great for party." The clerk grinned. "Come back by anytime."

Moreau pointed toward the door.

Danny didn't need to be told twice. He got out of the shop and took a deep breath. He was getting tired of the amount of shifterphobia they were dealing with.

"Well, if they keep East Coast banker's hours, probably won't do us any good to call them now." Moreau headed down the sidewalk toward the garage.

"So we call them first thing in the morning?" Danny asked.

"It ain't pretty, but it's our only option. Sure, they might pick up, but most likely we'll get a voicemail and won't get a call back for days. That's how these Hollywood types operate. On their own schedule."

A drag queen in bright pink and yellow taffeta skated past them with a huge bouquet of balloons. She made a pirouette halfway up the block, just past the garage, and headed into a store there.

Danny sighed as they started into the garage. "I really think this place is its own universe. You just don't see stuff like this in New Mexico."

Moreau laughed as they headed for the SUV.

Looking out the hotel window at the ocean, Connor sipped a glass of iced tea. It wasn't as good as his grandmother's Southern Peach iced tea, but it was better than a can of soda would've been. Thoughts of what they were dealing with swam in his head. He wished Lisa was there. They needed her observational skills, and there was a chance that the women they intended to interview might be more comfortable with a woman. There were too many factors and there just seemed to be more piling in. If the team was going to get to the bottom of what was going on, he needed them all together.

He set his glass on the table and swiped open Danny's phone. When he pulled up the contact list, he tried to find Lisa's number. It wasn't under Lisa. Why wasn't it under Lisa? He finally found it under Officer Collins. That was stupid. Connor pulled up the listing and changed it to Lady Bird. Maybe Danny would think next time he put a number in the phone and file it properly so Connor could find it. He tapped the listing to make the call.

"Hey, Dawg. What's up?" Lisa sounded tired.

"This is Connor. Danny and I switched phones for a while. I'll explain later." Connor paced in front of the window, hoping his nervous impatience didn't come through his voice. "How are things going with Steve and the divorce?"

"Just peachy." Sarcasm dripped through her tone. "With the big shifter scare that idiot Nelson caused with his press conferences, Steve and his mother have had a heyday making up stories about things I've done." She snorted. "Supposedly, you and I are having an affair, and Danny makes it a threesome. I tried pointing out that you and Danny are gay, so they changed the story to me and Kennedy."

Connor started to pick up the tea and then opted not to for fear of snorting some of it. "What did Kennedy say about that?"

"I didn't tell him. Didn't want to make any trouble between him and his wife. She's a nice lady. Add the fact the judge hearing our case is a total shifterphobe, and I'm coming out with the clothes on my back and nothing else. He even granted Steve full control of the house."

"You didn't get any equity or anything?" Connor had never had a close friend go through a divorce before. He wasn't sure what was fair and what wasn't. It sounded liked it wasn't fair.

"If you call $10,000 out of $50,000 equity on a $250,000 house something. Anyway, you didn't call just to ask about my divorce."

Relieved to have an opportunity to get to a subject he was more comfortable with, Connor answered her question. "We have a case. It appears someone is blackmailing shifters into doing stuff to keep from being exposed. One of them is Montezuma's granddaughter, and another is the boyfriend of Danny's cousin."

"What kind of stuff?" Lisa's tone was suddenly all professional. She'd been a policewoman with the Santa Fe Police Department for nearly ten years before

Connor had stolen her away from Chief Kennedy to be part of Shifter Force.

"Drug smuggling and prostitution."

Lisa whistled. "Do you need me?"

"It might help when we question the women if we had a woman on the team. Also, you're the only one of us who can blend in around here, animalwise. I mean you never know, Danny might be able to walk me around with a diamond collar and leash without raising any eyebrows, but that doesn't help with surveillance. When can you leave Santa Fe?"

"Definitely sounds like you need me." She didn't sound nearly as tired as she had when she answered the phone. "I'll get the first flight I can and will let you know what one. Give Danny a hug from me."

"Will do." He ended the call and took a drink of tea.

He looked back out the window. An uncalled vision hit him.

The sky outside turned dark, and stars fell from the sky into the ocean. Somewhere nearby, a woman's screams turned into a jaguar's yowl.

Connor shook as the vision cleared. The vision was short and unclear, but it came through strong and was more than he'd had in several days. At lease, it was from the future. Lately, all his visions had been of the past. It told him they were running out of time. They had to get moving and find the blackmailers and fast.

"Danny, where are you?" Connor asked through their mental link.

Visions of Stars

"Oh, now you bother talking to me. We're almost there." Danny's reply sounded a little hurt from Connor's earlier disconnect.

Then Connor remembered that he hadn't answered a call from Danny as well. He hoped the call hadn't been too urgent; Danny hadn't left a message.

The sound of footsteps and Danny's scent hit at the same time. It made Connor relax slightly, but also heightened his agitation. He needed someone to talk to face to face.

Rushing to the door, he jerked it open. "Where have you two been? You should have been back at least an hour ago."

"Hello to you too, Cat." Danny waved the printouts from the FBI lab in front of his nose. "We've been doing what you told us to. If you'll calm down, we'll tell you what we have." He handed the papers to Connor. Without so much as a quick hug or kiss, he walked to the small refrigerator and took out a couple of cans of soda. "Here, Moreau. Catch."

"Don't you dare throw that." Moreau dashed over, took the can from him, popped the top on it, and gulped down about half of the contents.

Connor sat on the bed and flipped through the paperwork. "So all of these actors are represented by this Kelly and Associates agency?"

"Looks that way." Danny popped the top on his can of soda and took a long swig. "I say we try to get in to talk to Jerome Kelly, Reggie Winters, Maria Lopez, and Lindy Lui."

"I've already spoken with Reggie. He sent me copies of emails he's been receiving." Connor got to the pages with the email printouts, then pulled out Danny's phone and compared them. "They match up with these sent to Wallace."

Danny's phone rang, the emails disappeared, and Lady Bird appeared, complete with the picture of a female kestrel Connor had found and added while waiting for Danny and Moreau to get back. Connor answered it. "Hello, Lisa." He clicked the speaker button to make it easier for Danny and Moreau to listen in. "Danny and Moreau are here also."

"I'll be at LAX tomorrow morning at 8 a.m. PDT." She gave him the flight and gate numbers. "I'm glad this went on your credit card and not mine. Damn. That's why I always book in advance."

"We'll see you then." He ended the call.

Danny frowned and crossed his arms. "Did you call her in?"

"I thought it might be easier to question the women if we had a woman on the team. Also we need her surveillance skills."

"What about her divorce?" Danny's frown deepened. He obviously wasn't seeing things the same way as Connor.

"It's over. Apparently, according to Steve and his mother, she, you, and I are having three-way sex, and she and Kennedy have also been heating up the sheets."

Moreau snorted soda out of his nose. "Don't they know you two are gay?"

"Didn't seem to make any difference to the shifterphobic judge," Connor continued. "Lisa said she was lucky to get away with the clothes on her back."

Danny sighed and shook his head. "We'll need to cheer her up."

Connor grinned. "I don't think she'll need much cheering up. She's just glad to have things settled." He handed Danny back his phone. "We can switch back now. Did the techs get anything off of my phone?"

"Timmons said the voice was very garbled, but he's going to check it against what they have." Taking his own phone, Danny handed Connor's back.

Sticking the phone in his pocket, Connor headed to the door. "I don't know about you boys, but I'm hungry. All I had was a couple of tacos for lunch."

"That's more than Moreau and I had. I'm ready for a steak and salad." Danny headed into the bathroom.

"Yeah, we didn't even get a chance to nab donuts out of the FBI breakroom," Moreau said. "Why don't we keep things simple and walk to that place a couple blocks away? Traffic is picking up."

Connor held up his hand for quiet. "Say no more. The less traffic we have to deal with the better." Danny was back and they were heading out for dinner. He could explain his adventures over food, and he hoped they had more than just the printouts to go off of. The repeat of the vision with the addition of the scream shook him. It was never good when a vision repeated. They had to act fast.

Danny cut into his steak. It was cooked just the way he liked it.

Connor placed a notepad on the table and scribbled some lines. "Tomorrow, we'll pick up Lisa at the airport. Then we'll see about going to meet Kelly and Lucas. Hopefully they'll be able to put us in touch with

Maria Lopez. With a bit of luck, while we see about some of the other people on the list, Lisa can go interview Maria." He laid the pen on the table and attacked his steak.

Danny had stopped eating and stared at him. Suddenly, his steak tasted like shoe leather, and he placed his knife and fork across his plate. This was not like Connor. They always talked things over before making plans. He didn't like what he was seeing and hearing. Connor was so on edge that he was reverting to his old habits. It made the need for them to talk all the more urgent, but he didn't want to rake Connor over the coals with Moreau there. That wouldn't be fair to Connor, and Moreau had already said he wanted to be on the other side of town when that went down. He figured he could start with something slow and tackle more when they were alone after dinner. "You know, Cat, you told me you'd tell me what you 'saw' at Wallace's apartment later. What was it?"

"I saw the murder." Connor finished his bite of steak. "It was someone Wallace knew enough to turn his back on. I think it was a man, but I'm not totally sure. After they shot Wallace, they picked up something from the dresser and left."

Moreau set his glass on the table. "That rules out suicide then. Think we should tell Lawrence?"

Connor snorted. "He probably wouldn't believe it." His phone rang. "Hello."

"This is Timmons at the FBI. Is this Lupan?" Timmons' voice was loud enough Danny heard it easily across the table. Thankfully Connor didn't put it on speaker so the whole restaurant, that was quickly reaching capacity, could hear.

"This is McGriffin." Connor motioned for Danny to take notes.

Reflexively, Danny pulled out his pad and pen to jot down what Timmons had found.

"I've matched the voice on your phone with the call that reported Wallace's body."

"I'm not surprised. Sounds like we need to interview Mr. Johnson some more."

"Might be a good idea. Oh, and you'll need to get someone else to go digging on John's List for you." Something in Timmons' voice sounded like he was pausing to look over his shoulder. "Mills keeps showing up at my desk for various things and it's not looking good for me doing more work for you guys. Just thought you should know."

Moreau leaned close to the phone as Connor turned it toward him. "Thanks, Timmons. I'll keep you out of this from here on. Don't need you getting on Mills' bad side."

"Knew you'd understand." Timmons sounded relieved. "Okay gotta go."

"Thanks for the help, Timmons." Connor ended the call. "Well, that's enlightening. You guys left out the bit about Mills being on a rampage. Mr. Johnson is apparently the one who reported the murder."

"I think Mills is getting pressure from above his pay grade," Moreau said and he leaned back in his chair. "Odds are, more than a few people on the hill aren't happy that there's now a government sanctioned group of shifters, and he's one of the main signatures on our papers. He's not a total shifterphobe, but he also follows whoever is shouting the loudest at him."

Danny waved off Mills. He'd had enough worry about him earlier. "Timmons' info would explain how Johnson knew about the bloody carpet."

"Moreau, get hold of Lawrence and have him bring Johnson in for questioning." Connor said as he cut another chunk of steak. "Also, have him get a warrant to search Johnson's bedroom and the girlfriend's house for the gun."

"I might have to talk nice to him," Moreau said. "You didn't make the greatest impression, and the whole 'we work alone' bit didn't inspire him to be helpful."

"Then what are we going to do? Just because we're a federal organization doesn't mean we can go waltzing into somewhere without a warrant." Connor paused and chewed his meat thoughtfully.

"Maybe if Moreau tells Lawrence you're not going to be the one serving the warrant, it'll go easier." Danny suggested, a bit relieved that the subject of Connor's behavior was being broached, and he might not have to follow up with a more in-depth talk later.

Connor rolled his eyes. "But I need to be there to get psychic readings. I can't do that through our link."

"And Lawrence isn't going to arrest anyone based on a reading," Moreau countered. "What if we let Perkins serve the warrants? He's human, so is Johnson, and probably Johnson's girlfriend. We approach it that way, it'll go over better."

"But I get to come along." Connor almost sounded like a petulant child.

"As long as you're on your best behavior," Moreau agreed. He looked at Danny and mouthed, 'you owe me' "No scaring the humans."

Danny let out the breath he hadn't realized he was holding when Connor nodded.

"I'll do my best not to scare, or traumatize the humans, even if Johnson did kill Wallace."

As they finished their meal with only light discussion about the traffic they'd seen and how Danny had been just blocks from the Hollywood Walk of Fame he hadn't stopped to see any of the stars, Danny hoped Connor would be able to stick to his word and behave himself. There was still something off about Connor, and Danny wasn't sure what it was, or how to fix it.

Chapter 5

As Connor pulled up in front of the terminal, Lisa was already standing on the sidewalk tapping her foot. It had taken them twenty more minutes than he'd figured to navigate the LA traffic and reach the airport. He was getting really tired of all the humans clogging the highways.

Before Connor could do more than bring the Jeep to a stop, Danny jumped out. "Here, let me get that." He picked up her suitcase and slipped it behind the back seat.

"At least one of you guys still has some chivalry left in you." She sounded tired.

"But always." Danny gave her a short, playful bow, then offered his hand to help her into the back seat next to Moreau.

She laughed weakly as Danny slid into the front passenger seat.

"What took you guys so long?" Lisa asked once she had her seatbelt fastened. "My plane landed half an hour ago."

Connor turned toward her. "Sorry, Lady Bird. I'm still not used to the traffic in this town." Behind them, a car honked, but Connor ignored them.

"What's the plan besides breakfast? I'm starved. All they serve on planes anymore is cookies."

Moreau leaned forward. "Cat, I saw a diner a couple exits back. Small place. Probably be able to at least get some bacon and eggs."

Danny chuckled. "Most places can at least cook decent bacon and eggs."

Lisa smiled. "As long as they cook the bacon well done."

Connor steered the Jeep out into a lane of traffic and abruptly came to a stop in the bumper to bumper line of cars waiting to get on the highway. He hissed. "I hate this town. Let's get this case over with so we can go home."

"That's fine for you guys," Moreau muttered. "At least you have a home to go to."

The traffic finally let up as they made it onto the freeway, but it was more than Connor was completely comfortable with, and he let the conversation in the back go with only a little input. He kept waiting for the small pastel blue Toyota in front of them to slam on its brakes and he'd have to be right on top of his, or slam into them. With his visions on the fritz, he wasn't totally sure he'd get a psychic warning in the case of something like that.

Lisa sighed, sounding like she was ready to hear someone else's problems for a little while. "What do you mean?"

"I've worked for the FBI for so long that I've never been in one place long enough to establish a home base." Moreau sounded a bit sad. "Never really had close friends, beyond Simone and her wife. Since her death, Becky's seemed distant every time I've gone by.

She knew I was a shifter, so I don't think it's that. I think she blames the job for losing Simone. Can't say as I blame her."

"What about your family?" Lisa asked.

"My folks are both dead. My sister and brother are in different parts of the world, the last I heard. Don't even know where they are." He let out a low huff. "The last thing my sister said to me was that she and her husband were going to find somewhere they felt safe raising a family. She wanted them to be able to be shifters and not have to hide. There are a few places like that in the world, but not many."

As he passed a pair of large leather babes on Harleys, Connor wondered where that would be. A lot of the more undeveloped countries had more backwards ways of thinking, although many shifters headed for places where their animal sides could blend in, like jungles and deserts, where the populations were low and natural cover high. The more domestic shifters were heading to European countries like Norway and Denmark that had always been years ahead of the rest of the western world in progressive thinking.

Lisa patted his knee. "Don't worry. We'll take care of you, won't we, guys?" *"You'd better agree, Cat. After all, he's one of us, now."* There was a feral, dangerous note to Lisa's mental voice that spoke volumes for her taking Moreau under her wing like a protective mother eagle.

"This exit, Cat," Moreau leaned forward and pointed over Connor's shoulder toward the next off ramp.

"Hope you like the mountains, Moreau," Connor said, not willing to argue with Lisa as he spotted a sign for a diner that looked like a train car and headed toward it. "I know a cabin you can get outside of Jemez. Not much nightlife, but peace and quiet."

Lisa chuckled. "Peace and quiet until the Cat finds a body."

Connor pulled into an empty parking space in front of the diner. It was surprisingly busy with so many of the locals seeming to be in a rush to get to their jobs. If it attracted so much tourist traffic, it must be a pretty decent place.

Danny moved his empty plate to the side, hoping the attentive waiter would come by and collect it soon so he'd have more table space, and pulled a folder out of his new briefcase. "With this thing, I'm beginning to feel like a real special agent." Spreading the papers, printouts, and photos, he chose the set of scene photos from David Wallace's apartment and handed them to Lisa. "Here's what we know so far." He told her about the dead raccoon and the people harassing Reggie. A couple of times, Moreau and Connor would throw in things in spots where Danny's account was lacking details. "We have an appointment with this Jerome Kelly right after lunch," Danny finished up. "Hopefully, he can shed some light on things."

"We need an appointment with Maria Lopez," Connor said. "She's Montezuma's granddaughter."

It seemed to Danny that Connor was trying to be a little less demanding since getting out of bed than he had been. More like himself.

Lisa looked up from the photos. "I suppose he's concerned about her in all this?"

"Diego, the jaguar Danny met at the border paid us a visit." Connor lifted his cup and nodded to the waiter. "Told us Montezuma was collecting on the debt we owe him."

The waiter refilled their cups and took their empty plates. "Are you guys visiting Los Angeles?"

Moreau smiled at him. "You might say that."

"Well, there're some maps by the register that will tell you some of the places you should see." He laid their check on the table, turned, and walked away.

Connor picked up the check. "I take it that's our cue to vacate the table since people are waiting." He stood and sauntered toward the register.

"Be right there, Cat. I need to powder my nose." Lisa walked toward the ladies' room.

Danny finished off his coffee and looked at Moreau across the table. "Is it just me, or do you have the feeling the quiet part of our day is done, at least for a little while?"

Moreau shrugged. "Hard to tell with you guys. Are Connor's powers rubbing off on you?"

"Oh, god, I hope not." Danny purposely shuddered. He knew what a torment his gifts were to Connor, he didn't want to have any of them impacting him. He was just as happy running off his policewolf instincts.

Setting his coffee cup down for the final time, Danny headed toward the counter where Connor was slipping his wallet back into his pocket and heading toward the door. Connor put his hand on the door to open it as the lady's room burst open and someone came running out. She was moving faster than a human.

It looked like Connor tried to sidestep, but the woman brushed past him. He got the faraway look that meant he was having a vision.

Lisa came behind her. *"Cat, that girl's in trouble, and she's some kind of cat shifter."* She was loud enough for all them to hear her as she followed Lindy.

Connor grabbed for her arm. *"We know. We've met her. Dawg, you and Lady Bird take after her. You can blend in. Moreau and I will follow in the Jeep."*

Lisa dodged Connor and slipped out of the door before it could close. Even in her human form she was quicker and more agile than a human would've been. She shifted before she'd taken two steps down the sidewalk. Her dress made a pile of cloth on the concrete with her purse on top of it.

Danny made it out the door as Connor held it open. He wanted to ask about the vision but didn't think they had time. "We're on this, Cat. You and Moreau keep our appointment. We'll either find you or call you to pick us up."

"Hurry up Danny, she just shifted and she's moving fast." Lisa said through the link.

Without a thought, Danny dropped his human form and found himself on four legs. He yelped as his paws hit the hot pavement of the parking lot. After two steps, he forced himself to ignore the pain and keep running.

"Be careful, you two," Connor called in Danny's thoughts. *"The vision I had when she touched me isn't good."*

"Then go find the bad guys, and we'll save the victim." Danny caught the scent of cat going down the alley at the end of the dinner. He ran as fast as he could on burning paws. He had to do something.

The dirt alley was cooler on Danny's paws than the pavement in the parking lot had been. He was thankful it was just late morning and not midafternoon. He doubted he could've endured that level of heat. There were shouts fading in the distance, and it sounded like Connor peeling out in the Jeep, but Danny kept running. It felt good to be on a trail and trying to do something more productive than just paperwork.

"Danny, she turned down another alley, but I've lost her," Lisa said from above a building a block down. *"There's too much garbage for me to get a clear field of view."*

"Then I get to dig through it." Danny didn't like the idea of barreling through human garbage in search of Lindy, but he wanted to find her, particularly if Connor had seen a bad outcome for her in a vision.

"I'll keep a watch from up here." A flash of brown told Danny Lisa had landed on the building overlooking the alley.

"Sounds good." Danny wrinkled his nose as he entered the alley. There was an oriental restaurant that dumped their garbage in the dumpsters lining the space. Stale soy sauce smelled worse than stale beer. All the garbage made it hard to follow Lindy's scent, no matter how fresh. It made him wonder if she might've recognized Connor and freaked out worse than when she had been in the bathroom.

"Any idea what set her running?" Danny paced from one dumpster to another.

"She was on the phone with someone. I figure it was a guy the way she was talking and crying. She didn't want to do something. Kept going on and on

about 'no. I'm done.' 'I don't care. I'm leaving town anyway.' 'This isn't working.'"

"*Yeah, sounds like she was talking to our perp.*" Danny reached through the link with Connor, thankful it worked at a greater distance than his pack link with Cortez. "*Connor. Was there a phone this time with Lindy's clothes?*" Sometimes dealing with shifters who weren't magically inclined to shift with their clothes was handy.

"*No.*" Moreau replied. "*Sorry, Connor just asked me to check the clutch she dropped and it's not there.*"

"*Then where is it?*" Danny made it to the end of the alley and didn't scent Lindy leaving the area. He turned back and started inspecting each dumpster individually. The one for the leather store was nearly as irritating as the oriental food place, and he didn't want to think about everything that was is in the bin behind the adult toy store.

"*Although I didn't see her throw it in there, I did see a trash can near the door of the café,*" Connor spoke up. "*If you don't find her, circle back there and check it out.*"

"*Yeah, more garbage.*" Danny muttered just loud enough to make sure everyone heard him.

"*And if Connor grabbed my stuff, you're going to be the only one with thumbs,*" Lisa piped in.

"*And we did,*" Connor replied. "*How do these people ever get anywhere on time? Dawg, you and Lady Bird handle this. I need to concentrate on my driving before I start treating these little economy cars like boulders.*"

"*Will do.*" Danny dropped out of Connor's mind and focused on trying to scent Lindy Lui. It was easier when there weren't three different voices in his head. He just hoped he and Lisa could find her before Connor's vision came to pass. With Connor's gift acting up for some reason, it was hard to say if they had a chance or not. He had to keep reminding himself that the future was mutable and they always had an opportunity to change everything Connor saw. Nothing was set in stone.

Chapter 6

Connor strode into the offices of Kelly and Associates and approached the receptionist. He did his best to ignore the brown stains on the dark carpet. If they were right about Kelly and Lucas, he probably didn't really want to know what they were from. "We're here to see Jerome Kelly and Damon Lucas."

"Do you have an appointment?" The woman glanced from Connor to Moreau and didn't seem impressed by either of them.

Leaning on the glass counter, Connor pulled his badge out of his pocket and showed it to her. "We do. Name's McGriffin."

The receptionist glanced at the tablet computer sitting on the counter. It was the most modern thing in the office. She scrolled down slightly, then nodded. "I'll tell Mr. Kelly you're here. He's expecting you. Mr. Lucas is out to lunch."

"Do you know where he went to lunch?"

She named a deli a couple of blocks away.

"If he's not back by the time we get done, we'll head over there. Unless you'd be so kind as to call him and let him know we're here." Connor put as much charm in his voice as possible, then wondered if maybe he shouldn't have let Lisa talk to her, woman to woman.

"Let me see if I can reach him." The receptionist picked up a cell phone and tapped it several times.

In an office just off the main one a phone started ringing.

With a frown and a sigh, the receptionist ended her call and laid her phone on the desk. The other phone stopped ringing. "Looks like he left his phone here. He does that when he wants to have a quiet lunch without all the clients calling him."

"I understand." Connor looked toward the office and wondered if either he or Moreau would have the opportunity to slip in there and grab the phone. It would be a fast way to find out if Lucas was their guy.

The receptionist's phone beeped and she glanced down at it before announcing, "Mr. Kelly will see you. His office is on the second floor." She motioned to the elevator.

Connor punched the button for the second floor. Various scents whirled around him, but the thing that hit him strongest was the orange cleaning smell. Someone was going out of their way to keep the place smelling better than it looked, or they were trying to cover something up.

When the elevator opened, it was a standard, nice elevator. Not overly dirty, and not looking like it came out of the last decade. As the door closed, the orange scent continued into the enclosed space making it hard to smell anything else. Maybe that was the reason for it.

The door opened into an opulent room carpeted in a lush green that cushioned their feet. It was a vast difference from the lobby and made Connor wonder if the firm handled different levels of clients and only the really important ones, or maybe the human ones were allowed on the second floor. The orange smell ended, and other than a few stray animal scents, everything smelled perfectly human. Pictures of elegantly dressed men and beautiful women encircled the room at eye level. Connor recognized several stars, both old-time and current.

A buxom blonde sat behind a desk facing the elevator. "May I help you?" She asked like the previous receptionist hadn't notified her of their impending arrival.

"I'm Agent McGriffin and this is Agent Moreau. We have an appointment with Mr. Kelly." Connor stepped closer to the desk and showed his badge while Moreau walked over to the pictures.

The blonde clicked a button on the phone in front of her. "Agents McGriffin and Moreau to see you." She listened for a second. Through her headphone, the male voice was garbled and difficult for even Connor's sensitive hearing to make out. "Yes, Sir. I saw their badges, but I don't recognize the agency."

After taping the phone, she motioned toward a door. "Go on in. He's expecting you."

The door to another room opened.

As Connor approached the door, the hair on the back of his neck tingled. Something was not quite right. If his gift was working right, he should be able to tell what was off, but beyond the tingle, nothing jumped out at him.

A stocky man of somewhere around sixty with roughly dyed black hair that didn't match his gray eyebrows, sat behind the desk. Smoke drifted up from a cigar in his hand. He took a drag from the cigar, blew the smoke toward Connor, and propped his elbow on the arm of his chair. "What can I do for you?"

Connor snorted the smell of the cigar out of his nose as he gestured Moreau toward a chair, and then sat facing the man. He held out his badge. "We're here about the murder of David Wallace. I understand he was represented by your agency."

"Murder." Kelly dropped his arm, and his eyes widened. "I thought the police said he committed suicide." He reached for Connor's badge and glanced over it.

"They're still trying to figure out how someone can commit suicide without a gun being found." Connor hoped that by revealing a bit more than was common public knowledge, Kelly might trip up on something that could help tie him or someone he knew to the murder. "Our agency is calling it a murder given Wallace's history of drug dealing."

"Drugs? I didn't know Dave was into drugs. He never showed any signs of being high." He tapped the cigar on the edge of an ashtray on the desk. "Anyway, just what is your agency? I've never heard of the Shifter Force. Are you like the FBI?"

Connor identified the scent of the cigar as a Cuban brand. "We're sanctioned by the FBI. We specialize in crimes involving shifters."

"Did you have something to do with that deal a couple of weeks ago with the condor shifters kidnapping kids?" Kelly returned the badge to Connor before leaning back in his chair. "That was some light show on the beach the night that went down."

"We're the ones who brought them down, yes," Moreau said. *"Cat, what's the matter? You're squirming like a worm on a hook."*

"Don't know. Something's not right here. Plus, I don't like cigars. They block too much of my sense of smell. I don't know about you, but it's way too strong. Surprised we didn't pick up on it in the entry way."

"So, Mr. Kelly, were you aware that Wallace was a shifter?"

He lifted the cigar to his mouth and took a puff. "Yeah. I knew. I have a lot of shifter clients." He stood, walked over to the row of pictures, and pointed to a couple from several years before. "Most people don't realize how many shifters there are in the movies." He returned to his chair. "Fans say they want to know everything about their idols, but they really don't. Susie Smith in Pocatello wants to dream about the possibility of meeting a movie star and marrying him. She doesn't want to know he isn't interested in women. Same with shifters. Fans don't want to know they aren't really human."

Connor bristled at his words. "I understand you also represent Maria Lopez, Lindy Lui, and Reggie Winters."

"Yeah. What about them?" He snuffed out his cigar.

"We have reason to believe they're in trouble. We've already spoken with Mr. Winters and Ms. Lui, but we'd like to talk to Ms. Lopez. Is there a way you can arrange that?"

Kelly pick up the phone. "Jessie, get me Maria Lopez on the phone." He laid the phone down. "I'm not sure she'll see you."

Connor quirked an eyebrow and smiled. "Tell her Montezuma sent us."

"Who's that?" Kelly pulled out another cigar. "She'll know the name."

The phone rang. Setting the new cigar on the edge of the desk, Kelly picked it up. "Good afternoon, Maria. There are some people here who need to speak with you. They said to tell you Montezuma sent them." He held the phone away from his ear as a loud female voice erupted in Spanish on the other end.

Connor was unable to understand the tirade. *"Do you understand Spanish, Moreau?"*

The ring-tailed cat smirked. "Enough to know she's not very happy. I took Spanish in high school, but they didn't teach us those words. I always let Simone translate for me when I didn't understand, her wife was Spanish."

"I know you've got that photo shoot this afternoon and the party tonight. How about if I send them around in the morning?"—another round of loud Spanish expletives—Tell you what. Come here about eleven, and I'll order in brunch." He replaced the receiver on the phone. "You heard the arrangement. Eleven tomorrow, brunch here. Is there anything you can't eat? I mean are either of you vegetarian or anything?"

"I was hoping to get this over with today, but tomorrow will do. No diet restrictions." Connor stood and waited for Moreau to do the same before heading toward the door. He paused and turned back to Kelly. "I just hope the delay doesn't cost anyone their life." Then Connor turned and walked toward the elevator.

As they entered the lifts, Moreau chuckled. "Okay, were you trying to show your acting chops and get a job?"

Connor frowned as the elevator doors closed and he tapped the button for the first floor. "No. I was trying to make a point."

"Good job. I guess we're going to try to find Lucas now?" Moreau stood in the center of the elevator.

"Of course." Connor wished Danny was there. Danny knew better than to ask so many questions. There hadn't been any communication from him or Lisa in a while, but he knew if there was a problem, he'd know about it.

Danny fumed as he dug through another pile of trash. He knew cats had senses of smell nearly as acute as wolves. How could Lindy handle the stench in the alley, let alone crawling around in the garbage itself?

"Dawg, I might have something," Lisa's voice cut through his internal grumblings.

"What've you got?" Danny looked up to where Lisa perched on the edge of the northern building.

She flew down toward the pile of garbage Danny had been working through. *"Can't really tell, but there looks to be some kind of small passage against the wall over here. There's a similar pattern here, and then along the wall between the next dumpster."*

Danny had to sit up on his hindquarters to see what she was talking about. A piece of plywood was there, it leaned almost like it was just tossed there, but the garbage hid most of it. From what he could tell, it ran from behind one dumpster to the next. It was like someone, or something had created a safe escape route for small shifters, or rat and cats. *"I wish Moreau was here, he might fit down there."*

"But why go to the trouble of putting it there?" Lisa returned to her gutter-edge perch.

Danny lowered himself back to his front legs. *"No clue. We don't really know any of the shifter community here in LA. Maybe they need to make clean escapes on a regular basis and they have these little roadways so they can move all over the place."*

"And it might be how some of them are moving drugs without the human authorities knowing," Lisa suggested. *"There are lots of other things small shifters could be doing unobserved if they wanted to."*

"So do we follow the covered areas, or do we head toward Hollywood to find Connor?" Danny closed his eyes and got the impression Connor was in an elevator somewhere.

"We're supposed to check the garbage at the cafe for Lindy's phone." Lisa scanned the sky. *"Why don't we do that real quick, then head north?"*

"Okay." Danny shifted to human and looked around. *"Guess having hands for that job will be easier."*

Lisa nodded and took to wing. *"Definitely."*

The pavement wasn't as uncomfortably hot walking across it in his boots as it had been on his bare paws, it was still hot, just not scorching. He really wondered how feral cats, dogs and coyotes survived in Southern California during the summer.

The parking lot was nearly empty, and Danny pulled out his phone to check the time. It was nearly noon. The place should've been filling up. Maybe their lunch wasn't as good as their breakfast and the locals knew it.

When Danny reached into it, the garbage can right outside the door was mostly empty. He frowned. "I guess they've cleaned up while things were slow."

Lisa was up on a light pole in the middle of the parking lot. *"You could go check their dumpster around back."*

The idea of digging through bags of half-eaten breakfasts and cigarette butts made Danny's stomach churn. He shook his head. "Why don't we just write this off as a wild cat chase and head toward the others?"

"Might not be a bad idea. How are we getting there?"

"Let me use my taxi app and I think I can get me to the same block they're in. Think you can keep up with us?" Danny pulled out his phone and brought up the app. He hadn't used it much since Connor normally drove everywhere, but Moreau swore by it when he was working cases in town and he didn't want to risk perps spotting his car.

"Probably, if traffic is as bad as normal, or maybe I can try homing in on Connor. The group link makes it easier for us to find each other. That way I can fly a straight line, acting more like a wild bird, and less like a shifter following a car, just in case anyone's watching us."

"Good idea." Danny put his info into the phone as Lisa took to wing.

"If you need anything holler." Lisa made a lazy circle around his head before heading north. *"See you in Hollywood."*

"*Yep.*" Danny waved her off, then hoped no one had seen him. He didn't want to let other people think he might've been talking to a bird shifter. It was silly since he'd been walking around the parking lot for a while, just talking to himself, but in the days of Bluetooth headsets, people going on when there wasn't anyone else around wasn't unheard of, it was commonplace.

It would've been nice to actually catch Lindy and find a lead on the person blackmailing the shifters. They needed a break before another shifter died. He felt like all he and Lisa had done was waste time digging through garbage, and he hoped Connor and Moreau had made progress with the talent agency.

Chapter 7

Connor fumed as he and Moreau walked toward the deli. "I wonder if Lucas thought he was being smart by not being in the office when we arrived. But are we supposed to walk into the deli and announce we're here to see Damon Lucas about the murder of David Wallace? I'm not opposed to doing that."

"Calm down, Cat." Moreau held up his phone and showed Danny a Facebook page with a photo. "Sometimes, FBI training comes in handy."

Lucas looked like a teenager with a smooth face, and a sandy-blond receding hairline was the only thing that belied the illusion. Connor didn't understand what it was with computer whiz-kids who looked like they shouldn't even be out of high school.

Scanning the patrons of the deli, Connor spotted the man at a table with two other men and walked over. He laid his badge on the table in front of Lucas. "We need to talk to you about David Wallace."

Lucas swallowed what was in his mouth. "Yeah? I heard he offed himself."

Connor pulled an empty chair to the table and straddled it. "That remains to be proven. It's kind of hard to shoot yourself if there isn't a gun present."

"Hey, look!" Lucas' eyes widened. "I don't know anything about that."

Moreau placed his hand on the shoulder of one of the men who started to rise. "Just stay where you are."

The man, who when Connor really looked at him, was the guy who'd taken his shirt off at the beach the previous day, glared at Moreau, but wisely didn't try to move away. "Don't involve me. I didn't even know Wallace."

"We still may have some questions for you. Just stay put." Moreau looked at the third man and included him in the warning.

Connor tilted his head and looked at Lucas. "You said you don't know anything about Wallace's death, but maybe you know something about his trips to Mexico."

Lucas huffed and crossed his arms. "You must not be from around here. Everyone goes to Mexico all the time. Open borders and all that. What makes you think I know anything about Wallace's trips down there? Maybe he's got himself a hot little piece he likes to tap from time to time."

Connor smiled slightly and kept his gaze on Lucas. He hoped he looked predatory enough to be scary. "Just the fact that some text messages were traced to pre-paid phones you purchased."

Lucas started squirming "You can't prove that!" He glanced to the two men at the table with him. The one from the beach was frowning heavily.

Letting his smile broaden, Connor moved in for the kill, hoping Lucas wasn't as tech-savvy as he appeared. "We have video from the Fast Shop where you bought them. After getting the serial numbers, we traced texts to Wallace and also to Lindy Lui."

Sweat glistened on his forehead as Lucas held up his hands with the palms toward Connor. "Look, man. I was just following orders."

"Whose orders?" Connor leaned in across the table.

"Lucas, you dumb fuck." Shirtless from the beach elbowed Moreau and lunged across the table. The other man reached inside his jacket.

Connor wasn't expecting the vision that hit him. *Everything shifted slightly. Moreau lay dead on the café floor and fire burned in Connor's arm. Lucas was also dead. Blood dripped from his forehead. Somewhere in the distance sirens rang out. People were screaming.*

He shook off the vision and lunged across the table at the guy pulling out his gun. Not caring that he was in public, he shifted, hoping it was going to be enough to save Moreau, and maybe Lucas.

The man with the gun's eyes widened as Connor came at him. His gun went off before it cleared his pocket. He yelped but pulled it free.

The glass of the café's front window exploded. Seconds later several more shots sounded from out in the street as Connor knocked the man down, cracking his head on the corner of the table next to theirs.

Moreau had Shirtless by the shoulder, as a red stain spread across the man's shirt. With a shudder, Moreau let him drop to the floor and glanced at his own chest that had a similar discoloration. "Shit. I hate getting shot."

"Cat, what's wrong?" Danny's voice rang in Connor's head.

"Drive by, I think." Connor glanced where Lucas had been, but the man was gone. He shifted back to human. *"Moreau got hit."* "Can you shift?"

"Yeah." A look of concentration crossed Moreau's features, and his face shrank in and grew longer. His human body fell away and a ring-tailed cat stood on the pile of Moreau's clothes.

"I'm still a few minutes away," Danny sounded frantic. *"You okay?"*

"Sure. I think you'd know it if I wasn't."

The ring-tailed cat wrinkled his nose at Connor, then started changing back to human.

In the distance sirens wailed.

"What did the car that did the drive-by look like?" Lisa demanded. *"I can see the café you're at. But there're lots of cars speeding away."*

Connor shook his head as he knelt down to pick up Moreau's shirt so he could cover his nakedness before some over enthusiastic cop tried to ticket him for indecent exposure. *"No idea, Lisa. We were focusing on Lucas and his buddies at the time. Lucas ran off. He's probably going to disappear on us, but the idea that the agency knows something about this is a fact. They're definitely up to something."*

Moreau shook himself as he took the shirt Connor was offering him. "Man, I hate having to do back to back shifts. Takes a lot out of me." He glanced at his chest as he buttoned his shirt. "At least they weren't using silver."

"Right." Connor picked up the gun the man had shot himself with and sniffed. "Unlike this guy. He was ready for shifters."

Putting the gun back on the floor, Connor waited for the police to get there and start the messy process of cleaning up from the killings. It was going to slow them down a couple of hours at least, even if Moreau could pull a few strings and get things moving. He didn't think the folks pulling the drive-by were anything more than hired muscle, but the question became, who had hired them, and pointed their guns toward Connor and Moreau? Once again, they'd stumbled into something bigger than they'd planned. He was really starting to miss the quiet simple cases he used to work, where there was just one perp and he just had to figure that out and go on to the next case. Child-molesting priests didn't tend to shoot at people.

At least his psychic powers were working well enough to give him a slight warning when he really needed it. He wanted to work that out too. It would make his life a lot easier, if he knew what was coming.

Even knowing Connor was okay, didn't help curb the urge to go running to him. By the time Danny's call-a-cab ride dropped him off at the record store he and Moreau had been in the previous day, the local authorities were swarming over the area.

"Man, this is as close as I can get you," his driver said. "I need to make a major detour to pick up my next fare three blocks down."

"This'll work." Danny took out his phone and looked at the app. He paid the bill and gave the man a generous tip.

"Thanks. Hope your day goes okay."

"We'll see." Danny slipped out of the cab and onto the curb.

The cab pulled away and turned the corner before getting to where the police had things blocked off. Danny glanced down the street and spotted the Jeep across the street from Kelly and Associates.

Lisa landed on top of the Jeep and stared at Danny. *"Well, if I can get dressed, maybe we can be of some help."*

"Oh, yeah." Danny hurried across the street and pulled out his keys. "Sorry."

He opened the door and Lisa flew into the SUV. He closed the door and leaned against it to give her a bit of privacy.

A minute later, she was opening the door. "You know this is getting messed up. We can't even get started on getting leads in this case, can we?"

Danny shook his head as she stepped out of the Jeep. "Nope. Well, there are a few, but somehow I don't think this one—" He gestured to the agency across the street "—is going to be easier to follow now. If they are our bad guys, they might be harder to chase down."

Lisa ran her hands down her dress. "Unless they think they're ahead of us." She frowned. "I think I'm going to have to give Connor, or Moreau, or both a quick lesson on folding women's dresses. Way too many wrinkles. This thing looks like I dropped it beside a bed and a cat nested in it while I was having a round of afternoon delight."

Danny chuckled. "Probably Connor. You know how those of us who can shift clothed can be."

"Never inconvenienced, so you don't think about it." She shook her hands, then reached back into the Jeep for her purse and shoes. "Yeah, I get it."

"Cat, what can we do out here?" Danny asked as more police vehicles pulled up. He counted at least three agencies there, none of them were folks they'd dealt with to that point. There was also a growing number of people lining the street across the way from the café.

"Keep your eyes open," Connor replied. *"If this was more than just a random drive-by, our perps might be in the crowd of looky-loos. Moreau's doing a great job handling things, but we're still going to have to go to Hollywood PD and fill out a report, unless the FBI can get us off the hook."*

"The way Mills feels about us, and you in particular, don't count on it." Danny really wished Connor didn't rub so many people the wrong way, it would make working with other agencies so much easier. He was getting tired of explaining that to Connor. Just because he could see the future, it didn't mean he was always right, or that he didn't have to work with others.

"You don't think it would help if Moreau told him that this delay might mean more people die?" The level of naiveté in Connor's tone reminded Danny that Connor just didn't get what they were all trying to tell him. He wondered what it was going to take for them to drive that point home.

"At this point, I don't think Mills cares," Moreau added, breaking his silence in the conversation. *"He might be waiting for us to fail, I don't know. I think a lot of folks are hoping the great and powerful Connor*

McGriffin will end up with egg on his face when the curtain is pulled back."

"Not going to happen," Connor replied. *"Okay, let's talk to these folks some more and try to get out of here and back on the trail."*

Danny doubted they were going to be on the trail any time soon. Down the street, Connor and Moreau were escorted into police cars and headed away.

"Come on Lisa, let's follow." Danny hurried around the Jeep and opened the driver's side door. He made sure to adjust the seat. Connor was just taller than he was and would complain if Danny forgot to put it back, but particularly with using the clutch, it was necessary.

"We're in for a long day, aren't we?" Lisa buckled her seatbelt.

"Probably." He started the car. "Hey, do you know if Connor got with Larea at the Santa Fe office to follow up on John's List?"

"Might be worth checking with her." Lisa pulled out her phone. "Or you could ask Connor."

"He's got his mind on other things right now." Danny pulled the Jeep out into traffic, but due to the police barricade a short distance away, he had to turn the way his cab driver did. Luckily, due to his link with Connor, he had no fear of losing track of him, unless something nefarious happened.

"Hey, Larea, Lisa here, any chance you've found out anything about John's List?" Lisa held the phone a little away from her head.

Danny was thankful for the move since it didn't muffle the response the way it might've if she'd had the phone against her skin.

"Hey, Lisa. Yeah, I called and left Connor a message a little while ago, but he hasn't called me back."

"Probably due to dealing with the Hollywood PD because he was in a café during a drive-by."

"Really? Wow, a real Hollywood drive-by. How cool is that?"

Since he'd never met Larea when he'd been in the Santa Fe PD, Danny could only guess what she looked like, but she sounded young and perky. During the case with the missing kids, she'd always been ready to help in any way they needed her to.

"Connor's not too happy about it," Lisa relayed. "It's slowing down our investigation here. They've hauled Connor in to fill out a statement."

"Ooooh. I bet he's not happy about that. Connor hates doing stuff like that. If we ever didn't just take his word, he got mad."

"Right. We're trying to work on him about that. So, what about the website."

There was a bit of clicking from a keyboard in the background. "Yeah, about that. I got with Kennedy and managed to get a warrant for the records, since it's interstate we had to go through the federal judge to make that happen, but we got access a couple of hours ago. We're trying to narrow things down, but it might take a couple of days. I didn't realize that shifter sex workers were in such high demand."

"High demand?" Danny asked as they stopped for a red light he had nearly run. The car behind him honked loudly as the driver rolled down his window and flipped Danny off. With a frown, he stopped watching through Connor's eyes. He needed to focus on Larea and his driving.

"Yeah, almost half of the listings on the site are for shifters across the world who are willing to sleep with humans. Nearly sixty percent of the requests for sex are from humans wanting a first time with a shifter. I didn't know getting your shifter cherry popped was even a thing."

As the light turned green and Danny pulled forward, he glanced at Lisa with raised eyebrows. "News to us too. I guess there's all sorts of different kinks out there."

"And you've sent me to the kinkiest site I've ever seen. There's even pictures."

Lisa almost dropped her phone as she waved her hands in negative. "Nope. Please don't."

"Alright, this time, but just remember I've got them and if I need leverage on you guys they might come out again." Larea chuckled. "Okay. But seriously, it's going to take a while to go through all this. I'm trying to narrow things down based on the location, time, and date Connor gave me, but even then, there's a lot going on. Oh, and I thought you might like to know, there are people offering seven figures to sleep with a female jaguar out there."

Danny whistled as they came to a stop again. "Seven figures? That's some serious cash. See if we can follow that up if there are any responses."

"Already set up a script to monitor that," Larea said. "Figured it might prove useful."

"Particularly if the jaguar in question turns out to be Maria Lopez," Danny said as he turned right.

"The movie star?" Larea replied. "Wow."

"She's also the granddaughter of Montezuma," Lisa added.

It was Larea's turn to whistle. "Okay, that gets serious. I wonder if the bad guys know her connections."

"No clue." Lisa pointed toward a building that said Hollywood Police Department on the side.

Danny had to circle the block to try to find a parking spot.

"Alright. We don't need him getting mad at us. I'll stay on top of this and let you know when I get done sorting through things." There were more clicks on Larea's side of things. "Oh, and Kennedy wanted to let Connor know that he needs to stop pissing off the locals. Kennedy was having a bad day when he had to field a call from someone out there."

"Sounds right," Danny muttered as he settled the Jeep into a spot between a Rolls Royce and a Porsche. "I'll be sure to pass that along."

"Thanks. Okay. I do better not multi-tasking," Larea said. "Should I call you, Lisa, or Connor?"

"Call me," Lisa replied. "It'll be easier."

"Will do. Enjoy sunny California." Larea hung up.

Lisa sighed heavily as she put her phone back in her purse. "Kennedy must've been having a really bad day to pass that along through Larea. He normally wants to fuss at people himself."

Danny turned off the Jeep and rolled down the window, wondering how long they were going to be parked there waiting on Connor and Moreau. "Yeah. Guess we're going to be having another talk with Connor, soon." He wasn't looking forward to that in the least.

Connor wasn't happy as he and Moreau walked out of the Hollywood PD. He hated answering endless questions about something he was only trying to piece together himself. He'd had to offer to cut the Hollywood PD in on things to get them released. They were getting too many fingers in his pie.

As they approached the Jeep, Danny and Lisa got out and scrambled around to get in their customary seats. Danny took a second and adjusted the driver's seat back. He gave Connor a wide welcoming smile, that Connor didn't feel like returning. After a moment, Danny walked around the Jeep to the passenger's side.

When Connor slid into his seat it felt much better than the hard chairs the police department had kept them sitting in all afternoon. "We need to go over what we found out from Kelly and Lucas. Let's get something to drink before we go back to the hotel."

Danny fastened his seat belt. "I think you need to talk to Lawrence about what you *saw* at Wallace's apartment."

"And whatever you *saw* about Lindy when she brushed past you at the diner this morning," Lisa said. "I hate that we weren't able to catch her."

"Danny's right," Moreau said. "We need to touch base with Lawrence."

After spending several hours at the Hollywood PD, Connor wasn't in the mood for more stale coffee, hard chairs, and bad attitudes, but he started the Jeep and drove to the Venice Beach police station.

Chapter 8

As they walked into his office, Captain Lawrence rose from his chair and glared at them. "Moreau, I thought I told you to keep him away from me." He pointed at Connor.

It was all Connor could do to hold his tongue. But since the words were directed at Moreau, he opted to let his teammate handle the situation, at least until he needed to give his input. Thinking back, Moreau had said something about Lawrence not being happy with him. But he was used to people in authority being uncomfortable with him, until he proved to them he had useful gifts.

Moreau held up his hands in a resigned motion. "Sorry, Captain. We have some information to share, and questions to ask."

Danny stepped forward. "Did you call that number I gave you?" He was using his mellow cop voice. "What did Kennedy say?"

"Yeah, I called." Lawrence screwed up his mouth and plopped down in his chair. "He said McGriffin is an arrogant S.O.B., but he knows things no one else does. Said I was lucky to have him on my team. If I could put up with his rudeness and attitude." He looked over at Connor. "I'm not sure I believe in psychics. My mother taught me to believe only what I see. I don't like you, but if you're right, we need to work together." He leaned forward and tapped a button on his phone. After a ring, he said, "Perkins, you need to be in on this also."

Danny touched Connor's arm. *"Cat, let me do the talking. We don't want to antagonize Lawrence any more than he already is."*

Lawrence leaned back in his chair and waved his hand to the chairs in from of the desk. "Have a seat, gentlemen and lady. We'll give Perkins a moment to come in before you start telling me what you know that you think I should know about."

Connor ignored the invitation to sit and walked to the window. He was a little surprised at the change of attitude. There were a lot of things about Lawrence that didn't make sense.

"Cat." There was a quiet soothing feel to Danny's mental voice.

"It's okay, Dawg. I'll be good. Not enough chairs for everyone." He leaned against the wall and crossed his arms.

Perkins walked in and stood just inside the door while Danny took up a position on the opposite side of the doorframe. Lisa and Moreau took the chairs facing Lawrence.

"Have you had any luck finding a gun?" Danny asked.

"No." Lawrence picked up a pen and fiddled with it. "I've come to the conclusion that you were right about that. It couldn't be a suicide if there was no gun."

Connor snorted. There were times the way human logic worked amazed him.

Lawrence turned his head and looked at him.

"Connor." Danny's tone was just shy of a warning growl.

"Sorry." Connor shrugged and tried to look innocent.

"We've found out a bit more about the victim," Moreau said. "He'd been receiving texts from pre-paid phones telling him where to go in Mexico and where to drop the items he brought back. He had texted back the last few weeks that he wanted out, and the messages got menacing."

Lawrence placed his arms on his desk. "Menacing in what way?"

"They warned they were going to reveal his shifter status if he didn't do what they wanted," Danny said. "Another shifter has also been receiving messages from the same burner phones with similar threats."

"Who?" Lawrence asked, sounding like he didn't believe them.

"A starlet by the name of Lindy Lui," Danny said. "She's being forced to perform sex with men she doesn't know on threat of being outed."

Lawrence turned back to Connor. "So. You're supposed to 'see' things. What do you have to say?" His face was closed, like there was no way he was going to entertain the idea of believing what Connor had to say.

Connor took a deep breath, choosing his words carefully and keeping his tone level. "Regarding Wallace. The shooter was someone Wallace trusted enough to turn his back on them and get shot. Description: about the same height and weight as Wallace. Indistinguishable if male or female." He walked around to the front of Lawrence's desk and stood behind Lisa. "Timmons, the tech at the FBI identified the voice that called in as Wallace's roommate, Jack Johnson. He knows things he didn't tell us. He could be the person I saw shoot Wallace."

From near the door, Perkins sneezed.

"When did you see this, and how?" Cutis squinted as if he mistrusted what Connor said.

"In Wallace's bedroom when I touched the carpet where the body was." Connor gripped the back of Lisa's chair, determined to not reflect the negative energy flowing off Lawrence. The man was making the very air in the room hostile. "You say you don't believe in psychics, but we do exist. You need to call him to be interviewed, and also his girlfriend. He said he spent the night with her."

Lawrence glanced over at Perkins, as if making sure the man was taking notes. It was similar to how Connor and Danny often worked. "How did the FBI identify him?"

"I recorded his voice, and they compared it with the phone call 911 received." Determined to be good, Connor kept his voice level, even though he hated people questioning what he did.

"That's an illegal recording." Lawrence tapped a pencil on the desk. "We can't use it."

"We don't need to say how we know he made the call." He walked back to the window and looked down at the street. Pacing would've made him feel better, but it also would've shown his agitation. He couldn't let Lawrence get to him. "The next victim will be Lindy Lui. You're going to find her in an alley. I don't know where the alley is or how or when she'll die."

"You're sure of this?" Lawrence looked skeptical.

"You can check with Kennedy on the accuracy of my visions. I will say that if we can, we may be able to stop Lindy from being killed, but it isn't likely. Usually when I 'see' a death, it happens. It may not happen the way I see it, but it still happens." He glanced at Lisa. "She's a cat shifter and very good at avoiding us."

"I spoke with Chief Kennedy." Lawrence pursed his lips as he frowned. "He told me about the man who was killing boys and about the bear shifter who was killing prostitutes. Said your visions usually play out."

"One correction to what you said." Connor shook his head. "Hernandez wasn't a shifter. He was a werebear."

"What's the difference?" Lawrence tilted his head as if he were a dog trying to hear better.

"Moreau, Collins, Lupan, and I are shifters. We are natural born shifters. Hernandez was turned by a natural bear shifter." Connor couldn't believe he was having to explain this to the man. For years, shifters had been explaining this to humans, but they never seemed to get it. He'd hoped being in a metroplex like LA, Lawrence would understand the difference, especially as chief of police.

"And Wallace?" Lawrence continued.

"He was a shifter." Connor was rapidly losing patience with the man. There was no point in putting a guy this stupid in as chief of police.

As if picking up on Connor's growing agitation, Moreau took up the narrative, "We know that there is some connection with a talent agency called Kelly and Associates. Both Wallace and Lui are clients along with a couple of other people we've identified."

Lawrence nodded toward Perkins, a clear indication he wanted Perkins to get the information for him. "What are their names?"

"Maria Lopez and Reggie Williams," Moreau replied. "We know that Williams has been approached by the blackmailers."

"I've spoken with Williams," Connor said. "As far as I can tell, he hasn't given in to the blackmailers' demands yet. However, I got a strange vibe from him."

Perkins spoke up, "Have they asked for money?"

The captain said, "Not all blackmailers want direct payment. It sounds like these guys get their money from the drugs and from men who want to have sex with a movie star." He turned back to Moreau. "What do you know about Williams and Lopez? Will they help us apprehend these men?"

"We know Williams because he's my cousin's boyfriend," Danny said. "My uncle, who is the prominent wolf alpha in New Mexico, asked us to look into what was happening to him. Lopez is related to someone in Mexico who is very powerful and is worried about her."

Moreau looked over his shoulder at Perkins. "Can you check to see if a man named Damon Lucas has a record? He's a computer whiz. We think he may be the one behind the burner phones."

Perkins turned and left the room.

Lawrence again consulted the file. "You say there's nothing we can do to protect this Lindy Lui?"

Connor shook his head. "If you put 24-hour-a-day protection on her, maybe. But I've found that if I stake out the place I think the death will occur, it happens somewhere else. Although I can see possible futures, sometimes fate plays a role in deciding if people die or not. It's one of the things I hate about my so-called gift."

Perkins returned, blowing his nose and quickly shutting the door behind him. "According to police files, Lucas has been arrested several times for cyber-crimes. Mostly hacking and on-line bullying. Started in high school. Looks like he himself is the victim of bullying because of his looks. Twenty-seven and looks about twelve."

Connor chuckled, hoping the happy sound would cut some of the tension in the room. "We noticed he looked younger than his position warranted. But if you look closely, you can see his age."

"Same with Timmons at the FBI," Moreau added. "If working with computers makes you look so young, maybe I need to change occupations."

Lawrence leaned forward, putting his elbows on the desk like he was ready to accept their help in the case. "What do you propose as the next move?"

"We have an appointment tomorrow to speak with Maria Lopez. We'll find out if she's received any threats." Connor walked toward the door. "In the meantime, have your guys keep an eye on Lucas and Lui and call Johnson in. I'd like to be here when he's interviewed. I might be able to pick something up he isn't saying."

"Okay." Lawrence pointed to Perkins. "Get on it. But if you guys say Lui is being able to shake you, and you're shifters, what makes you think human cops can follow her? I might have to bring in other departments if she travels outside of Venice Beach."

"And Lucas is currently wanted in Hollywood, something about a drive-by." Perkins looked up from the tablet he'd brought back into the room with him. "But you already knew about that didn't you?"

Connor nodded. "Moreau and I were there for that, yes. We aren't sure if it's related to the case or not."

"But Lucas is in the wind at this point," Lawrence said with a scowl. "Perkins, work with Hollywood on this." He looked at Connor, a level of distrust in his gaze. "I don't know where, besides Santa Fe and Phoenix, you guys are used to working, but things get complicated here in LA. There isn't just one police force, as you may have figured out. We have to all work together on things. Sure, we sometimes get in a snit when Santa Monica works a case that bleeds over, but if we've got more than neighbors running into each other, we try to communicate. Moreau, you're former FBI, you should understand this. We get too many fingers in the pie and we're all screwed. Communication is key."

"Then just let us handle things." Connor sauntered over from the window. "We tell you what we need, and you provide it. If the big boss turns out to be human, then we hand him over to you. If he's a shifter…" Connor paused. Although they'd dealt with other cases where the perpetrators were shifters, they'd always died by the end of the case. Traditionally shifters didn't hand shifters over to the human authorities, they handled things among the packs and other groups that had been wronged. If they were going to be an official force between the humans and the shifters, they were going to need to get something worked out. He didn't want to be judge, jury, and executioner. They were in America. Things didn't work that way there.

"We'll handle the shifters," Moreau finished for Connor. "The FBI has been working on a special containment facility."

"Really?" Connor asked mentally, so as not to show Lawrence his surprise.

"Yes," Moreau supplied.

"Okay. But just remember, we get the humans." Lawrence stood. "Now, if you don't have something more for me, I suggest you go and do whatever it is that you do to have your visions so we can try and save as many people as possible."

Although he didn't like being dismissed by the captain, Connor graciously nodded to the man and offered Lisa a hand up from her chair. "Thanks for your time."

Connor walked with the others out of the police station. He felt like every cop there was watching them as they left. The growing distrust of shifters was making their work that much harder. It would be nice if people would just mind their own business, put their fears aside and stop worrying about who could change into what. But then the world would be a nicer place to live and there wouldn't be a need for the Shifter Force.

Danny kissed Connor as they walked into the hotel room. "I'm proud of you for not getting too high and mighty with Lawrence. You're making progress."

Connor huffed as he closed the door. "Hard not to with you right there. You're my conscience."

Laughing, Danny took a couple of hopping steps, then turned and crouched down raising his voice in a high approximation of a cartoon character. "Do I look like a cricket to you?"

"No." Connor laughed too. "You look like a silly wolf trying to be a cricket."

Hearing Connor's humor helped Danny relax a little. Connor had been so volatile since the case started. He wanted to help him out, but he wanted Connor to ask for the help, not just have Danny force it on him.

Rising out of his crouch, Danny caught Connor in a big hug. It felt so good to have his arms wrapped around his cat.

As Danny went to kiss him, Connor stiffened. "Get down."

Connor shoved Danny toward the floor as something smashed through their hotel room window. Glass flew everywhere as a bottle landed on the bed and everything exploded into flames.

Danny's first instinct was to shift and dash out the window. They were on the second floor, it would be a far jump.

"*No,*" Connor shouted in his mind. *"Through the hall."*

Turning, Danny ran to the door. With the multiple locks, chains, and deadbolts, it took him nearly a minute to open it to the fresh air of the hall as their room was consumed in smoke and flames.

The smoke followed them down the corridor. Danny shifted with a thought, and seconds later Connor was running alongside him, his longer puma legs eating up carpet as they went.

"Lisa, how far are you and Moreau?" Connor called through their group link.

"What's happening?" Her mental voice was tinged with worry.

"Molotov cocktail into our motel room window." Danny replied as they reached the stairs and ran down, thankful for the open-air passage that didn't have doors.

Connor reached the parking lot first, then jumped back as bullets hit the side of the hotel. *"And shooter."*

"Lisa, call 911 and get back here." Danny didn't want her or Moreau in the line of fire, but they needed backup.

The motel's fire alarm finally went off, making Danny wonder if the place had been up to code or not. It had been a fairly nice place, especially for a rent-by-the-week location.

"They better not be hurting my Jeep." Connor crouched low and peered around the edge of the building.

"Stay here, Cat, I'm going to see if I can get around to the other side." Danny didn't wait for a reply, but just ran down the center hallway of the first floor of the motel. All down the hall, doors flew open and patrons in various states of dress were running for the outside. There was also the heavy odor of gasoline. He wondered if the rooms facing the parking lot were putting innocents in the line of fire.

Danny reached the far end of the hall just as cars started leaving the parking lot. In the distance sirens wailed. Staying low to the ground, he worked his way around to the parking lot, hoping to see men with guns getting into cars and speeding away. Shouts and screams were growing louder and more frequent around him.

"Help!" a woman shouted above Danny.

He glanced up. On the fifth floor, the top, a woman clutching something to her chest stood on a balcony. She was right above the room Danny and Connor had been in. The flames had already reached the fourth floor and were dancing around the balcony.

"Cat, I need a hand here. I think the bad guys have already left." Danny shifted and looked up at the woman. "Ma'am, drop your baby to me. I'll catch it."

"You can't. We're going to die." Her voice was just loud enough to reach his sensitive ears over the roar of the flames that were quickly consuming the old building.

"I'll go after her," Connor said, suddenly human next to Danny. "You catch the baby. I'm not sure I can get both of them down." He ran a couple of doors down, then jumped up and caught the rail of the second-floor balcony. He pulled himself up with the grace that only cat shifters possessed.

"Ma'am, please. I'm a police officer. I'll catch your baby." Danny didn't mind bending the truth if it would help save the baby.

Smoke billowed around the woman making her bend over coughing. The baby's cries were so loud to Danny, they drowned out the fire engines pulling in.

"Please, Ma'am." Danny held out his hands, hoping the woman would listen to him.

Connor had made it to the fourth floor, but the flames forced him to change his route by two rooms before he could make to the fifth floor.

Flames roared up, blocking the woman and baby from view. The woman screamed and the baby was suddenly flying through the air, tumbling end over end toward the ground.

"Oh my god, I can't catch a baby!" Lisa screamed in Danny's head as her high-pitched kestrel scream of distress came from above the motel.

"I've got him…her…" Danny backed up, trying to follow the baby's trajectory. He was going to need to time everything perfectly. "It!" He jumped. Hoping he had everything right, he used his wolf shifter strength to give him an extra push off. At the peak of his jump, his hands found the baby's towel. Scrambling to hold on, he brought it to his chest as the baby cried even louder.

When he landed, his knees hurt, but it didn't matter. The baby was still crying, so it had survived its journey down.

Around them, people cheered.

A fireman rushed up to Danny. "That was incredible. You saved the baby."

"I'm a first responder too." Danny handed the baby over to the man. There was a big lump in his throat. Somehow saving that little human life was so powerful. They chased criminals and did all the police legwork he was used to, but saving a life with a split-second decision was so much more powerful.

"There're three more people up here," Connor's thoughts cut through Danny's moment of glory. *"I can't get them all down. Get the firemen to put up a net, or whatever they use nowadays. We're going to have to jump."*

The old building creaked and groaned.

"Connor's still in there." Danny pointed up. "He says there're three other people still up there."

"That building's about to fall," the fireman replied. "We don't have time for the ladder truck to get here. We need the pad, people!" He shouted as other firemen dashed back to the truck. They were just getting the hoses connected to the fire hydrants down the block. The water hadn't started to flow yet as they unfolded a ten-foot square cube that seemed to instantly inflate. It barely fit in the open spot in the parking lot next to Connor's Jeep.

"Jump now!" the firefighter holding the baby yelled. "You'll be fine."

"Getting hot up here," Connor said. *"But I'm staying until everyone is down."*

Danny knew he was doing the right thing and knew that as long as Connor wasn't killed outright, he could survive breaking some bones or being burned, but he didn't want to take that chance. As irritating as Connor was, he was Danny's partner, in more ways than one. They had barely found each other; he didn't want Connor to die. *"Be careful, Cat."*

The mother of the baby hit the inflated square. It dipped drastically, but not all the way to the pavement.

"Come on, lady, get off there so the others can jump too." One of the firefighters offered her a hand just as another fire truck roared into the parking lot.

"Danny, we should get out of the way and let the firefighters do their job." Moreau appeared at Danny's shoulder.

"When Connor makes it down." Danny muttered, staring up at the balcony that was engulfed in flames.

A man jumped off. He looked older and screamed as he fell. He hit the inflated square hard and screamed louder.

"Let's go, sir. We've got to the get the last one down." The firefighter who'd helped the mother off reached for the man, who was lying in the middle of the square moaning.

"I can't." His voice was soft and tight with pain. "I think I broke something."

"If you don't move the other people who were up there with you are going to die." There was a harsh edge to her voice, but it allowed for no disobedience. It was almost like an alpha wolf ordering his pack away from danger.

The man started rolling toward the edge of the square when the last person jumped, followed by the sleek form of Connor in his puma shape.

Danny and Moreau moved as one, dashing to the square and yanking the injured man out of the way as the final person from the room hit the center of the square.

Connor landed gracefully in the parking lot, after hopping off the top of the first fire truck. He shifted instantly, and Danny ran to him.

"You're okay, Cat." Danny kissed Connor before he could answer. It wasn't the first time one of them had been in danger, but he was always relieved when they managed to get out of it alive.

"I think the building's clear," Lisa called as she landed on a fence behind Connor.

"Good." Danny gave her a thumbs up as he let go of Connor and they turned toward the firemen.

"That should be the last of them," Connor said. "The fire started in the room we were in. Someone threw a Molotov cocktail through our window."

"There was also the smell of gasoline in the hallways," Danny added, he pulled out his badge. "We're with Shifter Force. We believe this might be related to our current case."

"Believe." Connor huffed in Danny's head. *"If it isn't, then this town really is crazy. Of course, my vision as the window broke was of bullets, not a bottle. Not sure what's real and what's not anymore."*

"The fire chief is going to want to talk to you," the fireman said, then pointed across the road. "Wait over there."

"Any chance I can move my Jeep out of the way?" Connor asked. "It would make your job easier."

"Make it fast, we've got more trucks coming in, but please, just to across the street so we can get the reports accurate."

"We'll do that," Danny assured the man. "Connor, you move the Jeep. I need to check on the baby."

"Okay." Connor didn't argue. He just went and got in the Jeep and quickly moved it as Danny walked over the ambulance that had arrived where the mother and baby had been put, along with the man who'd been injured in the fall.

The mother sat on the ambulance's bumper, cradling the baby who'd finally stopped crying.

"He's going to be okay, ma'am." Danny stopped a couple of feet away from them.

The woman looked up. "Thank you so much for saving her. The flames came so fast, and our door… it got stuck and we couldn't force it open." Tears made rivers down her soot-coated face.

"It's okay. It's what I do. I save people."

"He really does." Lisa patted Danny on the shoulder and leaned over to peer at the little baby. "And one day, maybe she'll grow up to save people too."

"I hope so." The woman smiled. "You're a shifter aren't you, like your…ah friend?"

Danny nodded. "Yes."

"I don't care what the news says. Shifters can be good people. You're both heroes in my book." She stood up and wrapped her arm around Danny's shoulder, holding the baby between them.

Heat rose in Danny's face that had nothing to do with the fire behind them. "Thanks, ma'am." In all his time as a deputy sheriff, he'd never had anyone so thankful for something he'd done. Most of the work they did as Shifter Force was done in the shadows, where the public might not know who did it. He felt good, like he had earlier, at being able to help save lives.

When the woman finally let go of him, Danny and Lisa walked across the street where Connor, Moreau, and the rest of the refugees from the fire watched the building collapse. For Danny, it had just been a temporary home while they were in LA and waiting for Connor's vision of falling stars to come to fruition, but he knew for some of the other residents, it had been the only home they had.

Moreau took his phone away from his ear. "Lawrence is getting us the traffic cam footage from this area. Also seeing if the motel had a live feed to off-site cloud storage for their security. We might be able to get license plates, or maybe faces."

"We need to see what Kelly and company know about this," Connor muttered. "But I bet they won't tell us."

"We're going to need another hotel," Danny said. "It's going to take Lawrence time to get us the info. And we've got to talk to the fire chief."

Connor nodded and pulled Danny into a hug as they leaned against the front of the Jeep. "Yeah. Let's see about finding some place to sleep while we wait. It's going to be a long night."

After Connor kissed his neck and released him to use his phone to find a new hotel, Danny watched the firemen do their job. He wondered just how close they were to finding the person responsible for blackmailing shifters, and how much money that person stood to lose if they were willing to risk killing potentially hundreds of people, if the motel had been full for the night.

Chapter 9

Danny suppressed a yawn. Their new hotel was a lot better than the old one, even if it did stretch Connor's pocket book a bit more than he liked. The room was an interior one that didn't have any windows. They'd discussed it and decided that if they could wrap up the case, they wouldn't have to deal with it very long. Like before, they'd stayed away from having the same hotel as Lisa and Moreau, as a safety precaution.

A sharp knock, followed by a sound of a swipe key passing through the reader, made Danny turn toward the door just as it swung open.

Lisa walked in with her arms full of bags.

Danny jumped up and dashed over to her. "What's all of this?"

She cocked her head and stared at him. "You did realize you're still wearing the same clothes you had on yesterday, right?"

"Oh." Danny glanced down at his jeans that still had some musty smudges on them from the explosion and fire.

"You were in the shower when Lisa called and offered to pick up a few things." Connor got up and headed for the small coffee maker that had just finished brewing the second pot of the morning. "Although this looks like more than a couple of things."

Dumping the bags on the closest bed Lisa moved her sharp look from Danny to Connor. "And unless the two of you are going to take time out from the case to go shopping, I figured you'd both need several changes of clothes at least until things slow down."

"Very practical, Lady Bird." Danny picked up the first bag and glanced in to see a couple of dark pairs of slacks, along with some jeans.

"And not from a store I've ever had to deem to shop in." Connor wrinkled his nose.

"Yeah, I kinda thought that." Lisa strolled over to the chair near the far wall. "But I also figured your bank account would appreciate it if I kept the cost down."

"That it does." Connor sipped his coffee.

"So I hope someone has been working the case while I was out." She crossed her arms and glanced between the three men.

Danny pulled a robin's egg blue button up shirt from one of the bags and tossed it at Connor. "I think this one is yours."

"Okay, here's what I've found out," Moreau said, holding his tablet out for all of them to see, drawing their attention away from the new threads. "Okay, not me, but Lawrence's people. I just got the report a few minutes ago."

Connor put down his coffee cup. "Cut to the chase, Moreau. Did they find out anything useful?"

"We have names on the license plates of all the cars that came and went from the motel within fifteen minutes before and after the attack. Lawrence says he's going to put someone on following up with the list."

Moreau tapped the screen. "But here's the interesting one." He enlarged one name on the list. "Reggie Winters."

"Reggie?" Danny put down the orange he'd just picked up. "Why would Reggie's car be in the parking lot of our hotel before or after the attack?"

"Maybe he had information for us," Lisa suggested as she looked at Connor. "You did give him the name of the hotel and room number you guys were staying at, yes?"

"Yes." Connor blew out a long breath. "I figured if Cortez vouched for him, he'd be safe."

"We're going to need to dig into him farther, aren't we?" Danny picked the orange back up. "I mean he wouldn't be the first so-called victim who really wasn't. But if he was there to pass along something useful, maybe he saw the guys throwing the firebomb and rabbited."

Connor gave Danny a sad smile. "You're always ready to give people the benefit of the doubt. It's one of the things I love about you."

Danny smiled back as he peeled the orange.

"All right, before we get sappy in here," Moreau continued. "I also heard back from the Hollywood PD. We've got names on Lucas' associates. They weren't the most wholesome guys. No current warrants, but they'd both served time for extortion, harassment, assault, and a few other things. Don Dottery, the bigger of the two, had the longer rap sheet, going back to his teen years. At that time, he didn't seem to care who he hurt, he just liked causing pain."

"Don?" Connor nodded thoughtfully. "I was just thinking of him as Shirtless. On Venice Beach he was the one who took his shirt off and headed toward the beach."

Danny looked at Connor with an orange slice dripping juice down his fingers. "Anything I should've been worried about?"

"No." Connor laughed. "He was human. You're my wolf, and always will be."

"Focus, guys, these folks have tried to kill us…you…twice now," Moreau drew their attention back to him. "This gets serious. The other guy, Fred Miso, had a similar sheet as Dottery, looks like they met in prison about five years ago and have run together with a couple other repeat offenders ever since. Speaking of prison, didn't you guys say your bear shifter from a couple of cases ago was in federal prison in Colorado?"

Danny popped another orange slice in his mouth. "Yeah, that's right. Is there a connection?"

"Maybe." Moreau tapped the tablet again. "I'll have to do some digging."

Danny didn't like the idea that there might be a connection to multiple cases. He was used to simple speeders he had to stop, not criminal masterminds.

"Do we have names of the other offenders?" Lisa popped a soda open. "Might give us an idea of who to keep an eye out for."

Moreau pulled up several pictures on his tablet. "As a matter of fact, I do. Penny Tito, she isn't one of the members who met in prison." He pointed to an elegant Asian woman with a gold dragon tattoo spiraling down her left arm "But her brother, Tam Tito, is." Tam's picture was a bulky man who looked like he could be a sumo wrestler with just a few more pounds on his ample frame.

"That's one of the guys from the taco stand." Connor tapped the tablet. "So at least one of them is still alive."

"Right," Moreau scrolled on. "Tam is known around town as a powder keg, but only toward shifters. His record is very one-sided as far as his crimes go. He started off assaulting a turtle shifter in college, then has gone on from there. He served time for shooting a wolf shifter, then decapitating him."

Lisa set her soda down and yanked the tablet away from Moreau. "How is he even still on the street?"

"Crimes against shifters often get lighter sentences than crimes against humans." Moreau sighed and walked over to the mini fridge. "You know that."

"Yes and no." Lisa shook her head and passed the tablet to Connor. "In Santa Fe, we're a fairly liberal area. Everyone is treated equally."

"Sometimes being from a small town, particularly one that's the center of a major alpha's territory, is a good thing." Danny finished off his orange. "The county judge for Jemez Springs always treated everyone equally."

"Then you're in a good area," Moreau said. "There aren't a lot of places in the world where that can be said. Most law enforcement, and judges…hell, people, let their personal prejudices ride over the rules. Maybe I've seen more than most, being in the FBI." He turned off the tablet and looked at them. "Maybe that's why I took you all up on the opportunity to be part of all of this. We have a chance to help other shifters. That's bigger than any of us by ourselves."

Danny nodded. Although he was likely to always follow Connor, he liked the idea that they would be able to make the world better for shifters while solving the crimes waged against them, even if they were often fighting against the shifters who were preying on their community.

Connor's alarm on his phone went off. "Okay, gang, we need to get on the road. They're expecting us at the talent agency to meet with Maria."

Picking up his orange peel, Danny headed toward the garbage can first. "We don't want to be late for that. If we don't do what we can to protect her, Montezuma is going to have our hides." Having dealt with Cortez for years, Danny was well acquainted with the level of possessiveness alphas had over their family and group members.

Connor stepped off the elevator in front of Kelly's office. The place still smelled too clean. He went straight to the second-floor receptionist, since they'd not had to deal with the first-floor woman. The main door had been open, but no one was at any of the desks there. It had felt strangely deserted. After that, he was pleasantly surprised to find someone on the second floor. "Good morning, Jessie. I believe Mr. Kelly is expecting us."

She frowned and looked down her nose at him. "How did you know my name?"

He smiled hoping to throw her off a little. "I could tell you it's because I'm a psychic, but I heard Mr. Kelly call you that yesterday."

She clicked the phone. "Agent McGriffin and party are here. Yes, sir." Standing, she walked around the desk toward a hall. "Follow me. He has the meeting set up in the conference room."

"Something smells good," Lisa said.

"Mr. Kelly has a brunch set up for you all." Jessie opened a door and a white-coated waiter motioned them in.

A man and woman, wearing white coats that matched the table covering, stood behind a long table that was covered with a white cloth and loaded with food.

The first waiter motioned to the table. "Help yourselves. Mr. Kelly will be here shortly."

Lisa walked toward a pitcher of orange juice and some glasses.

"May I help you?" The serving woman picked up the pitcher, filled a glass, and handed it to Lisa.

Delicate china sat at one end of the buffet which held eggs, bacon, ham, fresh fruit, and croissant sandwiches.

A smaller table held linen napkins and sets of silverware.

"Thank you." Lisa took the glass. She set it down, picked up a plate, and placed a croissant filled with ham, eggs, and cheese on it.

The woman behind the table gestured toward a microwave. "Would you like the croissant heated?"

"That would be nice." Lisa handed her the plate.

She heated the sandwich and handed it back to Lisa. "Be careful, the cheese might be hot."

"Thanks." Picking up the glass of juice, she walked over to the other table and sat. "I don't know about you guys, but I'm hungry. I didn't have as much breakfast as you guys did."

Danny walked over and followed her example of the croissant. Setting his plate on the table beside Lisa, he walked back and helped himself to a cup of coffee.

Moreau soon joined them.

Connor, however, walked to the window and looked down on the street below. He always wanted to see where he was in connection to his surroundings. The view wasn't much, just down the street. He could see the boarded-up café that had been shot up the previous day. People hurried past it, like it wasn't even there. He was a little surprised that no one stopped, but figured they were in Hollywood, and no one had time for something like a shot-up café. Even if it inconvenienced their plans for a second, they could just go on to one of the many Starbucks scattered around the area.

Danny spoke in his mind, *"Are you okay, Cat?"*

"Just worried." He was still trying to figure out why his gift was on the fritz. The previous night, he'd had only a second's warning like he'd had at the café. If he'd not learned to act reflexively, he'd have been dead, and worse, in the motel, Danny would've been dead. He already carried a bit of guilt about not seeing when Danny had been kidnapped by the serial killer; if he'd not reflexively gotten them both on the floor when he saw the window shatter a mere second before it did, he wouldn't be able to live with himself. Connor just didn't want to burden Danny with his internal fears about his powers not working right.

The door swung open and Jerome Kelly walked into the room carrying his ever-present cigar. Trailing smoke behind him. "I see the staff has made you at home. I know I told Maria 11 o'clock, but I don't expect her before 11:30-11:45." He accepted a cup of coffee from the man behind the table.

Connor wrinkled his nose at the scent of the cigar. That smell bothered him. There was something about it. He finally came away from the table and got a cup of coffee. "Tell me, Kelly, what do you know about an employee of yours named Damon Lucas?"

"Lucas. Lucas. Oh right, he's in the tech department I believe. Does a pretty good job." He chuckled. "Looks young but has a great brain for computers. Why do you ask?"

"We have reason to believe he's involved with the people blackmailing shifters. We've traced some texts and emails sent through burner phones he purchased to Wallace, Williams, and Lindy Lui," Danny answered between bites of his croissant.

Kelly turned to Connor. "Did you know this yesterday when we talked?"

"No. The information came to light shortly after our discussion." He debated how much to tell the man. There was still something about him Connor didn't trust. It would be nice to know what was in the damned cigar that put him on edge.

An intercom beeped. "Mr. Kelly, Ms. Lopez is here."

"Fine, fine. Send her in." He hurried over and opened the door.

The woman standing there was dressed in a pair of wide-legged black pants and a full-sleeved red tunic. Her raven hair was fluffed around her exquisitely made-up face.

"Good morning, my dear." Taking her hand, Kelly gave her 'air kisses' on both cheeks.

Maria Lopez sauntered into the room followed by two beefy men. "You two may eat if you want to. I'll just have coffee." She waved toward the table of food like a member of royalty dismissing servants.

The woman behind the table filled a delicate cup with coffee, added sugar and cream, and handed it to her. The move made it obvious the serving staff were used to taking care of the agency's clients.

Maria took the cup without a 'thank you' and turned to Connor. "My grandfather told me about you a couple of weeks ago. I don't see why you're here. Doesn't he realize I'm a grown woman? I don't need him to babysit me."

Connor shrugged. "He thinks we owe him a favor, and he's worried about you."

"Why?" Her face remained neutral, making her hard to read. "Oh, I know he saved your butt in Mexico a few weeks ago, but why is he worried about me?"

"Because you could be in danger." Connor forced the trickle of irritation that started up in him to back down. He should've realized, before she entered the room, that she was going to be hard to get along with. She was the granddaughter of a very powerful shifter with a large territory. On top of that she was one of the biggest actresses in the country. To say she was going to be a spoiled brat was an understatement.

She lazily waved at the two men sitting at a table eating. "That's why they're here. To keep me safe."

He looked at the men and back to her. "They may be able to keep you physically safe, but they can't protect you from blackmail."

"What do I have to be blackmailed about?" She squinted at him, the first hint of emotion she'd displayed since she entered the room, but it was only a quick flash, then it was gone, hidden again behind her chilly exterior. "I haven't done anything."

"It isn't something you've done. It's what you are." Connor felt like he was having to explain the obvious to her. There was no way she could be so dense.

"And just what am I besides a movie star?"

Connor stared into her eyes. "You're a shifter. Given the public feeling about us, how would your fans react it they knew you were a jaguar?" He tried to probe her mind, but a very powerful shield resisted his attempt. It had been years since Connor had encountered a sane mind who could resist his efforts.

"Are you going to tell them?" She raised her chin haughtily.

Giving up trying to see into her thoughts, he shook his head slightly. "Not me. But so far, we know of three shifters who have been threatened with exposure if they don't do as they're told. Two of them have been forced into illegal acts. One of those is dead, and if my *sight* isn't wrong, the second one soon will be."

She gasped. "Who? Do I know them?" Her cold exterior didn't instantly return, but the mask slowly lowered as she sipped her coffee.

"David Wallace was found with a silver bullet in his brain. The police were treating it like a suicide, but they haven't found the gun. He was smuggling drugs into the country from Mexico. Lindy Lui has been forced into prostitution. My visions lead me to believe she's going to also be killed."

Danny stepped next to Connor. "Reggie Williams has been threatened but hasn't done anything yet."

"And my grandfather thinks they'll come after me?" Maria sighed, then glanced at her bodyguards who were enjoying their food a short distance away. "What are you going to do about it?"

Connor handed her a card. "We can't do anything unless they contact you. Call if they do."

She reached for the card and Connor grabbed her wrist. *"What are you hiding?"*

Maria reacted with a speed only a cat shifter had. She slammed her hand into Connor's chest. The blow caught him off guard as he stumbled backward into Danny.

Maria sat in the middle of a bed, her knees pulled up to her chin crying as a door opened and a man walked in. There was a glowing leather collar around her neck.

"Don't *ever* touch *me* again." The words were verbal and mental, carrying a level of pain with them Connor had never felt. It shattered the vision that hadn't finished.

"Cat?" Concern clouded Danny's voice.

Connor didn't respond. He straightened and marched over to Maria. "Look. You think you can avoid these people. You can't. The vision you just destroyed, showed me otherwise."

Maria squared her shoulders and glared at him. Dark rosettes and dark fur suddenly appeared on her face. "Get away from me."

"Cat, come on." Danny put his hand on Connor's shoulder. "You've done enough."

The vision shook Connor. "Dawg, she's got to listen."

"No, she doesn't." Danny turned Connor toward the door. "We need to go."

"She's in danger." Connor jerked free of Danny and started toward Maria. "You know you're in danger. Don't you?"

The bodyguards had dropped their plates and were heading toward him.

"Connor, go." Danny's voice was a bark of anger. "Lisa, get him out of here before he makes this worse."

"Come on, Connor." Lisa took his arm.

"No." Connor jerked out of her grasp. Didn't anyone understand what was at stake? Were they all against him?

"Oh, I think you're all leaving." Kelly was there, blowing that foul smoke in Connor's face. "You've overextended your welcome. Mateo, Phillip, remove them."

The jaguars grabbed Connor's arms.

Two big cats lay in pools of blood on white carpet. Somewhere nearby, someone laughed, and Maria screamed louder and more desperately than in any of her movies.

Danny wanted to punch the bodyguards, but knew it wouldn't do anything except make the situation even worse. Connor had been erratic the past few days, but he'd never lost it to the level he did with Maria Lopez. He wanted to sit Connor down and talk it all out, but unless they wanted to be hunted down by Montezuma and his men, he was going to need to fix things with Maria Lopez as fast as possible.

Connor hit the elevator door hard enough to dent the metal. "Damn it. Why don't people ever listen to me?"

"You're coming on way too strong, Cat." Danny said as Lisa and Moreau backed off a safe distance. "You need to calm down."

"Or maybe you need to take this seriously." Connor pointed up toward the floor they'd just left. "She's going to get kidnapped and those bodyguards are going to die in the process. If people don't start paying attention to me, she might die too." He shook his head. "I know what I'm talking about."

The elevator opened to the dingier office and Connor stormed across it, pausing at the first receptionist. "They're all going to die. You know that?"

She stared at him as her phone beeped.

Connor shook his head. "We're leaving."

Danny put his hand on Connor's shoulder. "Come on, Connor." He started to steer Connor toward the door, hoping they could get out onto the sidewalk without further problems. A constant flood of anger washed through their telepathic link. It felt like Connor was about to fly apart at the seams.

"Connor, calm down." Danny opened the door out onto the street. "I'm going to try to repair things with Maria."

"How? She wouldn't listen to me, why would she listen to you?" Connor turned to face him, sneering.

"Because maybe I'm not going to come off as a raving lunatic." Danny somehow managed to push back the anger welling up inside him. For the first time in months, the antagonistic nature wolves felt toward cougars flared up. He wanted to punch Connor. He forced it down.

"You two need some space," Moreau said, drawing both their attentions.

"Stay out of this!" Connor snapped.

Danny didn't think it was going to do their cause any good to have people catch them yelling at each other on the street. *"Connor. You're overstepping right now."* He pulled out his keys and tossed them to Lisa. "Can you drive him back to the hotel? I'm going to see about salvaging things with Maria."

"Sure." She didn't sound positive about the prospect.

Taking Connor's face in his hands, Danny stared deep in his blue eyes. "Connor, go with her. We'll talk later."

Connor shook with anger, but his eyes got a faraway look, like he was having another vision. Frowning, he nodded and let Lisa lead him away.

With a deep breath, Danny looked at Moreau. "Okay. How are we going to fix this?" He hated sending Connor away, but lives were on the line and letting Connor stay was just going to make the situation worse.

"You don't ask for much do you?" Moreau glanced up and down the street, then gestured toward the spot in the wall that divided the agency from the record store next door.

Understanding they were still standing in the middle of the sidewalk, Danny nodded and followed Moreau out of the flow of pedestrian traffic. He glanced down the street just in time to see Connor and Lisa disappearing into the parking garage where they'd left the Jeep. It was going to take some effort to make Connor see that he'd crossed a line by grabbing Maria and trying to scare her into listening to him. If that was the way Connor was going to run Shifter Force, they were going to have to really talk about things, and he was going to have to do some soul searching.

"I don't know about you, but I'm not picking up any hint of Maria's scent out here." Moreau gestured around them. "I think the agency must have a way into a different parking garage than the one we use."

Taking a deep breath, Danny didn't catch the scent of any cats beyond Connor. If Maria and her bodyguards had walked through the main doors, it wasn't showing, and it didn't make any sense for the agency to have one of their top clients come through the less-than perfect lower floor. "So where is it?"

"I'm not sure, but I think I know someone who can help us." Moreau headed for the music store.

It didn't take Moreau long to talk the old hippie behind the counter into letting them out the backdoor and into a separate garage. There were several high-dollar cars parked back there, and an elevator that the man assured them led up to the offices above the other part of the agency.

"Sniff around," Moreau suggested. "Let's see if we can figure out which car is Maria's"

Danny laughed and pointed to the sleek black Jaguar sitting nearest the elevator. "What do you wanna bet that's hers?"

Moreau shook his head as they walked toward it. "No bet. Man, I don't know if she's arrogant, or what."

"Or what." Danny stopped as the elevator dinged.

Maria Lopez and her two bodyguards stepped out and started toward the Jag. With a snarl, she stopped and stepped behind the large men. "What are you doing here?" She glanced around, obviously looking for Connor.

Danny was definitely getting tired of covering for his screw-ups. "Connor's not here. Since I'm the one who actually accrued the debt with your grandfather, I was hoping I could smooth things over."

"I don't ever want that cougar near me again. Do you understand, wolf?" She all but spat the word at him. "If word of his actions reach my grandfather, he'll hunt all of your Shifter Force down and kill you. I doubt he'll care what your alpha has to say. Montezuma controls more of the Americas than any realize."

"I'm not here to exchange threats, Ms. Lopez." Danny kept his voice level, hoping to smooth things out. "I'll keep Connor away from you. That won't be a problem." Inwardly he wondered if it would even be possible. "We just want to make sure you don't end up like the others who've run afoul of the blackmailers." Standing there speaking with the actress he'd seen so many times in movies and interviews felt unreal, but the danger was real. He had to do what he could.

Maria nodded. "I'm sorry for what has happened. I've worked with Lindy. I tried to call her after you left and just got her voicemail. I hope the cougar is wrong. She's a good actress and could go far, if she gets the chance."

Danny nodded. "I know. We want to give her the chance."

"So far, I haven't been contacted by any blackmailers." She took a long breath. "I hope I won't.

I know my grandfather can't help me much in this, but Mateo and Phillip are loyal to me. They will protect me. If I am contacted, I will contact you." She pointed at Danny. "Not the cougar. I will get as much information as I can. But only a fool would threaten to out me. I've been so careful with my—" She looked up at the bigger of the two guards. "—our secrets. Other than Kelly and the agency, nobody knows. Until your cougar so stupidly said his name, they didn't know about grandfather. Some things we like to keep quiet."

"I understand." She didn't need to spell out everything for Danny for him to get the drift of what she was saying.

"Keep the cougar away from me, far away, and I won't tell my grandfather of his indiscretions. When you catch the people doing this, I'll call Grandfather and let him know your debt is paid." She gestured to the bodyguards, nodding toward the car. "You are a very brave wolf to come down here. If I hadn't failed to reach Lindy, I might not be so believing of your story. Something is wrong with her. Find her. Save her." She continued walking toward the car.

Danny watched her go. With the graceful way she moved, he wondered if she went to great lengths to hide that from her audiences. Had learning to be human been part of her acting lessons?

Chapter 10

Connor slumped in the passenger seat and glared out the window as Lisa pulled them out into the Hollywood traffic. Danny had never dismissed him. Nobody understood what he was doing. He was trying to save people's lives; it was why he'd been given his sight to begin with. Over the years he'd never tried to use his powers for anything more than the benefit of others. None of it made any sense. His powers were malfunctioning and Danny was turning on him.

"You're being really quiet over there," Lisa said as she pulled onto the highway. "Not that I want to listen to you screaming at me."

"I wouldn't scream at you." Connor sighed and shook his head.

"You were screaming at Danny back there, you realize that, don't you?"

"What?" Connor tried to replay the scene in his head, but the two visions kept popping up.

"And everyone else in the room who wasn't Connor McGriffin. I've never seen you like that." Lisa slowed down as traffic congested around them. "There's something going on. What changed while I was gone?"

"That's just it. I don't know." Connor hadn't even realized he'd been yelling at anyone other than Maria Lopez. If she wasn't careful, the arrogant jaguar was going to get herself killed, or worse. "I was shouting at Danny?" A cold knife twisted in his gut. Danny, of all people, didn't deserve his abuse.

"Yes. Cat, talk to me. What's going on?"

With a heavy sigh, Connor began explaining how his visions weren't working right. How he was having to touch people to see their futures, and how his precognitive flashes were only for a few seconds ahead.

"Wait, so you're saying that's why you grabbed for Maria, to try to get a better vision." Lisa accelerated again as they clear an accident that had been blocking the left lane.

"Yes. Maybe if she hadn't hit me, I might've been able to read more, or at the very least gotten an idea of time or location." He hung his head and rubbed his temples. "I have a reason for everything I do, you know that."

"I do." Lisa nodded and patted his shoulder. "I bet Danny's learned that by now too, but he's been trying really hard to get you to cultivate a more professional attitude than you've had in the past. What we all saw back at the talent agency was so far from professional that it can't really be called anything more than a child having a temper tantrum. I say that as your best friend." She pulled her hand away to downshift as traffic slowed again.

"I've been trying." Connor sighed again. "I really have. Maybe things would be different if I could figure out why I can't see everything I'm used to seeing."

"Then talk to someone about it." Lisa changed lanes with the rest of traffic. "I don't mean just me, someone who knows what it's like to have visions. Maybe your grandmother will have some insight for you. She's been a seer for longer than you have. Didn't you say she helped train you in the use of your gift?"

Connor couldn't help but chuckle. "As if my gifts could be trained. They've always just led me around by the nose. Grandmother did teach me how to filter out things I shouldn't be seeing, and how to accept things like death as part of what we witness." Connor hadn't heard from his Grandmother since she'd headed back to Florida after they'd stopped the vultures. Although he didn't talk to her all the time, she could normally sense when he needed her advice, or just a listening ear. He wondered if part of what was wrong with him might be impacting her too.

"I don't pretend to understand what it's like to see the future, particularly things like violent deaths, and little boys being forced to do things no little boy should endure, but maybe you need to stop a bit and think about what it's doing to you, and to the rest of us."

Connor frowned and looked at Lisa. "Not getting what you're saying, but it sounds like you're suggesting that I stop being psychic for the sake of all of us."

"No." Lisa shook her head violently as she angled the Jeep toward the off ramp. "That's not it at all. Your gifts save people, maybe not as many as you'd like, but that's out of your control. I'm just saying that maybe, instead of just letting the visions control you, and cause you to lash out at those who love you, maybe you need to find more filters."

"Filters? What kind of filters?"

Lisa shrugged as she stopped the Jeep at a light. "Not sure if 'filters' is even the right word for what I'm trying to say. But I'm betting if you hadn't had those visions back at the agency, you wouldn't have acted so strongly. Am I right?"

Connor pursed his lips and sighed. She was hitting close to home, but she'd always been good at that. Lisa wasn't known for pulling her punches and that was why they'd become closer than anyone before her. "Maybe. Maria was pushing my buttons, and there's something about Kelly that's not right."

"The damned cigars?" Lisa nodded as the light changed and she headed down the block toward their new hotel. "I'm a kestrel and don't operate on scent, but I had been wondering if he was trying to mess with the shifters who do."

The swing of discussion toward the case make Connor relax a little. He had to figure out how to make Danny forgive him for losing it. He hadn't meant for it to be as harsh as Lisa made it sound. He trusted her to tell him the truth, and if she said he'd been acting up, she was right. He was going to have to pick up the pieces.

"You're sure about this?" Moreau asked Danny as they got out of the cab at the hotel Moreau and Lisa were staying at.

Danny sighed. In that moment, he wasn't sure about a lot of things. "I think this'll shake him up a bit." They hadn't talked much during their drive from the talent agency. It might've been different if they'd been in Moreau's SUV, but they didn't want to risk the driver not being friendly, or Connor listening in since his telepathic ability was the source of the link between the team.

"I know I'm the new guy on the team, but a shakeup will be good for him." Moreau opened the lobby door for Danny. "I'm not sure how you and Lisa have managed to put up with him for as long as you have. You both have law enforcement training…"

"And he's not very well trained." Danny resisted a chuckle as he pushed the elevator button. "Yeah, I know."

"Right. I'm trying to be polite." Moreau followed Danny into the elevator as the doors opened.

As the mirrored doors slid closed, Danny half expected to see a dent in the shiny surface, but it was perfect, even looked like it had recently been cleaned.

"You don't have to be polite. You're part of this team." Danny leaned against the wall.

"I had hoped after our short talk the other day, things would be better." Moreau stood near the front of the lift.

"And I think they were," Danny said. "But there's something wrong. Connor's not opening up to me about what it is."

"Who knows? I wonder if he's worried if he's less than perfect, it'll affect things with you, and maybe with the team."

The elevator arrived and dinged before the doors slowly opened. Danny pushed off the wall and headed for the hall. "He is a bit of a perfectionist,"

"I've noticed that," Moreau agreed.

"You might be on to something." Danny stopped behind Moreau as they reached his room.

Before Moreau got the door open, Danny's phone rang. His cousin Jime's howl rolled out of his pocket and down the hall.

Danny pulled out the phone and answered it. "What's up, Fuz-Cuz?"

Moreau got the door opened and Danny followed him in. The AC was a little stronger in the room than it had been in the hall, and goose bumps rolled across Danny's arms.

"Hey, that's no fair," Jime complained. "I can't call you that anymore. I'll have to think of something new."

"Yes, you will." Danny walked over and looked out of the window. He almost chastised himself for doing the same thing Connor had been doing, but then he spotted the outline of their hotel a few blocks away and wondered what Connor and Lisa were doing. It would be easy to open the link between them and look and see. "What's going on? We're trying to solve a case here in sunny California."

"Yeah, yeah, hanging with stars and all that," Jime teased. "Look, Trina was asking me if you guys had found Reggie yet. He's stopped answering her calls."

Danny frowned and turned from the window, catching Moreau's gaze and pointing at the phone to his ear, indicating that Moreau didn't need to be polite and try not to listen in. "What do you mean he stopped answering her calls? Connor went and talked to him yesterday."

"Cuz," Jime's tone rose. "You didn't let your cat go talk with him, did you?"

"Moreau and I were working a different lead at the time." He didn't figure his cousin needed all the details.

"But really, Cuz. Your cat's not known for subtlety. For all we know he scared the poor dog so badly he's shifted and run all the way back to Canada. He probably isn't answering the phone 'cause he doesn't have thumbs anymore."

"I doubt that's the case." Danny sat on the edge of the bed, hoping Moreau was doing something useful as he booted up his laptop.

"Cuz, you've got the hots for the guy, so you're immune to the vibes he sends out to the rest of the canines. I'll tell Trina that Cat saw him yesterday, and that he was fine then. Did Cat say anything about *seeing* anything? Maybe he saw Reggie dead or something."

"Not that he said. There was something about a trio of muscle following Reggie, but two of them are dead. Not sure what happened to the third."

"Dead? Really. That's cool."

Danny rolled his eyes at his cousin's enthusiasm about dead people. "It was a drive-by. Connor and Moreau almost got caught up in it too."

"Oh. Yeah. Drive-bys aren't cool. Kinda cowardly if you ask me. Glad shifters don't do shit like that."

"Me too. Tell Trina I'll call her as soon as we make contact with Reggie again."

"You do that. I don't think Rusty would like it if I have to take a couple days and come out there to keep you straight and all."

"I know Rusty wouldn't like it." Danny knew Sheriff Calloway wouldn't be happy at all if Jime up and took off on him. Sandoval County only had three active law enforcement officers, and being down one put a strain on the other two.

"Right, so find Reggie and get something done. We don't want Trina getting mad at us either."

"No, we don't want that. Okay, Jime, I think Moreau's got something pulled up here. I need to get off the phone." Since they weren't face to face, Danny didn't worry overly much about his cousin picking up the partial lie, but Moreau did have something pulled up on his computer.

"Right, Cuz, you have fun out there. Oh, and if you meet her, I want Maria Lopez's autograph. She's hot."

"She has her moments." Danny wondered how Jime would react if—when he told him Maria had punched Connor and proved to be the biggest cat in the room. "Bye, Fuz-Cuz."

"Bye…damn it. I'll think of something." Jime ended the call.

Danny slipped the phone back in his pocket. "What do you have, Moreau?"

"I just logged into an FBI backdoor into the cellphone network." Moreau glanced over his shoulder at Danny. "This doesn't officially exist, but it's faster than getting warrants every time we need track a phone. It also only allows for real time data, their system backs up every hour or so to keep it from bogging down."

Danny walked over and looked over Moreau's shoulder. "So we can't tell where he's been, but we can tell where he is."

"Right, and how long his phone's been pinging off a particular tower." Moreau hit enter on the screen. For over a minute, silence descended on the room, as the circle on the laptop spun.

Then data appeared. Just a single line.

Moreau frowned. "He's not left the area of his home tower. That doesn't mean he's not left home, but he hasn't gone far if he did."

"Can we see activity?" Danny pulled his phone out of his pocket and started to call Connor, then stopped himself. It might be better if they let Connor stew for a little while.

"Just inbound calls. But a fair number of them, and not all from the same phone number."

"We've got Reggie's address." Danny put his phone back in his pocket. "What do you say we go see what's going on?"

"And what are we going to tell him when he answers the door?" Moreau closed the laptop.

"We'll sort that out on the way." Danny headed for the door. "At least we can talk in your truck on the way over."

"Definitely." Moreau followed.

It felt good to be doing something rather than worrying about Connor. Danny hoped it turned out better than going after Lindy Lui had.

Chapter 11

The hotel door closed behind Lisa as she headed out to get some dinner for the two of them, when Connor's phone rang. Caller ID showed it was his grandmother. His fingers shook slightly as he swiped the screen to answer it. "Hello, Grandma."

"What have you done now?" Her voice was even, almost emotionless. It sent a chill through him. "You're transmitting anger and hurt clear to Florida. That's nearly 3000 miles. I've never known anyone to reach that far. So, your wolf left you. What are you going to do about it?"

"How do you know he left?" Connor stumbled over the words. He hadn't even thought things had gotten that bad. Had Danny taken him losing it at the Kelly agency that badly?

"Bairn, have I taught you nothing? Of course I know." She sighed. "Things are a little foggy, but there aren't many options for the future where he hasn't left—at least for a little while."

Connor's heart tightened. He'd never known his grandmother to be wrong about something so important. "Why did he leave?"

She chuckled. "Probably for the same reason your grandfather left me too many times to count. You're just like I was when I was younger. Arrogant, bull-headed, stubborn."

"I didn't know Grandpa left you." He knew she couldn't see his frown. He wondered what other useful information about his family he didn't know. For a group that was prone to having psychics, they tended to be a little closed-mouthed about a lot of things "But he came back, didn't he?" He knew the answer. His grandfather had always been at family gatherings when he was growing up. Until that fateful night when he'd suffered a massive coronary. Connor had woken up in a cold sweat and instantly flown to Florida to be with everyone else. There hadn't been the need for phone calls; they'd all just known.

"Always. He was like that cat in the song that couldn't stay away no matter what the man did. Your wolf will be the same, but you'd better think about why he left. Just because you have 'the sight', it doesn't mean you're better than everyone else. You're just different. You make mistakes sometimes too. Learn to be a little more humble. I love you, Bairn."

"I love you, too, Grandma." He glanced at the dark screen of the TV he hadn't bothered to turn on. "Can I ask you a question?"

"Always."

"Have you ever had a time when your gift wasn't working right?" Asking for her help made him feel instantly better. Her call had warned him that Danny might leave if he didn't make an effort to be better. He could deal with that, but he had to get his powers back to where they should be.

"Like what? There's a lot of ways our gifts can be thrown off the rails for a while. At least you don't have to worry about being pregnant."

"It's been going on for a few days, or maybe longer." He thought back about how he'd had the vision of stars, then nothing for weeks. "We're still here because I saw stars falling into the ocean, then nothing for a while, which isn't too unusual, then I bumped into a cat shifter, had a vision, and since then I've either had to touch someone to see their future, or get little flashes seconds before something happens."

"You're still in LA?"

"Until this case is solved, yeah." Connor stood off the bed and started pacing the hotel room. At least no one was watching him.

"Too many people, too many futures." She hummed. "You're probably not overly-emotionally invested in things like you get when there's kids involved."

"But I've been in big cities before and things worked right." He had always considered Santa Fe and Phoenix big cities.

"No. Well, not exactly. Think back, Bairn. Those cases involved kids. There's a lot more emotional energy put out by kids when they're in danger than there is when it involves adults. The bear was killing adults."

Connor shook his head. "But that was in a small town."

"And if you'd be quiet and let your grandma finish what she was saying, I would've gotten to that."

Chastised in a way only his grandmother could do, Connor stopped pacing and looked in the mirror, thinking that for a moment he could see her face, still fairly unlined even as her hair was gaining more and more gray.

"When we're away from so many people, it's easier for us to pick up on more things happening around us. I think it's a survival technique. My great-grandmother told me things were so much easier in Scotland when everyone was still living in villages and clans. When we knew most everyone, and cared about them, it was easier to see what was coming, and do what we could to prevent it."

"I can see that."

The mirror illusion of his grandmother grinned. "But we can't remove millions of people from the planet, so we have to do what we can to adapt. Have you ever wondered why I moved to Florida?"

Connor shrugged and started pacing. He understood the need to not have a window for safety, but it would be nice to stand and stare out while he was one the phone. "I figured the weather was better for your joints."

His grandmother laughed loud and long. "Bairn, wait until you're a hundred and fifty and see how much you enjoy humidity in your bones. Not to mention those damned hurricanes. No. I moved here for the water and the people. Between the two, I've managed to limit my visions to our family." She sighed. "I know it's selfish of me, but with you out in the world, and others coming up, I figured I'd stop seeing so much of other people's disasters and focus on the things I wanted to and the ones I love."

"Water and people." Connor nodded to himself. "There's a lot of both around here."

"Exactly. Now, I want you to do two things for me."

"Anything." There wasn't anything his grandmother could ask him that he wouldn't do.

"Go apologize to Danny. You need your wolf. He's a good balance for you."

"As soon as I can." Connor had been about to try to find Danny through their link when she'd called.

"Good. But first, you need to go open the door and let Lisa in. Enjoy your dinner, me bairn." With a laugh, she ended the call.

Connor stared at the phone, then a knock came from the door.

"Open up, I've got my hands full." Lisa's voice was loud in his mind.

Feeling better than he had in days, Connor went over and opened the door. He didn't think he'd been on the phone long enough for her to have gotten to the restaurant and back, but maybe there hadn't been any traffic or lines, then he chided himself they were still in LA. Of course there had been lines and traffic.

The rush-hour traffic was slowing them down as Danny rode in Moreau's Explorer. Actually doing something as opposed to sitting around trying to figure out what he was going to say to Connor when they finally saw each other again. He wanted to make sure Connor understood how far across the line he'd gone, and that they were going to need to take steps to fix Connor's attitude if they were going to make the difference in the shifter community that they really wanted to make.

"You know, you two really do have something unusual," Moreau said. "I mean, I'm not Connor's biggest fan, but I'd hate to see him if he didn't have you."

"He'd probably still have Lisa," Danny looked out the window at the palm trees and yearned for the pines around Jemez Springs. "She was around before I was."

"But I bet she doesn't have the same level of influence as you do. I know with Simone and her wife, Simone always said Brenda was the most influential person in her life. I might be her sounding board and even her good right hand, but Brenda was her heart and soul."

Danny chuckled. "And you think I'm Connor's heart and soul?"

Moreau maneuvered the Explorer into a parking spot that was nearly too small for it. "Maybe…Probably. We don't all find that."

"Are you even looking?" Danny unbuckled his seatbelt and tried to turn the conversation away from him and Connor.

"Not in the traditional sense." Moreau got out of the Explorer. "You know I'm ace, but that doesn't mean I don't want someone to come home to. Someone to worry about me if I get hurt. Someone to cuddle."

Danny chuckled again as they started walking toward the beach and the boardwalk that wasn't. "Yeah, cuddles are nice."

"Exactly. But most people want to find someone that wants to play poke with body parts and that's just not me." Moreau put his hands in his pockets as the stream of people walking and skating grew heavier. "I don't know why, unless it's just our animal sides being so strong, but I haven't run into many other ace shifters. The couple I have come across were just totally not compatible. Honestly, that's one of the reasons I jumped at the idea of joining Shifter Force."

Danny frowned. "Moreau, you're cute and all, but-"

Moreau laughed. "Gods, no. That's not what I'm suggesting. Family. I can see this as a family unit. A lot of law enforcement, even humans, have trouble finding family outside their working environment. I like the idea that I might have a chance to have something like that with you guys. You, Lisa, even Connor care what happens to me. That means a lot." He sidestepped a tall woman skating between them. "I've been thinking about this the past day or so, as Connor's been getting worse and worse. I'm going to fight to keep Shifter Force together. We might be all different sorts of shifters, and come from different backgrounds, but that doesn't matter. We're going to help other shifters. That's huge. The thing is, I think we're also going to help each other find a place in the world."

As they turned off Boardwalk, Danny nodded. "I can see that. It's my place to sit Connor down and talk to him. We're the central core of this group, and yeah, we need to stick together as much for us as for the shifters we're going to help."

"Good. Now, let's see what this malamute has to say about what's going on around here, or at the very least why he isn't answering your cousin's calls." Moreau started up the stairs.

"If that's all we accomplish with this little trip, I'll be happy." Danny trailed after Moreau.

When they reached Reggie's door, Moreau knocked.

The door swung open.

"This isn't good." Moreau pushed it a little farther, but didn't step over the threshold. "Reggie Winters, this is Agent Moreau with Shifter Force. Please come out."

Danny listened for all he was worth. Two doors down someone was playing heavy metal music too loud. He blocked that out and tried to focus on Reggie's apartment. A refrigerator buzzed a short distance away. There was no sound from the air conditioner. He didn't pick up a heartbeat, or the sounds of anyone moving around in the small space beyond the door.

"I've got nothing." Danny reflexively reached for his gun but stopped himself. He knew the apartment was vacant of life. There was no danger.

"Same here." Moreau slowly entered the living room. "Not smelling anything out of the ordinary. Bad aftershave, someone vaped here a while back, but not recently, dog shifter, cat shifter, Connor, humans, pizza a few days back."

Danny blinked at him. "You're getting all that? Your nose is a lot better than mine."

"Different species, different skills." Moreau paused. "You realize that we don't have a search warrant? Anything we find won't be admissible in court."

"Yeah." Danny nodded. He wished they'd thought to bring gloves or something so they wouldn't leave evidence of coming in, not that Reggie wouldn't know they'd been there as soon as he came home…if he came home. "So we don't tell anyone what we find, or make sure we backup anything we find as legally as possible."

"Now you're thinking like an FBI agent." Moreau guffawed. "That's what we do when we have to. Not cool to a lot of people, but sometimes it's the only way to get criminals off the street. Goes back to getting rid of people like Al Capone."

"Not sure I like it." Danny walked from the living room into the bedroom. Everything looked fairly clean. Reggie wasn't perfect, but at least he wasn't a slob.

On the nightstand lay three smart phones. Danny wanted to pick them up, check the numbers, see if any of them were the burner phones that had been texting Lindy Lui, find out which one was the phone Trina had been calling. Then he paused and pulled out his own phone. Jime had texted him Reggie's number. Danny found it and called it. The phone in the middle came to life with a standard factory preset ring tone.

Danny leaned over and saw his phone was the one calling. He ended the call. "I found his phone."

"I realized something in here too," Moreau said.

Hurrying back to the living room, Danny slipped his phone back into his pocket. "What?"

"Look around." Moreau put a pen back in his pocket. Most of the drawers in the room had been opened. "Tell me what's missing."

"Sneaky little thief shifter." Taking his time to check each drawer and cabinet Moreau had so carefully opened. For the most part, they were all empty. One drawer had a bottle of lube and some condoms. There was a small stack of take-out menus in a different drawer.

Stepping to the middle of the room, Danny shook his head. "Doesn't look like he spends a lot of time here, but beyond that?"

"There's no mail. Sure, maybe he dumps most of the junk mail in a garbage can near the mailbox, but there should be things like an electric bill, a phone bill." Moreau ticked things off on his hand.

"But Connor said Reggie was here when he came by the other day. Trina said they lived here. She's expecting to come back here when Reggie tells her it's safe." Danny sighed. That might be why all the scents were old. "Maybe he doesn't feel safe here after those thugs followed him as he was leaving the meeting with Connor. But why would he leave the phones?"

"Especially the one Trina calls him on," Moreau finished for him. "There's something wrong here. More than just the door being open when we arrived."

Danny ran his hand through his hair and glanced around, not seeing anything new. "I wish Connor was here, he might be able to get a vision that might help us out." Since they'd met, he'd gotten so used to Connor being right there underfoot, that it felt really strange without him there.

"We should at least tell him," Moreau said.

"Yeah." With a deep breath, Danny reached out to Connor, not using their personal, private link, but the wider one Connor maintained with Lisa and Moreau.

"Connor, we've stumbled on something."

"What do you have?" Connor sounded just like normal, although there was the sensation that he might be eating.

"We're at Reggie's place and his door was open, and he has three phones, and no mail." Danny made

sure to put in mental pictures of things, not sure if that would help Connor or not.

"Three phones—that's a bit suspicious," Lisa added and the sensation of eating made Danny's mouth water. *"Why would anyone have three phones?"*

"He might like to play games where it helps to have multiple players," Moreau suggested.

"People really do that?" Lisa sounded doubtful.

"Yeah, burner phones make it really easy, or some people only have one active phone and just use the others as minicomputers running off the hot spot," Moreau added.

"That sounds like you've done it," Connor said. *"Why did you guys go over to Reggie's again?"*

"Jime called and Reggie hasn't answered Trina's calls in a couple of days," Danny felt odd standing in a strange living room having a mental conversation but he didn't want to walk out if Connor needed to see something that was there in the apartment.

"Curious," Connor muttered.

"We also checked the cell phone tower and the phone's not moved in over a day—at least, it hasn't left the coverage area for the local tower," Danny walked over and shoved the door almost closed with his toe. He didn't want to leave any more evidence than they already had that they'd entered the place without permission. As the sensation of eating continued to flow from Connor and Lisa, Danny's stomach growled reminding him that he and Moreau hadn't had anything to eat since the brunch at the agency.

"Do you want me to come over and see if I can get anything?" Connor's tone was a bit off, like he didn't

really want to do that. *"If Reggie's not there, it might be tricky."*

Danny stared at Moreau. Had Connor just admitted he wasn't perfect? Something was up.

"Why don't we keep that as an option if we need it later?" Moreau said. *"We could get a warrant and make things official if we need to."*

"A warrant might be a good thing," Lisa agreed.

"Definitely. Are you two heading back over here?" Connor asked.

"Not sure about later, but we've got a couple other leads to check on tonight," Danny said, doing his best to keep things as close to truthful as possible. *"If we end up closer to Moreau's hotel, we might just crash there."*

"I'm sorry about earlier," Connor's mental voice was suddenly louder, more intimate. He'd dropped Moreau and Lisa out of their conversation.

Danny nodded and pointed to his head to let Moreau know the discussion was still going on. *"I am too. I need to think about some things. Okay?"*

"Okay." Connor's voice lowered. *"I love you, Dawg."*

"I love you too." Danny broke the connection and looked at Moreau. "They were obviously eating and that made me hungry. What do you say we go down to the boardwalk and see if we can find a good steakhouse and take a long walk on the beach?"

"You do realize that we're more apt to find seafood around here and not steak." Moreau went over and toed the door open again.

"Please, tell me there's at least surf and turf. I know you and Connor like fish, but I'm a canine."

Danny went out first and let Moreau close the door back to the state it had been in when they arrived.

"Let's go find out." Moreau walked past Danny and down the stairs.

Following, Danny thought back on the conversation. Connor had seemed more subdued than normal, like maybe he realized what he'd done and was sorry, even if he hadn't come out and said anything. He hoped that was the case. Although he didn't want to make a scene with Connor, he did want to make sure *his* Cat understood things were going to have to be different.

Danny woke with a start and sat up. He looked over at the other bed in the motel room. Moreau lay not moving and softly snoring. It wasn't anything as loud as Connor's purring.

He swung his legs over the edge of the bed, stood, and walked to the bathroom. After relieving himself, he washed his hands and slinked back toward the bed.

The neon light of the motel's 'vacancy' sign blinked off and on through the thin drapes. There was constant noise from the cars and trucks going past, even after midnight. It had made it hard to get to sleep. If there was one blessing to Connor's purring, it helped block out the sounds of the city and had become comforting enough to lull him to sleep even as he complained about it.

Danny sat on the side of the bed and looked out at the traffic flowing past and thought about the dream he'd had of a day spent along the Jemez River with

Connor. He could still smell the pine trees over the exhaust of the city.

Danny lifted his nose and took a deep breath of the pine-scented air as Connor parked in a pullout on Route Four.

Connor shifted as he jumped out, landed on four paws, and took off running.

Danny followed, twisting in mid-air as he dropped his human form for his wolf skin and ran full out after Connor.

When they got to the river, Connor stepped into the clear stream and lapped at the water.

"Don't you know it isn't safe to drink out of the river?" *Danny asked, rubbing up against him.*

"Been doing it all my life," *Connor said.* "Of course only in cat form."

Danny lapped at the water. "Tastes pretty good."

Connor lay down and rolled in the cool current.

"Never knew a cat who liked water as much as you do."

Connor stepped out of the stream. "Come on." *He shook the water from his fur and ran into the brush.*

For half an hour, they chased each other around. First one in front and then the other.

Finally, Connor flopped down on the grass with Danny beside him.

"This has been fun." *Danny rubbed against Connors side.* "We should do it more often."

Connor licked Danny's nose. "We could call this 'our place'."

"Yeah." *Danny put his paw over Connor's back, then laid his head on Connor's rib cage. The rise and fall of Connor's chest and his gentle purring soon lulled Danny to sleep.*

The dream woke Connor enough that he turned first to one side, and then to the other trying to get comfortable. Although he and Danny had only been together a short time, they hadn't voluntarily slept apart since the first night they spent together at his house in Santa Fe. They'd never had a fight. Well, at least not a serious one. His heart warmed as he remembered the time right after they met when he asked Danny to hold his hamburger, and Danny took a bite of it. He'd hissed at Danny. "I told you to hold it, not eat it." But that wasn't really a fight.

He finally got out of bed, went to the mini-fridge, and got a bottle of cold water.

Sitting in a chair, he thought about all of the times with Danny. Soaking in the hot tub at his house in Santa Fe. The feeling when Danny was abducted by Hernandez, and he'd thought he lost him. What would he do without Danny? His grandmother said Danny completed him. In that moment, he felt as if part of him was missing.

He stood, walked back to the bed, and shifted into cat form. Maybe he'd sleep better. Lying with his head on his paws, he started purring. He could almost hear Danny complain about the noise.

Chapter 12

The piercing yowl of a Siamese cat penetrated Connor's sleep causing him to leap from the bed shifting as he did. He landed on his feet and immediately sat on the side of the bed with his head in his hands.

The twisted body of the young girl lay on in a pile of garbage in an alley. The streetlight gleamed off a silver necklace set with dark green stones that encircled her neck. The human-shaped shadow stood over her, reached down, and removed the necklace. The person walked to the street end of the alley and got into the passenger seat of a running car. A neon light across the street blinked the name of the diner where they'd had breakfast the day before.

He reached out to Danny mentally. *"Dawg. Trouble. We have another body. Get Moreau and meet us at the diner we had breakfast at."*

"Do you realize what time it is?"

"Sorry." He looked at the clock. *"It's three a.m. I just saw Lindy's murder. See if Moreau can contact Lawrence or Perkins and have them meet us at the alley behind the diner where we had breakfast."*

As he pulled on his jeans, he called Lisa. "Come on, I know where Lindy is."

Lisa rolled over and groaned. "You do realize I'm not an owl. It's still dark out."

Connor wrinkled his nose as he yanked a t-shirt over his head. "How do you know that?"

"Birds have an excellent sense of light and dark. It's still dark out there." She eased off the bed. "And what about Danny and Moreau?"

"They're on the way." He sat on the bed to pull on his shoes. He really hoped that Danny would be willing to listen when they got together. Maybe he could get Lisa to ride with Moreau when they left the scene and he and Danny could talk things out in the Jeep. He really didn't want to spend another night without his wolf at his side.

Connor slammed down the brakes for what felt like the hundredth time since he left the hotel. "Does this traffic never let up?"

"I always thought New York was the town that never slept." Lisa yawned. "Either that, or all these people have early jobs to get to. At least we're almost there."

"I know." Connor could feel Danny ahead of them, already at the crime scene. A knot formed in his stomach. He couldn't believe he was nervous about seeing Danny. They hadn't even had a real fight, but with his grandmother's warning, he wanted to make sure he didn't do anything to make the situation worse.

He swung through the parking lot of the diner to the alley behind it causing Lisa to grab her 'oh, shit' bar on the dash in front of her as he angled toward the dark Explorer that blocked casual access to the alley.

"You can slow down a bit," Lisa muttered.

"Sorry." Connor pulled the parking brake as he turned off the car.

Danny and Moreau stood in front of the Explorer, looking down the alley. Moreau was squatting down, looking across the area as Danny slowly panned a flashlight around illuminating the area. The added light caught things even their night sight wouldn't catch.

The girl's twisted body lay roughly three feet from the entrance to the alley. Her unseeing eyes stared from a face contorted with pain.

"She was dumped here," Moreau said.

The sound of sirens rose above the noise of the city. A patrol car swung in behind the Jeep, and Perkins got out of the passenger side. Another came in close behind it.

A female officer exited from the driver's side.

"What do you have, McGriffin?" As Perkins stepped closer to Connor pulling on a pair of gloves, he sneezed. "You realize this is outside of our jurisdiction, but we called in the LA folks."

Inwardly Connor groaned. The complexities of dealing with so many different forces were getting on his nerves bigtime. Things were so much easier in areas with just one law enforcement branch to deal with. He started forward, and Danny put out an arm to stop him.

In his hand were a pair of purple rubber gloves. "Be professional. Respect their crime scene."

"Thanks." Connor took the gloves. *"Sorry I've been an idiot lately."*

"We'll talk." Danny's softly brushed Connor's fingers, sending tingles through him.

The simple gesture gave him hope there was time to make things right.

Putting on the gloves, Connor knelt and let his arm make contact with her hair. "Lindy Lui."

Lindy stood on a street corner. A car pulled up. It was an older model sedan, not even a color came through the vision. A door opened.

Lindy got in, even as her heart raced. "I've done everything you've asked. When will it be over?"

"When I say it's over." A man in the back seat said as the human woman driving pulled away from the curb. "Why did you send Shifter Force after us?"

"I don't know what you're talking about." Lindy started to turn but the man behind her hit her in the back of the head.

"I don't believe you, bitch. Why are you actor types so hard to deal with?"

Metal coiled around Lindy's neck and jerked her backwards.

"No." Lindy clawed at her neck, her fingers becoming claws as the heavy necklace chain tightened around her. "Not silver!" It burned.

The pain was so much, Connor rocked back on his heels, breaking contact, ending the vision. Even with his grandmother's explanation of what was happening with his visions, the limitations made it hard.

Connor raised his head and sniffed. Something didn't smell right, but there was so much else in the alley, he couldn't pin it down. "Dawg, do you smell something?"

Danny shifted, placed his nose to the ground, and sniffed around the alley.

"Agent Moreau, I thought you'd left the FBI." A tall dark police officer with an LA badge walked forward. "I was sorry to hear about Agent Reed."

"Yeah, still getting used to her not being around. Good to see you, Tully." Moreau shook the man's hand. "Not sure if you know Perkins and his partner?"

Tully glanced at Perkins, "Venice Beach, yeah we've crossed paths before." He nodded to them. "Perkins, Black, what brings all of you to the west side of LA, a bit out of your area?"

"A murder that might be connected to one of ours, and to that shootout in Hollywood yesterday." Perkins wiped his nose on the back of his hand like he was trying to stifle a sneeze.

"And because it crosses all sorts of jurisdictions, you called Moreau, got it." Tully pulled out a pair of gloves.

"Actually, Captain Lawrence called Moreau in because the first victim was a shifter." Perkins pointed toward Lindy. "As was this one."

"Shifter?" Tully glanced at Connor as if just seeing him.

Connor pulled out his badge and handed it to him. "McGriffin with Shifter Force. We're Moreau's new partners."

Tully glanced at the badge and nodded. "You're what, like the FBI, but for shifters? Might be a good time for you guys. More and more crimes we can't always explain." He handed the badge back.

"That's one of the reasons we're doing this." Connor put the badge back in his pocket.

"Male." Danny said through their link. *"Smells familiar, but I can't place it."*

After a sneeze, Perkins wiped his sleeve across his face. "Murder weapon?"

Danny shifted back to human.

"Whoa, dude, warn a guy." Tully took a couple of steps back. "Thought you were a crime scene dog."

"Sorry." Danny smiled. "Agent Lupan." He glanced at Moreau and Lisa. "Let's see if there's anything else here, but we went over the area earlier and there's way too much garbage."

"And I'm not about to be flying around in the dark giving air support," Lisa said, pulling out her own mini-flashlight from her purse. "If we're going to need night air support, we're going to need to find ourselves an owl."

Danny chuckled. "We'll talk about it, if we can find an owl with police or investigation experience."

"Training Con-" Moreau's statement was cut off as Danny gave him a big flashlight a little more forcefully than need be.

"I'm sorry I'm a lot of trouble. Thanks for bearing with me," Connor said through their link before focusing on the humans.

Connor looked at Perkins. "It was a silver necklace. I think he took it with him." He sighed and shook his head. "The vision cut out before she actually died, but it's not here with the body."

"A necklace? How did he kill her with a necklace?" Officer Black asked as she also donned a pair of gloves.

"She was a shifter. The silver seeped into her body through her skin." Connor stood. "It's not an easy death. Very painful, even when the victim isn't being strangled while the silver eats into them." He took a deep breath. There was something odd about Lindy, and the silver was covering it up. Careful not to touch the body, or move anything, he leaned over her cooling form and inhaled as strongly as he could to confirm his suspicions. With a soft growl, he straightened and looked at the gathered police officers. "We might be able to charge the killer with two counts of murder. Lindy was pregnant."

"Are you sure?" Officer Black asked. "What makes you think so?"

Connor stood and stepped away from Lindy "I'm sure. A pregnant female gives off certain hormonal scents that alert everyone to her condition, although most humans can't smell them. They're faint enough, I don't think she knew it yet. Maybe the ME can determine who the father is with DNA."

Perkins took an inhaler from his pocket and sprayed it into his mouth. "We'd have to have men to test to match DNA. How'd you know she was here?"

Connor realized he probably shouldn't lean against anything in the alley and took a couple of steps away to prop himself on the hood of the Explorer. "I had a vision. I told Lawrence the other day I'd seen her body in an alley. This time I knew where the alley was."

"How?" Perkins asked.

Tully straightened from where he'd been kneeling next to Lindy's body. "This wound is consistent with silver poisoning. The CSIs had training on it recently. With more shifters around, they thought we should know."

Resisting the urge to say something coy, Connor pointed to the neon sign of the diner. "We had breakfast there. Lindy was in the diner. That's when I had the first vision."

A man wearing a white apron came out the back door of the cafe. "What's going on back here? I heard the sirens." He looked toward the body. "Oh, my God." He covered his mouth with his apron. "That's Lindy. What happened to her?"

Officer Black stopped him from approaching the body as an ambulance pulled up behind the patrol cars and two EMT's got out. "Please, Sir. Just stand back and let us do our job." She took a notebook out of her shirt pocket. "Did you know the deceased?"

"Yeah." He lowered the apron and turned from Lindy's corpse. "She lived just around the corner. Came in here every morning for breakfast. Usually about two or three o'clock after a night out."

"Was she here this morning?" Black asked.

Connor stood back and let the officer do her job, just listened to everything, hoping some of it would give them a clue to go on with their investigation.

"Yeah. About an hour ago." The man glanced at the empty parking lot as if he could figure something out by looking there.

"Was she alone?" Black continued to probe him, as Perkins was making notes in a notebook, just like Danny carried all the time. Since Perkins had done that in Lawrence's office the day before, it made Connor wonder if he was always taking notes while other people were talking.

"No." He shook his head. "She was with a young kid. Looked about 15 or so."

"Had you seen him before?" Black continued interrogating.

"Yeah." The cook nodded. "He's been in here with her several times."

Black smiled for the first time. "Do you know his name?"

"She never introduced him. I thought he might be her younger brother or something. She called him Lucas."

"Thank you. May I get your name and address?"

Danny came back and touched Connor's shoulder, drawing his attention away from Officer Black and the cook, or dishwasher, whatever he was.

"What's up, Dawg?"

"We've covered this alley, unless we want to spend all morning dumpster diving."

Connor shook his head. "If the humans want to do that, they can. A silver necklace should stand out to us. What do you say, you and Moreau shift and do a quick sweep of the surrounding area. I wish I had more to go on."

"Me too." Danny smiled. "I'm proud of you for letting Officer Black handle things. I know you would normally be the one asking the questions."

"Yeah. Give me a chance and we'll see about me doing more listening and less talking."

"That's good." Danny shifted. *"We'll keep talking."*

"Thanks." Connor did his best to not let his relief, at Danny seeming to not still be mad at him, show too much. He didn't want to be like his grandparents and have Danny leave multiple times because he was too arrogant.

The pads on Danny's paws were dirty and gritty. He had to force himself to not stop and lick them. He and Lisa had spent hours checking the alley behind and adjacent to the café for Lindy less than twenty-four hours before, and he didn't look forward to doing it again.

"It smells worse down here and with my human nose," Lisa muttered as she walked between Danny and Moreau.

"It might be better with a human nose," Danny replied.

"I second that." Moreau trotted a little faster to keep up with their longer legs. *"I've been in some nasty alleys over the years but damn."*

"Oh, trust me, there are cans you want to stay away from out here." Danny paused as they reached the road at the end of the alley. *"You know this might be easier if we had air support."*

"To find a necklace in a pile of garbage?" Lisa huffed. "You realize what a longshot that would be?"

"It's an idea." Danny jogged across the street as an opening in the traffic presented itself.

"We could only hope." Moreau caught up to Danny as Danny started sniffing around the first dumpster. *"Although we have to check, the odds of actually finding the necklace our killer used are minimal. That would almost be too easy."*

"You probably have more experience with this than I do," Danny said, trying to avoid the smell of rancid beer that filled his nose. *"But that was my thought."*

"Too many speeding tickets and not enough bodies over the years, Dawg?" Moreau chuckled, then backed up sneezing and rubbing his long nose.

"Could say that." Danny headed for the second dumpster.

"I bet the LAPD will have people going over the area too." Lisa looked into the dumpster as they sniffed around it.

"That's a safe bet." Moreau stopped sneezing and trotted after them. *"Seriously people are disgusting."*

"No arguments there, Thief." Danny tried out the nickname for Moreau. He liked the way it sounded.

Lisa paused and looked at Moreau as he sniffed the tighter parts of the dumpster where Danny's larger wolf body didn't fit as well as his smaller ring-tailed cat. "Thief? You do look a little bit like an anorexic raccoon, with a long nose."

Moreau slipped out of the other side of the dumpster and glared at Danny. *"I'm not sure I like it."*

"I wasn't sure if I liked Dawg at first, but I got used to it." Danny gave him a wolfish smile. *"We'll bounce it past Connor when we get back. Since he's not piped in, I'm guessing he's not listening."*

"He's playing nice with the locals," Lisa said. "That'll be taking more of his attention."

"Yeah, why's he being so nice with everyone today?" Moreau stopped glaring at Danny and moved to the next dumpster.

Lisa shrugged as she followed. "I know yesterday really shook him up. Not sure if you knew it, but his *sight* is on the fritz."

"I knew something was off, but he hadn't gone into it. He's just been more of an asshole than normal."

Since it was just them, Danny didn't mind telling Lisa, and if Connor was listening in without their knowing, it would serve him right to get a mind full.

"Yeah. He explained it to me, and then his grandmother called." Lisa shook her head after lifting a box and backed away from the dumpster. "Ah. No. Not this one. But after he spoke with her, he's been more worried about the way he's been acting and not as worried about his gift."

"I'd love to know what she told him." Danny caught a whiff of something that defied description beyond nasty and gagged leaving that dumpster to the LAPD.

"You could ask him," Moreau said, racing toward the next dumpster.

"After all this is over." Danny tried to catch up to Moreau, hoping the next trash bin was going to be somewhat more pleasant. *"He's a bit mellower in between cases."* Danny hoped Connor's more co-operative self would remain that long and they'd have the opportunity to sit and talk. It was really nice to see Connor playing nice with the authorities.

They reached the end of the alley and Danny paused. *"We're two blocks south of the café. How far do we want to go?"*

"Normally if perps are stupid and drop evidence soon after committing a crime, it's within a two-block radius," Moreau said. *"We can eliminate the highway side, we could check the alley to the east and head back toward the café."*

"That FBI knowledge of yours comes in handy," Lisa said. "Let's head east then. Maybe the locals have thought to go west and look."

As they headed down the next alley, Danny wondered what Connor's grandmother had talked to him about. Miranda McCay was a force to be reckoned with. If she had called Connor, the odds were she'd seen something and had to warn him. Though honestly, if it helped improve Connor's general attitude, he didn't really care; she'd helped make their situation better.

Connor stood beside Lindy's body trying to do as Danny had told him and not interfere as he watched Tully and Officer Black look for clues.

"We've got this scene as catalogued as we can until the CSI team shows up," Tully said as he headed toward Connor. "They just let me know they're still half an hour out. Something about a gang shooting closer to downtown."

Officer Black held up Lindy's purse. "Tully, while you're waiting, I think I'm going to see if we can find another lead in here. This is an inter-departmental case."

Tully sighed. "Don't lose anything. I don't want to hear anything about evidence getting misplaced."

"Sure." Officer Black started pulling things, handing them to Perkins who had a large Ziploc bag and was carefully putting things into it as they glanced at it. For the most part it was all regular stuff, lipstick, condoms, Kleenex.

As she extracted a wallet, Connor stepped closer. He'd been doing good at letting the police take lead, but the wallet might be more useful. "Hold on, what's in that?"

Perkins tucked the bag under his arm, and sniffled. "Let's see. Standard things, debit cards, most look like prepaid…that's odd. Oh, here's a driver's license."

Black pulled out a scanner. "Let's see that." She swiped it and stared at the small screen. "No warrants, a couple of minor tickets that she paid."

Perkins glanced at the license. "That address is just a couple blocks away."

"While Tully waits for the CSI, can we check it out?" Connor sighed, it was so much easier to just charge ahead, but there was too much of a chance of the locals getting bent out of shape and upsetting Danny. He didn't want his grandmother's vision to come true— Danny sleeping at Moreau's just one night was harder than he expected it to be.

"Actually, Perkins or Black should stay with the scene," Tully interrupted. "That address is in my jurisdiction."

"And we don't need to upset the locals," Connor muttered softly enough he hoped the humans didn't hear him.

"Connor be nice," Danny said as he, Lisa, and Moreau came across the parking lot.

"I said it softly. I doubt they even heard me." He couldn't believe he was defending himself, but he wanted to make Danny happier with him.

"I know." Danny shifted and grinned at him as Moreau jumped into the Explorer to complete his own shift and get dressed.

"You guys got back just in time." Connor returned Danny's smile. "Find anything?"

Danny shook his head. "Nope. Unless you count way too many smelly dumpsters, a dead rat, two homeless people having sex, or an illegal chop shop as something."

"Can you give me the address of the chop shop?" Tully pulled out a notebook and pen.

It made Connor wonder if most beat cops carried Danny's standard accoutrements.

"Sure." Lisa pulled out her own pad and gave him the address. "Thought you might like that. Lots of unused parts in the dumpsters out behind it. Should be enough evidence there to close them down."

Tully smiled. "Thanks. Now, let's go check out this address."

"Sure." Connor went to the Jeep. "Danny, do you and Moreau want to ride with us?"

Danny glanced at Moreau who nodded. "Sure."

Seconds later, they were all in the Jeep following Tully and Perkins as they headed for Lindy's apartment.

Connor pulled into the circle drive of the upscale apartment building behind the patrol car. They piled out and the four shifters followed Perkins and Tully into the building.

A security guard just inside the door stopped them. "What can I do for you officers?"

"I understand Ms. Lindy Lui lives here," Tully took the lead.

"Is there a problem?" The guard glanced from the two police officers to the shifters in street clothes.

"Ms. Lui was murdered early this morning," Tully explained. "We need to check out her apartment."

"Do you have a warrant?" The guard looked like he was prepared to block them if need be.

"No, but since it's a murder investigation, it won't be hard to get one." Tully gave the man a stern look. "Actually, Agent Moreau, doesn't the FBI supersede warrants in cases like this?"

Before Moreau could respond, the guard gave in. "FBI? I'm sorry, didn't mean to slow down your investigation. I'll have to call up and see if Ms. Alexander will see you without it."

Connor frowned. "Who's Ms. Alexander?" He so wasn't in the mood for another complication. Small town cases were never so convoluted. Although the more they found out, the worse things looked for the people at Kelly and Associates.

"Ms. Jessie Alexander." The guard pulled out his phone. "She and Ms. Lui share the apartment."

"We'd rather you not call," Moreau said. "It's better to let us announce ourselves." He took the lead headed for the elevator. "Perkins, stay here and don't let anyone on the elevator. Also watch if someone tries to leave the building."

"Interesting… Kelly's secretary rooms with Lindy. Strange they didn't tell us that when we questioned them," Connor said.

Danny shrugged. "They probably didn't think it was important."

"Or else they wanted to hide it." Lisa chuckled. "It's hard to hide things from the Cat, though. I'm surprised you hadn't already figured that out."

"Things are a little fuzzy out here." Connor flashed her a look. "Everyone, stay alert. I'm not sure what we're going into."

"We got it," Moreau said.

"You guys are fairly organized, aren't you?" Tully hit the elevator button.

"We've got to be," Danny replied. "If we aren't, we look bad, and the way the country feels about shifters, we have to set a good example." He gave Connor a look that quietly told him to behave.

The elevator arrived, and they all piled in.

Tully glanced at his notebook. "Says here they're on the sixth floor."

As the door started to close, Connor stopped it. "Agent Collins, do you mind staying down here? If something happens, you can reach us faster than Perkins will be able to."

She stepped out of the elevator. "Sure, Agent McGriffin." She flashed him a grin, as if she found it funny they were sounding official.

Connor figured it might help people treat them better if they started calling themselves agents when other agencies were around.

As the elevator door completed its close, Connor looked at Moreau. "Agent Moreau, I'll let you cover the hallway when we come out of the elevator, if you don't mind."

Moreau's eyebrows rose. "Sure. I'm up for it."

"Thanks." Connor took a deep breath. Trying to keep things professional was going to take some effort, but hopefully Danny would continue to help him and they could get the credit Shift Force was due.

As the elevator door opened on the sixth floor, Danny sniffed. "I smell something familiar."

Connor stepped off behind him and took a deep scenting inhalation. "Me too. Perfume I've smelled before."

Tully went down the hall and stopped at a door. He double-checked his pad before knocking "Ms. Alexander, this is the police."

After a few seconds, he rapped again. "Open up, or we're coming in." His words carried the power of command most people associated with the authorities.

The door opened. Ms. Alexander stood there clutching a robe around herself. "What's going on? What do the police want with me?"

"We need to search the apartment," Tully said.

She didn't look like she was ready to step aside as she looked past Tully to Connor, Danny, and Moreau. "Do you have a warrant?"

"Not needed when we have a dead body and the FBI's involved."

"Whose body?" Jessie's gaze darted between them. "There's no body here. And none of these men are FBI. They're Shifter Force."

Connor hoped he could shock her into at least letting them in. "Lindy Lui was murdered a couple of hours ago. We need to check the apartment for possible clues."

"Lindy murdered?" Jessie stumbled a couple of steps back until she braced herself against a wall. "When? How? Where?"

Tully went through the door first. "That's part of what we're trying to figure out. We'll need to get a statement from you about her activities the past couple of days."

"I'll give you what I can."

Not wanting to intrude on something it sounded like Tully had under control, Connor headed down the narrow hall, toward the two bedrooms at the end. One door was closed; the other open. It made sense that the closed one was Lindy's.

Jessie pushed past Tully and tried followed him. "Wait a minute. You aren't police. You can't go in there."

Tully acted fast and stepped between her and Connor. "He's with me and has the authority to search the premises."

"By what law?" She sounded more like a secretary who was used to keeping people from getting to her boss.

"We have significant cause and a dead body." Tully took her by the arm and led her to the living room. "If we need to, I can haul you down to the precinct and we can question you there as a suspect for murder."

She objected, but Connor did his best to block her out. He hoped Tully could handle her until he found out what he could and then send the LAPD back with search warrants to properly catalogue anything he came up with.

The room was quite a mess. It looked like it was normally well-cleaned and cared for, but clothes were scattered on the bed, on a chair by the window, and across the floor. Several days' worth of them, if Connor had to guess.

He picked up a discarded dress from the bed and images instantly flooded into him.

Lindy was glaring at Jessie, the dress wadded up in her hands. From the fact she was in her bra and panties, she'd just removed it, or was about to put it on. "I don't want to do this, Jessie. Why does he make me?" Tears ran down her cheeks, streaking her mascara.

Jessie walked over and took hold of the dress, as if to pull it away from Lindy. "It's in your contract to do what he says."

"But this is not part of my acting career." Lindy balled the dress up tighter and held it to her face. It softened her sobs.

"You do what you're told." Jessie jerked the dress hard enough to yank it from Lindy's grasp. "You know what'll happen if you don't."

Lindy glared at Jessie. "So he'll kill me? That might be better than this hell."

"It'll be fine." Jessie's face softened and she tossed the dress on the bed from where Connor had picked it up. "Just do what he says. It's probably only going to be a few more times."

"What if he makes me have an abortion?" She clutched her bare stomach.

"If he says so, yes." Jessie's voice was cold.

Having seen enough, Connor dropped the dress on the bed. Apparently Lindy did know about the pregnancy. Shifter children were precious. They weren't easy to conceive or carry to term. No one should be forced to have an abortion, particularly a shifter, not unless a doctor said there was no hope for either the mother or the baby.

Connor turned from the room.

Danny stood just outside the door, guarding as he so often did. "She knew she was pregnant didn't she?"

"What? Yes." Connor blinked at Danny. There was no way Danny could've seen his vision, no mental link was that tight.

"I'm sorry, Cat, I know that ups the stakes." Danny gave him a brief hug.

"Yeah it does." Connor let go of Danny and looked at him. "That wasn't very professional."

Shrugging, Danny grinned. "Well, nobody saw, and you needed it." He gave Connor a quick kiss.

It helped take the edge off Connor's fury at Lindy's death. "Yeah I did. Thank you." He touched Danny's lips with his, then headed down the hall toward the living room, knowing his wolf was with him.

He glared at Jessie where she sat coyly answering Tully's questions. "You're in on the blackmail, aren't you?"

She looked at him smugly. "I don't know what you mean."

Ignoring her denial, Connor pressed her. "What contract were you talking about when you and Lindy were arguing?"

Her eyes widened. "I don't know what you mean."

Connor stalked up to her. "You knew Lindy was pregnant."

"I know nothing of the sort." She turned away as if afraid he'd see the lie in her eyes. Then she grabbed hold of Officer Tully. "Officer, I need protection. This man is a lunatic. He was screaming and shouting in our office yesterday. He attacked Maria Lopez. You know who she is, don't you?"

Tully glanced from Connor to Jessie. "Did you?"

Connor swallowed. "It's complicated, but I didn't attack her. Agent Moreau can vouch for me."

"He already has, as far as Shifter Force goes, but I can't have you threatening humans." Tully took a step toward Connor. "Why don't you go with what you're already found and call that good for the moment? I'll get a CSI team in here to officially go over the place and we'll share our findings with you."

Danny put his hand on Connor's shoulder. "Come on, Cat, let's get you out of here. Officer Tully's right. Their team is more thorough than we can be."

Not wanting to back down, but understanding that Jessie had managed to outmaneuver him, Connor nodded. The secretary knew something, and he was going to find out what it was. The more they found out, the more it pointed to their blackmailer being someone at the agency, and she knew who.

Chapter 13

Connor sat out in the Jeep, waiting for Perkins and Black to finish in the Kelly agency. They'd been gone almost five minutes. He hated sending them in without him, but Kelly had made it clear the previous day that he never wanted to see Connor or any of Shifter Force ever again. Although he could've just buffaloed his way in, he was determined to act professional. If that meant him and Lisa sitting in the Jeep while Danny, and Moreau checked on things with the LAPD, and Perkins and Black did their part, then so be it.

"You're being quiet." Lisa put her hand on his shoulder.

"Thinking, and trying to be good."

Lisa chuckled and patted his shoulder. "You're doing a good job of being good. I'm proud of you and I think Danny is too."

"Then it's working. Grandma says I need to start watching my arrogance, or Danny might leave me." He spit it out, but talking to Lisa was going to make it easier to sit in the Jeep.

"Really?" Lisa's eyes widened. "I know Danny got frustrated yesterday, but I don't think he's upset enough to leave you."

"I hope not." Connor looked out the windshield and watched people walking along the sidewalk. Most of them were alone, looking into their phones like they knew the course they were traveling and weren't worried about missing their destination or stepping off into traffic. It was strange, and he never wanted to be one of those people. His life had gotten a lot better since he'd found Danny.

A rap on the window got his attention. Connor quickly unzipped the window and let the plastic fall toward him so he could talk to Perkins.

"They say they haven't seen Lucas in two days," Perkins said. "But they did give us his address."

"Then we'd better get a warrant and get over there," Connor replied. "Do you think we can do that quickly?" Being official was slowing him down and he didn't like it, but figured he'd have to get used to it.

"Maybe. But Moreau can probably—" Perkins turned and sneezed into the crook of his arm "—get that faster than I can."

"Give me the address and I'll call him on the way," Lisa said, taking her phone out of her purse.

As soon as she had the address, Perkins and Black hurried to their squad car a few spots ahead of the Jeep and got in. Connor zipped the window up and started the Jeep.

Lisa got off the call with Moreau. "Okay. He'll see what he can do. They'll head over as soon as they get the warrant. You know this is how normal police work normally works."

"Yeah, but it's slow, and our body count keeps going up." Connor muttered as he pulled the Jeep out into traffic and followed Perkins. He wanted to resolve things as fast as they could.

Danny stared at the marble floor and walls of the Federal Courthouse on First Street in downtown LA. The place was a lot fancier than the Sandoval County Courthouse he was used to dealing with. There were also a lot more people moving around it; potentially more people were coming and going from the building than lived in Jemez Springs.

It had taken him and Moreau almost an hour to get there from the Venice Beach Police department. Moreau knew the way but had Danny drive so he could be on the phone, laying the groundwork to make their getting the warrant faster.

"Thanks, Director. We're standing outside her office now," Moreau ended his call with his former boss and tucked his phone in his pocket and glanced at Danny. "They should be ready for us. All we have to do is give her the facts and she'll make the final judgement before issuing the warrant."

"Alright." Danny followed Moreau down the hallway. "I thought we've been sending her the information on the case."

"We have, but we'll have to assume she hasn't read most of it." Moreau paused with his hand on a doorknob that led to an office and not a courtroom. "Just remember, no talk about Connor's visions. We're law enforcement officers, not—" Moreau shifted like he was looking for the right words.

"Not crazies who've enjoyed a bit too many recreational drugs." Danny nodded. They'd been over it twice since heading across town, and he was used to people being skeptical of Connor's gifts. He'd been one of those not long ago.

Moreau pointed at Danny. "Exactly." He opened the door and they went in.

An older woman in a sharp dark suit was pulling a book off a shelf near a large cluttered desk. She turned toward them and smiled. "Agent Moreau, it's been a while since you've been in my office."

"Judge Williams, thank you for seeing us on such short notice." Moreau crossed the plush carpet and Danny trailed behind him. "This is my new partner, Agent Lupan."

"And with this new agency that's got everyone talking and scratching their heads. Shifter Force?" She carried the book over to the desk and set it to the side as she settled in her well cushioned leather chair. "This will be your first official warrant, although I understand you're prone to operating without one, and leaving everyone to sort out what can be used in court and what can't."

"Before we were 'official'—" Danny air quoted "—we did what we had to but tried to have the backing of either the local constabulary, or the FBI."

Williams nodded. "I've cleaned up after the FBI a few times too. Let me see what you have this time. Why do you need to go into Lucas' apartment?"

"Not just Damon Lucas' apartment, but we'd also like a warrant for the Kelly and Associates' offices." Moreau started even as he settled into one of the chairs across the desk from her. "At this point, we have two of their clients dead and another being harassed. Even if Damon Lucas is the source of it, we need to search his office as well as home."

"That makes sense." Williams took out a piece of paper and started taking notes. "Give me everything you have."

Between Danny and Moreau, they filled her in on the case, careful to leave out any of Connor's visions. They made sure to explain how they still didn't have the gun that had been used to kill Wallace, or the silver that had been used to strangle Lindy Lui. They covered how the last time Connor and Moreau had interviewed Lucas, there had been a drive by that killed two people and left Lucas in the wind.

During their talk, she nodded and murmured as she made notes. When they stopped, she put down her pen and looked at them. "Gentlemen, I'm impressed. This is all very interesting solid evidence, and not once have you mentioned Agent McGriffin's so-called psychic visions."

Her statement took Danny by surprise. He blinked at her.

She waved idly. "Young man, do you think everyone gets to walk into my office with just having to go through the metal detectors at the front doors and not having to clear my secretary next door? I've been on the phone over half an hour with different chiefs of police, and director Mills of the FBI. I heard their tales, and they believe in what McGriffin can do, even if it is hard to create cases based on those. He's prone to catch the bad guy first, then find the evidence to back things up. Makes people scramble, even if he's not aware of their efforts." She typed into her computer. "The fact that you've put together an actual case this time, is a good thing. As soon as it gets finished printing, I'll sign the warrant for a search of Damon Lucas' apartment and the offices of Kelly and Associates. I should warn you, that even though my warrant supersedes it, Jerome Kelly's attorney has filed a restraining order against McGriffin. Please keep a leash on him."

"Easier said than done," Danny muttered, and added that to the list of reasons to talk to Connor, and hope his good attitude continued.

"Do what you can, Agent Lupan. I understand that your agency isn't going to be just *my* pain, but will be operating across the country. With the way the public opinion of shifters is swinging right now, you can't always count on other judges being able to issue warrants for you, if they don't like you."

The door to the side of her office opened and a well-groomed young man stalked in with the grace of a big cat. There was the slight hint of musk coming off him, that was masked by his cologne. "Your printout, Ma'am." He put the paper down on the desk and turned to retreat the way he'd come.

Danny suddenly understood that Judge Williams was on their side. It helped having allies in high places.

She quickly signed the warrant, scanned it with her signature and handed it to Moreau. "There you go, Gentlemen. Go get the bad guys and do it with lots of physical evidence."

Moreau bowed slightly, like a knight accepting the blessing of a queen. "We'll do our best, Judge Williams."

"Thank you." Danny stood and gave her a brief nod. *"Cat, we've got the warrant. Be there in a little while."*

"Good. We're still trying to find a parking place."

Danny chuckled as he followed Moreau out of the building, some things were always going to get under Connor's skin, and Danny could completely sympathize with hating LA traffic and parking.

Connor paced the sidewalk in front of Lucas' building. "Danny's not that far away. They should be here by now." Spending almost two hours waiting for the warrant, nearly half of it parked near the high-rise apartment, was getting on his nerves. Even though Danny had let him know when they had the warrant, he still wished they could've used a picture of the warrant on a phone, or something like that to move things along. If they had resolved the case sooner, Lindy Lui might still be alive.

Lisa leaned against Perkin's patrol car. "Calm down, Cat. It takes time to get a warrant and get through the traffic. I bet the traffic bit was the harder part."

Moreau's Explorer pulled up behind the patrol car, finding a parking place a lot easier than either Perkins, or Connor. Danny and Moreau scrambled out.

Connor's heart pounded a little faster. He wasn't sure if it was the fact they could continue with their case, or the fact that Danny flashed him a smile. The past few days Danny hadn't been smiling at him much.

"Glad you called for this." Danny patted his shirt pocket that had a piece of paper sticking out of it. "We've got a friend in a federal judge's seat out here."

"Good, we can use friends." Connor stalked toward the building with Danny at his side, feeling like things might finally be going right.

"And we have to make sure to keep doing things right to keep them." Danny's voice didn't hold any harsh reprieve the way it had been.

As Connor opened the door of the building and entered the posh foyer, he hoped his good behavior was helping Danny feel better about things between them. They hadn't had time to sit and talk, and he didn't want to hash things out telepathically. It wasn't the same as looking into Danny's brown eyes while holding his hand. With a deep breath, Connor reminded himself to focus on the case. They were in the apartment building for a reason.

A security guard sat behind a desk. "Can I help you? Who are you here to see?"

Danny held out the warrant and his badge. "We have a warrant to search the apartment of Damon Lucas."

Lisa walked over and pushed the button to call the elevator with Perkins and Black behind her.

The guard glanced over the warrant. "This looks to be in order, I'll have to call and let Mr. Lucas know you're here." The guard pulled his phone out of his pocket.

Connor yanked the phone out of his hand and held it a couple inches away from him. "That isn't a good idea. This is a murder investigation. Don't want to spook our suspect. We'll need you to let us into the apartment."

The guard's eyes opened wide. "Murder? Ah-ah-ah." He opened the door to a key locker and pulled out a key. "I think you have the wrong guy. Mr. Lucas is a really upstanding guy."

"We'll see." Connor gestured for the guard to head toward the elevator and the group gathered there. When the elevator door opened, they all piled in.

Perkins moved to the back corner, as far away from Connor as possible and sneezed.

Connor moved to the opposing corner. "Perkins, sorry about the allergy. The sooner we get done here, the sooner you'll feel better."

"I'll be fine." Perkins sniffled and his reflection in the mirrored elevator walls wiped his nose on his shirtsleeve.

The door opened and Connor bounded out, then paused for the guard to lead the way toward Lucas' apartment.

After knocking on the door, the guard called out, "Mr. Lucas?"

There was no response, and he knocked again. Still no response. He glanced at Connor. "You're sure you want me to open the door?"

Connor rolled his eyes. "We didn't go to—" He stopped himself from being snide. "Yes, please."

"Good, Cat. Be nice to the scared human." Danny patted him on the shoulder.

It was all Connor could do to force back the growl that threatened to come out.

The guard unlocked the door and stepped to the side.

The reek of death filled Connor's nostrils as they walked in.

"Who died?" Moreau said before anyone else had a chance.

Perkins looked at the apartment guard. "Don't let anyone else in here."

The man nodded.

Connor continued into the apartment. There wasn't a mess like there'd been a fight. Everything seemed to be in order, for a bachelor's apartment. There were some wine bottles on a glass table in front of a big leather sofa. The huge television filled the wall opposite it. A box of Chinese takeout sat on the table, spreading its own aroma of souring soy sauce and fried rice.

"Living room's clear," Lisa said, going farther in than Connor did.

Following his nose, Connor headed down the hall, past the posters of classic geek movies. Just to be on the safe side, he glanced in the rooms as he went. The front bedroom was an office, full of computer equipment in various states of assembly. But the scent of recent death led him deeper into the apartment.

"Office appears clear," Moreau confirmed. "But we're going to need a tech squad in here, there may be more evidence on the drives."

Danny was just a couple feet behind Connor when he entered the master bedroom. The place was neater than the rest of the apartment. It looked like Lucas had cared about its appearance. There weren't any clothes strewn about. The drawers to the dresser and nightstands were all closed. The television, that was nearly as large as the one in the living room, was still on. A daytime game show had contestants spinning a huge wheel, but the sound was off.

Lucas lay on the bed on his back. He was still dressed in the clothes he'd been in when Connor had met him at the café. His blond hair was askew, and vomit covered his face and chest. The sour stench of it was almost enough to cover smell of the slow decomposition of his body that had only started hours earlier.

An empty pill bottle lay on the floor under his outstretched hand.

"People, remember your gloves. If you don't have them on yet, put them on." Moreau paused in the doorway. "Perkins, can you or Black call for a CSI team to get in here?"

"On it." Perkins withdrew down the hall before making the call, but he was still close enough for Connor to hear.

"Right. Let's not touch anything that might affect the case," Connor said as he pulled out his own gloves from his jeans pocket. They were just like the pair he'd used at the scene hours earlier where they found Lindy's body.

Lisa walked past Connor and looked at the nightstand. "We've got a suicide note. *I didn't want to do it. They made me.* It's signed Lucas."

Connor touched Lucas' shoulder.

Lucas paced his apartment. He stopped and looked at his cell phone. A text message filled the screen. You weren't man enough to do what we asked you to do, so we're going to clean up your mess.

There was a number at the top of the text screen, not a name.

After another swig of wine, Lucas threw the phone across the room. It hit the huge television and clattered to the floor. He picked up another phone and tried to call someone. "Damn it, Lindy answer." When he took the phone from his ear, he typed a text. "Lindy, run. I'll find you somehow."

The first phone chimed with an incoming text.

Lucas stared at it, not wanting to know what it said. Not being able to stop himself, he went over and picked it up.

There was a picture of Lindy, her throat burned by silver and her body draped amid some garbage bags.

Clean up your act, or you're next. *Appeared below the picture as the phone chimed again.*

"No. God no." Lucas threw the phone again. He grabbed the wine bottle and emptied it before pulling the cork on the next one. "Lindy. I'm so sorry. I should've told them no. We should've run away together. He's just a monster, and I helped him. Damn it, I helped him."

It was hard to tell how long it took for him to empty the second bottle of wine, then Lucas stumbled into the bedroom, back into the bathroom. He pulled a bottle of pain pills from the medicine cabinet. "Lindy, I doubt I'll join you in heaven, but I have to try. Do shifters and humans end up in the same place? I hope so." He downed the pills, gagging several times as the large medicine caught in his throat. He got a cup of water to help wash them down, then staggered to the bed.

Connor's shoulders slumped. "He loved Lindy. I saw it. Have your team check if that note's really Lucas' handwriting. It may be a forgery. I didn't see him write it."

Danny stepped closer and touched his arm. "Sorry, Cat."

"Job." Connor shook his head. He'd been all ready to see Lucas as a human manipulating shifters and willing to kill them, but he'd actually been in love with Lindy.

Moreau sniffed the air. "Do you smell that, Danny?"

Danny took a deep breath. "Yeah. Jessie's perfume."

"Perkins." Connor stepped out toward the hallway.

"Yeah, Connor." Perkins was slipping his phone back in his pocket. "The CSI team will be here shortly, and the coroner for the body."

"We need to get an arrest warrant out for Jessie Alexander."

Lisa came out of the bedroom. "On what grounds, Cat?"

"Anything." Connor paced toward the front door. "Charge her as an accessory to murder. Bring her into protective custody. I don't know all the ins and outs of these things. I just have a bad feeling that she's in danger. She might be the next victim. Or she might be our killer or working with him." He paused, wondering if there was anything else he could get from the place, but anything beyond Lucas' death might or might not be useful. He wasn't sure why he hadn't been able to see Jessie's last visit to the apartment. The easy answer was Lucas was totally focused on Lindy's death and his own. But they were missing something, something important, and he thought he might know where it could be.

"Dawg, Bird, let's roll. Moreau stay with Perkins and meet us back at the police station later. I want to question Jessie and Johnson this afternoon. Oh yeah, find Jack Johnson for me. He might also be in danger, or more likely, he killed Wallace."

Danny hurried after him. "Where are we going?"

"I want to talk to Reggie again. I hope he's okay." Connor hurried past the guard and toward the elevator. He paused. "There're going to be a lot more police in here real soon. Might want to clear an elevator for our use."

"Okay. I'll call the office and get more men over here to help out," the guard said, then broke out his phone while Connor, Danny and Lisa headed for the elevator.

Without having clear visions to guide him, Connor hoped he was making the right call. There was something about Reggie, but he couldn't tell if it was directly related to the case, or something else. He wished he knew exactly what was going on; it would make him feel more confident in what they were doing.

The only thing that worried Danny more than Connor's regular driving was his rushed driving. His frantic driving across LA would become something that would haunt Danny for years. He gripped the emergency bar so hard he was afraid he was going to tear it off the dash.

"Dawg, call Jime and ask him how well he knows Reggie Winters."

Danny looked at him. "Since he's just Trina's boyfriend, I doubt they've met. Jime's not been out to the coast in a long time. Plus, Reggie wasn't at his apartment last night when Moreau and I went by."

"I know that, but we're still going to start looking there."

"Did you have a vision of him?" Lisa asked from the back seat.

"No, but I'm trying to listen to my gut as well as my visions. They aren't working correctly at the moment."

Danny blinked at Connor. "Wait a minute. Is that part of what's going on with you?" The idea that Connor's gifts weren't working right would account for him being out of sorts, and more abrasive than normal.

"We'll talk about it later. But my grandmother gave me some pointers, okay?" He glanced at Danny as traffic around them slowed. "Please call Jime, he might know something."

"Okay." Danny pulled out the phone. It was the second time in a short while that Connor had asked politely to have something done.

Connor switched lanes. "On second thought, put him on speaker, so Lisa doesn't have to strain to hear him, and it'll make me talking to him easier. I hate this traffic." He slammed his fist on the steering wheel as he brought the car to a complete stop in the middle of the interstate.

After speed dialing the sheriff's office in Jemez Springs, Danny clicked the speaker icon.

After the second ring, Jime answered. "Sheriff's office, Deputy Mendoza speaking."

"Hi, Jime." Danny tried not to fumble the phone as Connor jerked the Jeep into another lane and rolled forward quickly, only to jam on the breaks again.

"Hey, Fuz Cuz. What's up? Have you met Maria Lopez yet?"

"Hey, Jime, it's Connor." Connor glared over the steering wheel at the green car only inches from their front bumper. "How well do you know Reggie Williams?"

"Don't. Never met him. Trina's the only one who knows him."

Connor straightened in his seat and drummed on the steering wheel. "So you don't know what kind of person he is?"

"Nope. Just what Trina says. What's Hollywood like? Have you met Maria? Do you need my help out there? I'll see if Cortez will approve me to come. You can introduce us."

"Jime, will you get a grip on your libido?" Danny said, not bothering to hide the irritation in his voice. There were times his cousin acted like he was still in high school. "We're trying to solve a murder here. Maybe two or three of them."

Jime's gasp came over the phone. "I thought you had a suicide."

"A suicide with a missing gun. Cat, be careful." Traffic was slowing down again, and Connor was right on the bumper of the green Toyota in front of them.

"Sorry." Connor swerved back into the center lane. "Apparently, the only person who knows Reggie is a love-sick woman."

"I wouldn't call her love-sick. She says they're getting married."

Danny snorted. "I can see Cortez allowing that. You know he doesn't like inter-species marriages." The only reason Cortez was 'allowing' his relationship with Connor was the fact that they wouldn't have biological children, not that Danny ever thought about them having adopted children either. Connor just didn't seem like the fathering type.

"Yeah, they've had some major growling matches over it. Right now, he's got her on house arrest, lockdown, grounded, whatever you want to call it. I only called you yesterday because she begged me to." Jime chuckled. "Sometimes I think if Cortez ever gets totally wise to the modern world, we're all in trouble. He hasn't thought to take away her phone. We've been getting cell coverage out at the den for almost a year now."

"Got a point there." Danny knew Cortez didn't use cell phones. It had been in the nineties, while Danny had been in school, when he'd finally gotten a land line out to the center of pack lands. "Would it do us any good to try and call Trina?"

"Probably not," Jime said. "She said she'd check in with me. I think she's smart enough to keep the phone turned off unless she's calling out, so Cortez doesn't get wind of it ringing or something."

"I can see that." Danny bit back a laugh. He'd done the same thing a time or two after he'd gotten his phone and didn't want their pack alpha to realize he had it when he'd been in trouble.

"Thanks for your help, Jime." Connor sped up as the traffic cleared. He sounded like he was done talking to Jime. "Dawg, watch for our exit."

"I've got that covered," Lisa said. "According to GPS, it's still a couple miles down."

"Thanks, Lisa."

"Guess I need to go hit the bricks and find a few tickets to write," Jime said. "Don't forget to get Maria's autograph for me."

"If we see her again, we'll do that," Danny promised. "Bye Fuz Cuz."

Ending the call, Danny slipped his phone back into his pocket. "It might be nice to talk to Trina."

"Probably don't have time for her to call us back." Connor said.

"This exit," Lisa pointed between them to the sign on the shoulder. "Then take a right."

Connor slowed, exited the highway, and turned right with the barest pause at the stop sign.

"You didn't stop." Danny growled, still worried he was going to snap the 'oh shit' bar off. "We don't need to get a ticket."

"I'm trying to stop the murders. No time to stop." He glanced at Danny and grinned. "Besides, there wasn't anyone coming."

Danny flashed his teeth. "This isn't a small country road. There might've been someone on a bicycle or something we could've really hurt. Or you never know when there are worse drivers than you are out there."

"This is LA," Lisa chirped from the back seat.

"And this is LA." Danny eased back in his seat as Connor stopped for the line of traffic at the next light. At least he was riding with Connor again and not with Moreau. Somehow, riding with Moreau felt a lot tamer than riding with Connor ever did.

Chapter 14

Connor felt at ease speed walking down Boardwalk with Danny and Lisa at his side. In the short time they'd been working together, he'd grown to depend on them more than he'd realized.

"You know not all of us have long legs," Lisa complained in between long heavy breaths after a couple of blocks.

"It would be easier if parking were closer," Danny said. "But you know some of us have wings."

"That's a good idea Lady Bird," Connor agreed. "What do you say to some aerial recon while we work ground support? We can cover more that way."

"Are you thinking Reggie's the killer?" Lisa touched their shoulders to bring them to a stop.

Connor gave her a sheepish shrug. "Honestly, I'm not sure yet, but with what Danny and Moreau found, or didn't find in his apartment last night, and the feeling I have in my gut, I just think something is about to happen and Reggie's involved. He might be the perp, or he might be the victim."

"Okay. I'll keep an eye out." Lisa shifted there out in the open.

Bending over, Connor scooped up her dress, clutch and shoes. He rolled them up and looked at Danny. "We need to start carrying shoulder bags or something for when she does this."

"It wasn't my idea." Lisa groused as she took to wing and landed on the top of a skate shop.

Danny held out his hand. "She's got a point, but it might be a good idea. I was thinking about replacing the briefcase, but we don't deal in papers as much as cops of old, so a messenger bag and laptop might be a good idea."

"Thanks." Connor handed him the clothes. "Yeah, and something like that might even be able to be carried in animal form. We'll stop and buy a couple when we get a chance."

They resumed hurrying toward Reggie's apartment.

"Guys, I've got someone matching Reggie's photos up ahead. He's approaching the apartment building, but moving like he's watching for someone," Lisa called as she flew ahead of them.

"Let me see him." Connor opened the link a little more so he could see through her eyes. Sure enough, Reggie was skulking around his own apartment building and not being very subtle about it. *"Yeah, that's him."* "Come on, Dawg, we've got a dog to talk to."

"Maybe he can explain where he was last night when Moreau and I stopped by." Danny kept up with him as they rounded the corner to the apartment complex.

Reggie leaned against a dumpster looking up toward the stairs leading to the walk in front of his apartment. He kept glancing back and forth. If two of the guys who'd been following him during their earlier meeting hadn't been killed in the drive-by, Connor would've thought he might've been watching out for them.

"Hey, Reggie." Connor stopped a few feet behind him.

Reggie whirled around, looking disoriented, but he quickly recovered. "Oh, hi, Connor. Didn't know you were coming."

"Obviously." Connor gave him a wide smile. "I haven't been able to reach you to let you know. Also, Trina called and said you weren't answering her calls, and she was worried about you."

"Really?" Reggie pulled out his phone. "I've had my phone on me the whole time."

"Dawg, can you tell if that's one of the phones from the nightstand?" Connor asked, not totally buying Reggie's tale. "So why are you hanging out here by the dumpster? Something I can help you find?"

Reggie frowned and shook his head as he scrolled through his phone before putting it back in his pocket. "No, it's not that. I got a call from a neighbor that some guys broke into my place last night. They didn't take anything, but I'm a little nervous. You know, with everything going on."

"Right." Connor nodded.

"Can't be sure, Cat," Danny said silently. *"So many of these smart phones look alike, and none of those had cases and this one doesn't either. Sorry."*

"So what *does* bring you out today?" Reggie seemed to lose interest in his apartment and focused on

Connor and Danny. "The call from Trina? Has there been another death?"

"This is Trina's cousin, Danny." Connor pointed over his shoulder at Danny who gave a small wave. "I was telling him about those great tacos we had the other day. Thought we'd stop and see if you were hungry."

"Dawg, something's definitely different in him today. Let me know what you think. Lady Bird, keep an eye on us. Make sure no one's following us."

"What? I wanted tacos too." A playful 'ki-ki-ki' kestrel laugh came from above them. *"Got my eyes open."*

"Sure. I can always eat a taco or two." Reggie headed down Boardwalk toward the eatery they'd been to a couple of days earlier.

As they walked, Connor causally placed his hand on Reggie's shoulder, hoping to get some kind of impression. Reggie jerked away. "Dude, no offense, but I don't like being touched."

Connor held up his hands. "Sorry. Thought you might like a bit of physical reassurance with everything going on." He wasn't used to trying to come up with a cover, he was used to just getting close to someone to get a reading. Limitations annoyed him.

Reggie stopped and put his waved his right hand between them. "I understand, and I know a lot of shifters who have to have physical contact all the time. I'm not one of them. It's one of the reasons I left the family years ago. I just couldn't handle the dog piles and shit. I'm my own dog. Got it."

"Got it." Connor nodded and they continued walking toward the taco stand.

They ordered tacos and sat at the same table Reggie and Connor had the other time with Reggie across from Connor and Danny.

"What's really up?" Reggie asked without touching his food.

Connor laid his taco on the paper tray. "I assume you heard about Lindy?"

Reggie shook his head. "Sad. She was so young and talented. Who would want to kill her?" Then he looked from Connor to Danny. "Hey, you two don't think I had anything to do with it, do you?" He picked up his soda cup and took a drink.

"I know you aren't the one who killed her," Connor said. "You'd have had to be wearing gloves, and I saw the killer's hands. No gloves."

"The news didn't say how she was killed." Reggie set the cup down and picked up a taco.

"Someone put a silver necklace around her neck and held it there until the silver killed her." Danny played with the straw in his cup. "Horribly painful way to die. I'd rather a silver bullet and get it over with."

"Did you know she was pregnant?" Connor asked.

Reggie's eyes opened in surprise. "I hadn't heard that. Who's the father?"

"We hoped you might be able to help us with that," Danny said.

"No idea. I know she'd been going on dates set up by someone. But, as far as I know, there was no one guy she was interested in. That makes two shifters dead. What's happening?"

Two men and a masculine-looking woman walked up and sat at the next table. They didn't have any food or drinks with them.

"Think you might have trouble there," Lisa reported in. *"They came from the road where Reggie's apartment is."*

Connor recognized one of the men from the last time he and Reggie had been here. "Two shifters, but three deaths." A strange feeling came over him. Something wasn't right. He wasn't getting a vision, so he hoped they weren't about to start shooting. Had they been the ones who'd done the drive-by? But if they were, why had they killed their associates? There were a lot of things that didn't make sense.

"Thanks, Lisa. Let me know if they start acting weirder than sitting here without eating." Connor took a bite of his taco.

"You realize there're several people sitting in this place without eating," Lisa said. *"I don't know if they've already finished and just enjoying the ocean view, or this is the place where walkers, and skaters stop to catch their breath. Beach people are strange."*

"Who's the third?" Reggie's eyes widened and he put his hands on the table on either side of his taco basket.

Danny swallowed a bite of taco. "An IT guy at Kelly Talent Agency. Damon Lucas."

"Damon? I know him." Reggie's face didn't divulge any emotion, and Connor wished again he could force his gift out of its shell and get a good reading. "Nice guy. Looks like a kid, but smart as a whip. Always ready to help program phones or laptops."

An idea hit, and Connor held out his hand. "Let me see your phone. Did Lucas help you program it?"

"Yeah." Reggie sounded just a little nervous while he took his phone out, laid it on the table and slid it across to Connor. "I was having trouble downloading an app, and he helped."

Connor opened the battery compartment on Reggie's phone.

"Hey, what are you doing?" Reggie started to get out of his seat then frowned. "Dude if you break that, you're buying me another one."

"Don't worry about that." Connor stared at the battery compartment. Nothing seemed to be out of the ordinary. "I was almost positive your phone was bugged." He put things back together and shoved the phone back across the table.

"Cat, you haven't been to a criminal tech class lately have you?" Lisa asked from above.

Connor frowned. *"No."*

Reggie took the phone back and turned it over a couple of times in his hand before putting it back in his shorts' pocket. "Seriously, if you damaged it, I'll let you know and you'll replace it."

"Criminals—hell the police—don't use physical bugs anymore," Lisa explained. *"He said Lucas helped him with an app, if the phone's bugged, he installed a bugging app when he installed the other one. You wouldn't be able to find it without a tech going over it and looking for a background app running."*

"If there's a problem, we'll take care of it." Danny sounded like he was trying to placate Reggie.

A strange, familiar scent hit Connor. It was odd, but something he'd smelled recently. *"Dawg, do you smell something unusual?"*

"Yeah. It's the same scent that was in the alley where Lindy was killed." He looked around as he bit into his second taco. *"Seems to be coming from that next table."*

That was Connor's take on it too. *"Reggie, very carefully, look behind you at the three people at the next table. Do you know them?"*

Reggie reached down and fiddled with the tie on his tennis shoe. *"I've seen one of them around Kelly's offices."* His mental voice wavered. He sat back up, but he didn't make eye contact with either Connor or Danny.

Connor finished his final taco and took the last drink of his soda. "Reggie, what do you hear from Trina? Jime says the two of you are getting married."

Reggie chuckled. "I'm not sure. Trina says Cortez might have a problem. I plan to go there next week and meet him."

"I'd like to be a fly on the wall at that meeting." Danny grinned. "It was hard enough getting Cortez to accept Connor. At least we won't be having any mixed offspring."

Lifting his phone up, Connor pointed it Reggie. "How about a picture to send to Trina and Jime? Danny, stand over by Reggie."

Danny chuckled. "Make Jime jealous. He wants to come out here so badly."

"Let me get next to you. Might as well get all three of us." Connor moved to the other side of the table and focused the phone camera on the three of them. "One more." He moved the camera slightly so the three people behind them were in the center of the picture. "That should do it. I got the ocean in the background.

Jime will probably be calling you trying to get you to say we need him.”

“You know Cortez won’t let him come.” Danny grinned. “He’s unhappy enough that I’m out of pack range on a regular basis.”

Connor stood. “This has been nice, but the Dawg and I’d better get back to work. Have a nice trip to New Mexico, Reggie.” *“Go today if possible. You could be in danger.”*

“I can’t leave for a few days. I’m up for a part in the sequel to a movie that just came out. My agent wants me here in case I need to go in.”

“Give Trina and Cortez my best.” Danny hugged Reggie. “Welcome to the family, Cousin.”

As Reggie walked away, Danny glanced at Connor. *“Anything?”*

Connor shook his head and made for the beach, putting a little distance between them and the people at the table behind them. *“Even as tight as we are, I didn’t get anything from Reggie when you hugged him, and he seemed to be trying to keep me from touching him, like he’s afraid of what I might see.”*

“The watchers from the table behind you are following both of you guys.” Lisa reported in. *“One’s going after Reggie and the other two headed toward the beach with you guys. They stopped at one of the benches. The man sat down, the woman is standing in front of him. Looks like they’re arguing, but I don’t hear anything.”*

“Follow Reggie and his tail. We’ll see if we can get the others to tell us something.”

“How do you want to do this?” Danny asked softly.

Connor glanced around. "I think my Dawg needs some shades, don't you?"

Danny grinned and hooked his elbow and started them toward the sunglass shop next to the taco stand they'd just left. Their path would take them past the couple on the bench.

"Does this mean you're going to stay with me?" Connor's heart pounded so hard as he asked the question. He didn't normally drop into personal conversations while they were on a case, but he needed to know. With any luck he'd managed to avoid his grandmother's vision.

"Hadn't given leaving a lot of serious thought." Danny patted Connor's arm. "You're my Cat. I'm your Dawg. We just need to work a little harder on the way you treat people."

Connor chuckled and took Danny's hand in his. "I know. Tell me when I'm being a complete ass and I'll try to listen."

"Good. That's what we need." Danny squeezed his hand. "Now it looks like our tails are getting nervous."

Connor glanced at the bench he'd been trying not to watch while he and Danny talked and sauntered toward the sunglass shop. The couple was standing, looking at them as they went past them.

"What are they doing?" the woman's voice was a low whisper, but still loud enough for Connor's sharp cougar ears to pick up.

The man's phone rang. "Yes. Okay. Do you want me—oh. Okay. On our way." He put the phone away as Connor and Danny made it into the sunglass shop.

Luckily the place was packed with people and the clerks didn't have time to pester them.

Connor swung Danny around so they could look out the front window and watch at the man and woman headed down Boardwalk, in the general direction of where the Jeep was parked.

"Let's follow." Connor started out of the shop.

"Do you think disguises would help?" Danny asked holding up a pair of sunglasses with the tag still dangling.

"No." Connor shook his head. "You're too handsome to disguise. Why don't we do this like shifters?"

"What do you have in mind?" Danny put the sunglasses back on their hook.

"I'll go high, track them from the rooftops, you take the beach. I know this isn't a dog park, so keep out of reach of humans."

Danny grinned. "Sounds like a plan." He shifted and took off out of the store. People stopped and stared at him.

Connor used the distraction to head out the back of the shop to a tight alley. Visualizing his cougar form, Connor shifted and jumped, bouncing off the buildings on either side of the alley a couple of times to make it to the roof.

"They still heading north, Dawg?" He took off running.

"No, they just turned east, heading down a street like they're parked over there or something."

"What can I spot from the roof?" Connor suddenly found a major flaw in his plan. It had sounded good in his mind.

"There's a purple dancing tube guy on top of the gym at the road they turned down."

"I see it." Connor altered course to bring him along that road a couple of buildings down.

"I'm heading down that street now. Who knew that a wolf running down Venice Beach would attract zero attention?"

"They're probably thinking some movie star lost a pet, or you're somebody trying to get away from a bad date."

"Right."

Connor stopped and scanned the street below him. A dark sports car roared away from the curb, somehow finding a clear couple of blocks to make a getaway.

"Guys, I've lost Reggie and his tail," Lisa called. *"They both went into a parking garage, then five cars came out at once and I couldn't make them out without swooping down and checking each one of them."*

Frustrated that everyone was getting away, Connor sat on the roof with a huff. *"Okay. Head back to the Jeep. We've lost them all. I can't believe humans are giving us this much trouble."*

"Reggie's not human," Danny corrected him.

"I know, but it's looking like there're humans at the core of this case." Connor jumped across the street onto the next roof and headed toward the parking garage, where they'd left the Jeep. There was something they were missing, and the people following Reggie were tied up in it, probably Reggie too. He hoped Perkins and Moreau had more luck getting Johnson and Jessie in for questioning. They needed a break in the case. If something happened to Maria Lopez while they were chasing their tails, he had no doubt that Montezuma would hold them responsible.

Chapter 15

As Connor pulled out onto the street, Danny called Perkins. "Connor wants to know if Johnson and Jessie are at the station." He tapped the speaker icon to make things easier for Lisa in the back seat.

"We brought Johnson in for questioning, but he's lawyered up." Perkins sounded tired. "His lawyer's in court and won't be free until this evening. We can only hold him for 24 hours without charging him."

"And Jessie?" Danny hated having to prompt for complete answers, but he understood that Perkins was busy. Since they left Moreau at the police station, it might've been better to call him.

"Black convinced her she could be in danger what with Lui and Lucas both dead. She agreed to let us put her in protective custody. She and Black are checked into a safe house for the night." Perkins paused and the sound of paper shuffling came over the phone. "That guy, Timmons, called Moreau. Said they pulled some footage from the CCTV at the Fast Stop around the corner from Wallace's apartment. Videos show Johnson purchasing a phone at 10:15 the night Wallace was killed. They also have videos of someone who might be Lucas purchasing burner phones that have been traced to the text messages sent to Wallace and Lui."

Connor came to a stop at a red light and leaned toward the phone. "Perkins, this is McGriffin. Did you get the warrant for Johnson's girlfriend's place?"

"Yeah. It wasn't easy, but Lawrence pulled some strings. The place is in LAPD's jurisdiction, so we've got to coordinate with them."

Danny hoped they'd send someone the team was used to dealing with. He was getting tired of trying to explain to people what Connor was like and someone they knew would make that a lot easier. It would also be nice if the person didn't have any shifter prejudices.

"Good." Connor grinned as he started forward. "Meet us there in about an hour."

"I'll try." Again, Perkins sounded tired.

"Don't try – do." Connor turned down a street full of cars waiting to get on the freeway. "We have at least one killer, maybe more to catch. Somehow, I don't think the same person killed Wallace and Lindy. I also don't think Lucas' death was a suicide any more than Wallace's was."

Danny looked at Connor, trying to put a little disapproval in his gaze. "He means, please, Perkins."

"Yeah. I know, I know. I'll be there as soon as I can if traffic cooperates."

Connor cast serious side eye Danny's direction. "Would you please have someone check to see if Reggie Williams has made any trips out of the country in the last few weeks?" He turned toward Danny. *"Was that polite enough, Dawg?"*

Danny ducked his head to hide his grin. *"Better."*

"You know, one thing I have to ask is what do these people out here in La La Land, consider a long-distance relationship?" Lisa spoke up from the back seat as they finally made it to the interstate onramp.

"I was wondering that too," Danny agreed. "I mean, I tried dating a guy from Albuquerque one time, that's like an hour from Jemez Springs, and after a couple of long drives, I was about over it. And that was without all this traffic."

"You know, I never stopped to think about it," Connor said as he managed to navigate into the center lane. "But you've got a point. Johnson and Wallace lived in Venice Beach, not far from Reggie, but from the address we have for the ex-girlfriend, she's…Danny how far away is she?"

With a smile, Danny looked at his phone that he'd put the information into. It was good that they were back on their regular pattern. It felt odd with Moreau. "Under normal traffic conditions, it would be about thirty minutes, we're looking at forty-five. She's got a place on the eastern edge of downtown."

"Near Chinatown, or the Arts District?" Lisa asked.

Danny looked back at her. "Chinatown. How do you know that?"

"While you two were taking moonlit walks on the beach, Moreau was showing me around. The food in Chinatown is incredible. That little place a block from the Santa Fe PD just doesn't compare."

"When we're done here, you've got to take us there." Danny did his best to not drool at the idea of incredible oriental food. "It's been too long since I've had the really good stuff."

"And maybe that's why Johnson was dating her, she was close to one of his favorite restaurants." Connor said as he slowed in the thick traffic.

"Maybe." Danny muttered. "But in my mind, it would be more than that."

"If we're lucky, it'll be something that doesn't involve the case," Lisa said.

The way the case kept taking twists and turns, Danny wasn't sure they could be that lucky.

A squad car pulled up beside the Jeep and Moreau, Perkins and a familiar figure got out.

The lanky man with long red hair moved his gaze from Connor to Danny.

Straightening from where they'd been leaning on the hood of the Jeep, Danny smiled and reached out a hand. "Bradford, good to see you. Didn't know you were around."

The man shook Danny's hand. "After that bust with the condors, and I got outed. They re-assigned me to regular duty. Can't have a shifter detective that everyone knows about, or at least not more than the token Harris is. When Perkins needed someone on our force to come out with him out here, since Tully's still dealing with that apartment you guys left him with on the south side, I volunteered. Thought I'd see what kind of trouble the Big Cat has gotten into now." He turned to Connor. "Glad to see you're okay." He pointed to Danny. "You had this one worried for a while there."

Danny had forgotten a lot of the time after the raid, when Connor had been unresponsive and Bradford had been there in the hospital, also wounded in the gun fight. The selkie had taken friendly fire when he'd tried to go after one of the boats the condors had hidden away and used for their escape. Luckily the seal shifter wasn't allergic to silver like most of other shifters were. During their time chatting in the shifter hospital cafeteria, and waiting rooms, Bradford make it clear that if they ever had need of a shifter who could swim, he'd be there for them.

"I agree, but it was an opportunity to work with you guys again." He gave a slight bow in Lisa's direction. "And the beautiful Lady Bird." Bradford headed to the door of the apartment building. "What are we waiting for? Let's check this place out."

Connor stood behind Bradford as he knocked on the door. "Mary Nelson? L.A. police. Please open the door."

Danny stayed back on the sidewalk, in case something came at them from that direction. There was something strange about standing there. It made the hair on the back of his neck stand on end, and he wondered if he'd inadvertently wandered into another pack's territory. There were rumors of Chinese shifters having recently taken over their main mob, a group that historically had major connections in Chinatown. He hoped they weren't going to have trouble before they could do the search with Ms. Nelson and get out of the area. He'd stay on guard until they left, just in case.

The door opened about an inch and stopped when it reached the end of a chain lock. A small, feminine hand slipped out. "Badge, please."

Bradford placed his badge in the hand, and it disappeared inside.

The door closed. The scrape of the chain being removed was loud. Then the door opened completely.

An attractive blonde stood in the opening. "I'm not sure why you're here."

"We have a warrant to search these premises." Bradford held out a piece of paper.

"What for?" She quickly scanned the paper. "I haven't done anything."

Connor stepped up beside Bradford. "Do you know a Jack Johnson?"

"Look, who are you? These officers have a warrant, but you don't. Get out of my home." She stepped in front of Connor to stop his path.

He pulled his badge out of his pocket. "I'm Connor McGriffin, head of the Shifter Force. We're working with the L.A. police investigating the death of David Wallace who was Jack Johnson's roommate."

She tilted her head and squinted. "What's the Shifter Force, and why are you asking questions about Jack?"

Danny moved up the steps toward the apartment door. Other doors along the front of the building remained closed, but the curtains in a couple of windows opened. Mere cracks, but enough for people inside to see out. He didn't want things to get nasty.

"We investigate when shifters are involved." Connor's voice was even and calm. A major step from the way he'd been acting. "Jack was a little evasive in answering questions, so we need to check farther. So again, do you know Jack Johnson?"

"Yes." She took a deep breath. "We used to live together, but we broke up a few months ago."

"Did he spend the night here a couple of nights ago?" Connor pressed, but didn't try to enter the apartment.

Her eyes blazed as she balled up her fists. "That's a personal question, and none of your business."

"He told us he was here when his roommate was murdered." Connor appeared totally relaxed as he kept talking. Even to Danny's eye, he wasn't letting her get to him "Was he?"

"Put that way, yes, he spent the night. Since I don't know when David was murdered, I can't say if he was here then." She stepped to the side and waved them into the apartment. "You might as well come in. There's nothing of Jack's here."

"Thank you." Connor quirked his eyebrow as they all walked in. "You just said you broke up, and yet he stayed the night?"

She grinned sheepishly. "Well, that part of our relationship was okay. But he cheated on me, and I kicked him out. We're trying to work things out."

"What time did he get here, and when did he leave?" Connor stalked around the living room like he was looking for something.

"He came after he got off work. He brought a pizza, we watched a TV show, and then he went out and got some ice cream."

Bradford asked, "What time was that, and what was he wearing?"

"It was around nine thirty. What do his clothes matter?" She frowned in thought. "Come to think of it, he must have gone home and changed. He was wearing his uniform that had pizza sauce on the front of it but jeans and a t-shirt when he came back."

"What time did he leave the next morning?" Connor asked, seemingly not minding Bradford's interruption of his interrogation.

"I don't know. He was gone when I woke up."

Leaving Connor and Bradford to continue questioning her, Danny motioned the others to fan out and search the apartment. There might be something Mary wasn't aware of, or maybe she was.

Danny went into the kitchen and rummaged through the cabinets. Everything seemed normal. Bowls, plates, silverware were fairly organized. There was a bit of dust in the cabinets themselves, but the dishes were clean. Nothing jumped out at him as wrong.

He was about to close the last cabinet, full of canned food and cereal boxes, when the smell of gun oil hit him. Danny frowned and started moving things. Nothing caught his eye until he glanced up.

A large canister set on the top shelf of a cabinet. He lifted the canister off the shelf. It was heavier than it should've been if it was just full of flour or sugar. The smell was stronger. He opened it and the barrel of a pistol stuck out of the flour. *"Found something."* He called to Connor.

Connor hurried into the kitchen. Danny tilted the canister so he could see the gun mostly hidden in the flour. "Perkins, we need an evidence bag."

A weight lifted off him as he set the canister down on the counter. It made him feel good to finally find the murder weapon. They would at least be able to put one case to bed.

Mary followed Perkins into the kitchen. Her eyes widened, and she placed her hand in front of her mouth. "Where did that come from? I've never seen it before."

Perkins looked at the scene. "Guys, leave that right where it is. We're going to need to get a team in here to catalogue everything." He looked at Mary. "I'm going to caution you not to say anything else." He recited the Miranda Rights. "You'll need to come with us."

"Shouldn't I call a lawyer or something?" Mary objected as Bradford put handcuffs on her.

"When we get to the station, you'll get your call." He glanced at Perkins. "I guess you'll have your CSIs send our CSIs the bullet so we can do ballistics comparing it to the gun?"

"Sure, or your guys could do the rifling on the pistol and send it to our guys for a comparison, since the murder happened in Venice Beach," Perkins countered.

Connor shook his head. "I think our part of the work is done as far as Wallace's death goes."

"You're sure the pistol is the murder weapon?" Bradford looked from Connor to the canister.

"Since I'm not supposed to touch evidence, as sure as I can be." Connor stood next to Danny. *"I'm trying to be good, Dawg."*

"Good enough for me." Bradford headed out the door with Mary. "I'll get her booked on accessory to murder."

The mental image of Danny patting him on the head came to him. *"Yes, you are, Cat. I'm very proud of you, and the CSI team will thank you for not getting prints all over the pistol."*

Connor headed for the door then stopped. "Perkins, any chance you can send the transcripts of Officer Black's interview with Jessie over to our hotel? There might be something in there that can trigger something for me." He wasn't sure if that would work or not, with his abilities on the fritz, but he had to hope.

"Why don't I just email them to you?" Perkins offered. "I know they have email in Santa Fe."

Connor bit back a retort. He was doing pretty good with Danny and didn't want to spoil it. If he was lucky, Danny wouldn't make him sleep alone for another night. "Yeah, we do."

"Try McGriffin at Shifter Force dot com," Danny said.

"Sure. That's easy. I don't even need to write it down." Perkins said. "So I guess you guys are going to leave the locals with another crime scene."

"Give me a couple of minutes to make sure there's nothing else that catches my attention." Connor walked out of the kitchen, not sure if he was going to be able to find anything else without contaminating the crime scene or not. He was going to have to get used to playing nice, even if it grated on his nerves something fierce. Keeping Danny happy would be worth it.

Chapter 16

Connor stretched as they walked out into the parking lot. The interview transcript between Jessie Alexander and Officer Black hadn't yielded anything useful. Sure, Black had been thorough, but Jessie either didn't know anything or was determined to keep her secrets. Connor couldn't help but wonder if his explosion in the office a couple days earlier hadn't caused some of the problems they were having getting information out of the secretary. Jessie had brought the confrontation up several times and Black reassured her Connor wasn't going to find out where she was.

Even though Danny had slept in the bed next to Connor and was as attentive as usual, he couldn't stop thinking there was something else wrong. Something outside of them. He wasn't sure if it was something he'd missed, or if there was a clue he'd missed, or a vision he could've had that being in the city was blocking.

If they were closing in on the culprits like he thought they were, things had been quiet over the night. No more shifters had died, at least none that they'd heard about. With all the cities in the area, that was possible, and he'd been trying not to think about it. He really wanted to make sure Jessie Alexander stayed safe. They needed to be at the Venice Beach PD to officially question Jack Johnson.

He stopped as he placed his right foot in the Jeep. "Bird, I'd like you and Moreau to check on Jessie Alexander. Stay with her, or at least near the safe house for a while."

"Do you see something?" Danny looked across the top of the Jeep.

Connor pursed his lips and shook his head before finishing settling into the driver's seat. "Just a feeling that we need to keep an eye on her. Things are too quiet."

Moreau dashed toward his car with Lisa close behind. "We're on it. Lisa, call Perkins and get the address."

Danny looked at Connor as he closed his door. "You sure about this?"

Connor nodded as he started the engine. "With my gift not working right, I can't be as sure as everyone is used to me being, but I'm going with my gut."

"Good." Danny patted his arm. "A lot of cops just go with their guts. That's okay."

"I can't wait to get back to a rural area where I don't have to worry about my senses being shut down like this." Connor backed the Jeep out and headed down the parking lot. "I don't know how most people deal with not knowing what's going to happen to them and the people around them."

Danny laughed. "We grow up with it, and thus learn to live with it."

Connor headed toward the interstate. "I get it, but I don't have to like it." Even if things didn't work out the way he wanted them to, with people either dead or in jail, if the bad guys got away, at least Danny was laughing with him again.

As they entered the police station, Danny put a hand on Connor's arm. "Let me do the talking, Cat. If you want me to ask something, mind speak it to me."

Connor's eyes flashed, and he tightened his lips as he gave a curt nod. *"I don't like it, but I'll try."*

Perkins came around a corner. "Lisa called and asked for the address where Officer Black and Jessie Alexander are. She didn't say why."

"Connor had a bad feeling about things." Danny followed Perkins down a hall with Connor close behind.

"We haven't heard anything from Black," Perkins said. "Must be a false alarm."

"Sometimes he gets these feelings before things go down," Danny said. "You might want to send someone to check it out."

"I told Lawrence, and he said to let you guys handle it until you call us in." He stopped at a door next to a two-way mirror. "Johnson's lawyer is with him right now. We're giving them half an hour together before we start questioning him."

"Tell me, Perkins," Danny said, "did you find any fingerprints on the gun?"

"No. It had been wiped clean, and the flour did a number to it as well. Even if it hadn't been wiped, the flour would've messed things up. However, it is registered to Johnson. It's going to be a few days before we have the ballistics test back comparing the rifling on the pistol to the marks on the bullet."

"Ask him if they found blood on the clothes."

"Was there any blood on the uniform?"

"Yes. It matched with the victim's blood type, DNA will take a while. The problem is, even though it was the crime scene, Johnson's claiming we entered the apartment without his permission, and without warrant. The lawyer said something about fighting the evidence."

Connor closed his eyes. *"Dawg, you know that if these big city cops would just listen to me, and if my gifts were working right, we'd wrap things up a lot faster."*

"I can tell you're restraining yourself, Cat." Danny grinned at him, not wanting to let Perkins in on how much self-control Connor was exerting in that moment. *"The more you do this, the easier it will get."*

"I doubt it."

Somehow, Danny did too. He just hoped they could wrap the cases up and get out of LA before Connor completely lost it.

Connor stood behind the two-way mirror as Perkins questioned Johnson.

Johnson's lawyer sat beside him at a table across from Perkins.

Perkins pushed a button on a small black voice recorder. "Questioning Mr. Jack Johnson regarding the death of David Wallace. Also present is his lawyer, Mr. Richard Abernathy. Mr. Johnson, you understand I am recording this conversation, and that you are not under arrest at this time. We are only questioning you. Your lawyer is present with us. Is that true?"

Johnson nodded.

"Please answer the question verbally so it will be recorded." Perkins frowned and pointed at the recorder.

"Yes, I understand." Johnson's voice was soft and bland.

"Now, Mr. Johnson, you said you spent the night Wallace was killed with Mary Nelson?"

"That's right."

"You said you went to dinner and a movie, is that correct?"

Johnson squirmed uneasily in his chair. "Yes."

The urge to storm into the room and grab hold of Johnson made Connor ball his hands into fist. A soft growl rumbled through his chest.

"Cat, chill." Danny put his hand on Connor's and gave him a soft squeeze. *"We have to let the humans handle this the way their laws say is right."*

"I know." He stopped growling and forced himself to relax and pay close attention to the interrogation on the other side of the mirror.

"Ms. Nelson states that you brought a pizza with you, and that the two of you watched a show on TV." He looked at his notes. "She also stated that you went out about nine thirty to get some ice cream, and when you came back, you were wearing different clothes. Which is it?"

Johnson looked at his lawyer, and sweat glistened on his forehead.

The lawyer shook his head.

"I refuse to answer that." The tiniest bit of fear crept into his tone.

"You realize that by refusing, you may be arrested on suspicion of murder."

Again, he looked at Mr. Abernathy who nodded. "I understand."

Perkins stood. "I have no choice but to arrest you on suspicion of murder. Court appearance date and time will be set by the judge tomorrow morning." He turned off the recorder, picked it up, and left the room.

Johnson and Lewis put their heads together and spoke quietly. Even with Connor's superb hearing, their voices were too soft for him to pick up everything that was said. He did manage to catch the words "shifter" and "evidence." Abernathy had sneered after saying "shifter".

The two got quiet as a uniformed officer entered the room a couple of minutes after Perkins walked out. He quickly led Johnson away, leaving Abernathy to load up his briefcase with papers he'd never made notes on, and walk out.

Connor stepped over to Perkins' desk and picked up a folder.

Perkins grabbed it out of his hand and sneezed. The Ziploc bag with the suicide note from Lucas's room fell onto the desk. "You aren't supposed to see that."

"Sounds like you need some more medication." Connor raised an eyebrow as he picked up the bag and handed it back to Perkins. "What about the handwriting on this note? Was it Lucas'?"

"We don't have an official report." Perkins opened the file and returned the bagged note to it. "However, preliminary tests say it was not."

"Any idea whose it is?" Connor wished he could touch the paper and get a reading off it. But his visions weren't admissible in court as evidence.

Perkins shook his head. "They haven't found a match yet."

"*Ki, ki, ki.*" The sound of Lisa's bird form warning cry echoed through Connor's head. It wasn't much. Just the sound reverberating through him.

"*Lisa, are you okay?*" Connor called through the team link.

"*Peachy. Everything's quiet here,*" she sounded slightly bored. "*You'd think these safe houses would be on the beach. Better view and less sides to cover.*"

"*You didn't just screech at me?*"

"*Nope. I don't tend to screech in mind speech.*"

"*Then it was a warning. We're emotionally connected—that makes sense. Stay alert. I just heard you screeching a warning.*"

"*Got it. I'll let Moreau know too.*"

"*Okay, we're on our way.*" Connor blinked and stared at Perkins.

Danny came around the corner carrying three sodas.

"Let's roll, Dawg." Connor ran for the door. "Lisa's in trouble. You drive. Perkins, you'd better come, too."

"What did you see?" Danny asked as he handed Connor a cold can.

"Heard. Made sure Lisa's okay right now, but something's about to happen. We need to get there."

They were wasting time and energy talking, but Connor understood. He didn't want to snap at Danny and make things worse.

"I'll call the Captain as we go," Perkins said a couple of feet behind Connor.

Danny slid uncomfortably into the driver's seat. "Why do you want me to drive? You usually won't let me behind the wheel of this thing."

"I don't trust myself right now." Connor got into the passenger seat and fastened his seat belt. "You know what happens when a vision hits. Hurry."

"Okay." Danny started the Jeep and pulled out of the parking place as a squad car pulled in front of them with lights flashing and siren squealing. If it weren't for all of the traffic, it would've felt a bit like the times he'd followed Rusty across the county to respond to a domestic disturbance call. There was occasionally gun fire at those too. He was glad he had a pistol in his shoulder holster, complete with silver bullets.

Danny's phone started ringing as they made their third turn. It wasn't a specialized ring tone, so he didn't automatically know who it was. "Cat, can you answer that?" He pulled the phone from his pocket and handed it to Connor.

"Sure." Connor took the phone and swiped it to answer. "Danny's phone, this is Connor." He put it on speaker and held it between them. "Danny's right here."

"Oh hi, Connor, this is Larea." Their tech support person sounded a bit nervous.

"Larea, Danny's driving at the moment, what's up?"

"Yeah, I needed to update you guys, it might be nothing, but I've been watching the Joe's List request for a female jaguar shifter."

Danny tried not to apply the brakes too hard as he engaged the clutch to slow as cars weren't getting out of Perkin's way. "Right. Do you have something?"

"Yeah, I'm still trying to track down the email, but they got a response. Somebody offering to set up an encounter this evening."

"This evening, are you sure?" Connor glanced at Danny. "That would mean Maria Lopez is cooperating with them. We'll need to talk with her soon."

They made it onto the freeway before Connor leaned back in his seat with the faraway look Danny knew was a vision taking him. All he could do was be thankful Connor hadn't been stubborn about driving—they would've ended up spattered against the back of Perkin's patrol car ahead of them.

Danny grabbed the phone as Connor's hand went limp. "Larea, try and track down that email. Connor just started having a vision. Need to go."

"Vision…okay. Right. Be careful." And she ended the call.

Danny kept driving, hoping the bouncing Jeep wasn't a problem as Connor was lost in the vision.

"The shadow of a large canine hovered over Officer Black who stood with her gun drawn.

To her left, Lisa loosened the drawstring of her dress and shifted. 'Ki, ki, ki.' The sound of Lisa's distress cut Connor to the core. She took to the air, staying close to the ceiling.

Jessie lay on the floor behind Officer Black screaming, 'He'll kill me.'

'Not if I kill him first.' Officer Black fired at the dog striking him in the shoulder."

Before the Jeep came to a complete stop in the driveway of a small, Spanish-style house, Connor leaped out. He started shifting as he threw the door open and completed the change in mid-air. Clearing the small, well-manicured yard in single jump, he bounded up the three steps to the front door barely touching the ground. With only a moment to decide, he chose the bay window instead of the solid door. In a shower of glass, he crashed into the living room, toppling the sofa that was on the other side of the window.

Something small and reddish brown flew toward the ceiling. Lisa's distress calls were drowned out as Officer Black fired three times in rapid succession at the big gray and white dog who was crouching to spring.

The dog howled in pain as bullets struck his shoulder.

Using the back of the couch to continue his race toward the canine he'd seen in his vision, Connor landed on the beast's back. The loud crack of its back breaking rolled through the room as Lisa stopped screeching. Grabbing the back of the dog's neck in his massive jaws, Connor sank his teeth into the flesh under the thick fur.

The dog tried to roll out from under Connor. Long bloody scratches ran from his ear to his nose, leaving his eye damaged.

"I would suggest lying still, Reggie, unless you want your throat ripped out." Connor punctuated his warning with a deep growl as the glass crunched near the window.

When Danny killed the engine of the Jeep, Connor was already out of the vehicle and running. Throwing the Jeep door open, before Perkins had a chance to move from his squad car in the street, Danny shifted and headed across the lawn. Gunshots came from the house, and he picked up his pace, hoping neither Connor, Lisa nor Moreau had been hit. Since he was in wolf form, he followed Connor through the window.

Moreau lay on the floor right inside the door next to a pile of clothes. Connor straddled a gray and white malamute. Officer Black had her gun out, still trained on the dog. Lisa was near the ceiling.

"Everyone okay?" Danny asked through the group link.

"I'm fine," Lisa responded. *"Might check on Moreau though."*

Danny shifted back to human and knelt beside Moreau. "Are you okay?"

Shaking his head as if trying to wake up. Moreau blinked a couple of time. "I think so. Although I may have a broken arm. Let me shift and heal." He slowly shifted into his animal form and crawled around in his clothes. Shifting back into human took even more time. He grabbed his pants and put them on. "I think that did it." He chuckled and looked down at his bare feet. "I'm not like you and Connor. I can't shift clothed."

"Not many shifters can. That's why Lisa has those dresses she wears."

Lisa had already landed in her dress and became human. She went to where Jessie lay curled up in a ball. "Are you okay, Jessie?"

"I think so. What's going on?"

Dropping her voice, Lisa started explaining everything that was happening.

Danny carefully made his way next to Connor. "You want to let him shift and heal? That bullet wound must be painful."

"I'm sure his broken back is more painful." Connor shifted and stood over Reggie. "Come on, Reggie. Shift and fix yourself. Just don't make any fast moves."

The dog writhed on the floor and slowly became human. It was one of the most painful shifts Danny could recall seeing, other than first time shifts where the shifter fought the change.

As Connor reached down and pulled a naked Reggie to a stand, the door opened, and Perkins came in. He glanced around at the glass shards and overturned sofa.

"Not sure why you went through the window, McGriffin, the door was unlocked," Perkins said.

Smirking, Connor looked from the door to the window. "I couldn't be sure, and the window looked like it would break easier than struggling to open a doorknob with my teeth. Time was of the essence. Either one of you guys have some silver cuffs on you? Maybe a spare blanket so he can cover himself before you walk him out."

Perkins reached into a pouch on his belt and pulled out a pair of rubber-covered handcuffs. "I think there's a blanket in the trunk. Might be moth-eaten, but it should cover most of him."

As Perkins pulled Reggie's arms behind him, Reggie cried. "Careful. That cougar broke my back. It's still painful. Shifting only heals so much. I need an ambulance. There's a shifter vet in the valley who can help me. I'm going to have scars."

"Don't worry. Scars look good in prison; they can up your reputation. You'll have plenty of time to heal the rest in jail." Connor looked at Officer Black. "Want to tell us how he got in here?"

"He knocked on the door and said you sent him. When Moreau opened it, he shoved the door hard, catching Moreau in the face. Then he tasered Moreau in the side. He shifted fast. Lisa clawed him across the face. By the time I pulled my gun, he was almost on top of me. The cougar hit him just as my bullets did."

"It's obvious whoever's in charge knows where Jessie is." Connor walked over to where Lisa had gotten Jessie into a chair. "Any idea how they found you? Did you call someone?"

"I called in work and told them I was sick and wouldn't be in." Tears streaked her mascara and she was shaking.

"Let me see your phone." He held out his hand.

Jessie glanced around the room. "I'm not sure where it is. I was playing some solitaire when he came in."

Danny squatted down at the edge of the couch and reached under. "Is this one yours?"

"Yes." Jessie reached for it, but Danny handed it to Connor.

The screen was locked. Connor walked over and held it out to Jessie. "Do you mind unlocking it?"

She looked up at Connor. "I still don't trust you, but he did just try to kill me." She glared at Reggie. "I thought I knew you, Mr. Winters. I thought you were a nice guy." With shaking fingers, she drew a design on the phone. "Without a warrant, nothing you find there can be used against me."

"I know." Connor turned the screen back toward him. Luckily it was an operating system he was used to. He pulled up the settings and looked at things. "Just what I figured. Your GPS is activated. All they had to do was follow the signal. Not really your fault as most phones come with GPS on as factory standard."

"But all I talked to was Mr. Kelly." She looked confused and betrayed. "I called his cell phone, not the switchboard."

"Perkins, you and Black need to get Mr. Winters and Jessie back to the station for questioning. If we don't get everything worked out quickly, I'll leave it up to your procedures if she gets a hotel room for safety or what." He handed Jessie's phone to Officer Black. "Might want to run this through your tech department to see if they can find anything. If they can't, check with Timmons at the FBI."

"And what are we going to be doing?" Moreau asked as he tucked his shirt tail into his jeans.

Danny's phone rang.

Pulling it out, Danny stared at it for a moment. "I don't recognize the number. Better not be a robo call for car insurance." He tapped to answer the call.

"They took her." A weak male voice came from the other side. "We were at home, and they took her." The phone clanked on something hard and went dead.

Connor frowned. "It has to be Maria Lopez." He glanced at Moreau. "Get us an address and contact the locals to meet us there. They aren't to go in."

"Will do, Cat." Moreau nodded. "We'll follow."

"You'll follow," Lisa countered. "I'll be there before any of you, unless it's a hundred miles away." She shifted and flew out the window before anyone could object.

"Follow that kestrel." Connor said as they raced for the door. "Perkins, take care of these two. Also, see about getting a warrant for Kelly and Associate's office, the whole place, not just Lucas' office." He wondered why they hadn't split up and looked in Lucas' office after they got the federal warrant. But they were going to need more than a warrant to get to the bottom of things.

"I'll get the warrant," Moreau offered. "The judge likes me."

"Good. Make it happen." Connor stopped at the Jeep. "I'm driving. Get me an address." He headed toward Hollywood, hoping it was the right direction. He should've gotten Maria Lopez's address days earlier. It would make things earlier in getting to her without delays.

Chapter 17

The ornate-iron gate was already open and squad cars occupied the long driveway as Connor roared into the circle drive in front of the Beverly Hills mansion with hedges cut like deer, gazelles, and parrots. He shut off the engine and jumped out of the Jeep with Danny hot on his heels. Somewhere above them, Lisa screeched to let them know she'd made it moments before.

He ran up the wide steps to the open front door where two cops in Beverly Hills PD uniforms came running out. A tall man with graying hair stepped out of the door as the two other cops bent over the porch railing and vomited. He held up a hand. "I need to see some badges. This is a crime scene." He let out a long breath. "A really nasty one. One of the worst I've seen in all my years on the force."

Connor stopped in his tracks and stared at him for a second before pulling his badge.

Danny beat him to it. "We're Agents Lupan and McGriffin with Shifter Force." He handed his badge to the man. "We were called by one of the victims."

The man tilted his head and frowned. "Shifter Force. You're new around these parts, but that explains some things."

"What?" Danny slipped his badge back into his pocket.

With a deep breath, Connor was positive there were more jaguars in and out of the house than just Maria Lopez. The place was probably the base for the local Jaguar prowl. Then the distinct metallic stink of blood mingled with fur hit him. "I think they were in cat form when this happened."

"At least one of them," The BHPD officer handed Connor his badge back. "I guess Ms. Lopez could afford some high dollar security, not that it helped."

"Is she here, Officer?" Connor asked.

"Hillside. Not that we can find." He stepped to the side. "Go on in, but please put on shoe covers and gloves. Don't touch anything. Our CSI team is on the way. Odds are so are the reporters. Maria Lopez is a big name around here. This'll make national news."

As he walked over to the box of shoe covers near the door, Connor groaned. They didn't need another case hitting the national news. Since Maria Lopez wasn't out as a shifter, if they slipped and gave away too much info, Montezuma wouldn't be happy. And the odds were, with the anti-shifter sentiment spreading across the country, having a rising star like Maria Lopez exposed in their midst, the anti-shifter folks would start lighting more torches than ever.

"You're being good, Cat," Danny said as he balanced awkwardly to put a shoe cover on over his boots. *"Thanks."*

"I'm trying." Connor twisted the shoe cover, trying to get it to fit correctly over his running shoes. He'd never met a cover that worked perfectly. *"We've got*

more dead bodies even after we got the warning from Larea."

"But we saved Lisa, Moreau, Black and Jessie." Danny reached for gloves. *"We can't be in two places at once, not with our current resources."*

Lisa swooped down and landed on one of the wrought iron bars covering the front windows. *"Nothing obvious when flying over the grounds. I hope you brought my dress."*

Connor didn't remember scooping it up on the way out of the Venice Beach safe house. *"I think there's a spare in the console between the front seats."*

"My phone and purse are probably being processed as evidence." She glared at him from her perch. *"That's going to be a pain to get everything back."*

Getting the purple latex gloves on, Connor shrugged. *"Sorry. We were in a hurry."*

"I'll check the console for you in a minute, Lady Bird," Danny said as he walked into the mansion.

"Thanks, Danny." Lisa roused, then took off again. *"I'll keep looking for things."*

Officer Hillside looked up. "Is that with you?"

Stopping at the threshold, Connor turned back to the cop. "She's Agent Collins. Best aerial support we could find."

Hillside huffed. "We're seeing everything nowadays. I'll go back in with you."

In the distance, more sirens wailed as more members of the constabulary arrived.

Although he'd seen dead bodies before, Connor wasn't prepared for what greeted him in the mansion's entry hall. One of the guards, it was impossible to tell which one since he was in jaguar form, lay spread eagle on the black marble tile. He'd been shot several times in the face. Most of his jaw was missing. After he'd been killed, someone had eviscerated him. His organs were reorganized next to him, into a parody of a human body.

"How did they have time to do that?" Danny asked, covering his mouth with his hand.

"No clue," Connor replied as his own stomach rolled at the stench of it all. "Unless they came back and did it."

"That might explain the phone call," Danny suggested. "Maybe they thought they'd killed the guards, left with Maria, then when she was secured, came back to leave a message."

"Where's the other guard?" Connor asked.

Officer Hillside raised an eyebrow. "How do you know there's two guards?"

Connor almost snapped at the man, but resisted. The guy didn't know Connor, or how he operated, and if he was going to keep Danny happy, he had to play nice. "We were worried about something like this happening and had a meeting with Ms. Lopez a couple of days ago. We offered her protection, but she refused. When she attended the meeting, she had two guards with her, both jaguar shifters."

"Fair enough." Hillside nodded and relaxed a bit. "The other one's in the kitchen. Looks like he had time to call someone… You people?"

"Probably." Danny turned from the macabre display and followed when Hillside walked down the hallway.

Connor took a final look at the guard, shuddered and hurried after them. He wasn't sure what kind of hatred would cause someone to mutilate someone to that extent. If this was the future shifters had to look forward to, it was going to get grim before it got better.

The clean hallway leading deeper into the house was a stark contrast to the horror in the foyer. Every surface was spotless, polished to within in an inch of its life. Connor wasn't sure if he'd ever been in such a clean home before. It made him thankful he had on shoe covers and gloves. He didn't want to mar the place any more than it already had been.

"I guess they didn't have as much time with this one." Danny squatted next to the other guard who was halfway through his change. Whether he'd been trying to change from human to cat, or vice versa, it was impossible to tell. Orange and brown rosettes mottled his skin. Short thick fur covered his limbs, but his hands were still human, and his face halfway between. A smartphone lay shattered a couple of inches from his outstretched hand. It looked like someone had smashed it with a boot. Blood oozed out from under the body from an angle that indicated a chest shot or two. A shot to the head must've been what finished him off when they smashed the phone.

"If they caught him on the phone with you, they might have realized their time was limited," Connor said.

"Officer Hillside, was there any indication where Maria Lopez was when this went down?" Danny said, controlling the conversation with the local authorities.

"There are signs of struggle in her bedroom, but also out on the deck, near the hot tub." Hillside glanced both directions. "Which way would you like to go first?"

Connor frowned. There shouldn't have been two areas of struggle, just one. That didn't make any sense, unless Maria had managed to get away from her kidnappers, and make it outside, or maybe she'd been outside and tried to get in to a phone. Connor wanted to go around touching everything, hoping to get some kind of reading from the area. Instead, he followed Hillside and Danny after Danny suggested starting in the bedroom.

Danny paced alongside Hillside as they went down the hall that was wide enough for three or four people to walk abreast. A fresh scent of lilac slowly got stronger as they closed in on the bedroom. To Danny's nose it wasn't enough to cover the musk of big cats. There were a lot more cats through the house than just Maria and her two bodyguards.

"The bedroom." Hillside stopped at an open door and gestured. "It's just like we found it. I don't want CSI crawling up my ass if we screw something up."

"I understand." Danny nodded, and tried to sound and look sympathy. The thing was, in Jemez Springs, he and Rusty had been the CSI team. If he screwed up something, Rusty would normally just gloss it over in the official report. Things were a lot different when there were a just a couple of people involved as opposed to a couple of departments, or even agencies who all wanted things done their way.

The bedroom looked like a tornado had exploded in it. The bed was overturned and shredded. Maria Lopez hadn't gone along quietly. There was an odd scent in the air, it was partially masked by the lilac that seemed to be coming from a plugin air freshener.

"Any idea what the smell is, McGriffin?" Danny glanced back over his shoulder as Connor entered the room.

Connor took a deep breath. "Lilac, Jaguar, several of them, and…" He took another deep breath and frowned. "Magic?" *"Dawg, we've got a bigger problem. Someone used magic in this room. I'm not good at it, but it does leave a distinctive odor."*

"That's what I thought, but I wasn't sure." Danny wanted to turn the bed over and properly inspect the room, but knew Hillside was going to have a fit if he tried something like that. He and Connor were going to be limited to what they could see, or what Connor could sense.

"Magic?" Hillside sounded doubtful. "Years ago, we thought shifters were going to be the strangest things we ran into on the job, but magic has started popping up more and more."

"Can't argue with you there," Connor said. "It leaves behind a particular stench. Might be why the bad guys plugged in that air freshener. Sometimes even humans can smell magic, but if they cover it up…" Connor spread his hands. "Might want your CSI to check that out. I bet it's only been going a short time."

Hillside nodded and pulled out a pad to make a note.

"I can smell Maria Lopez, but there're lots of other people too." Danny walked slowly around the room, careful where he stepped. He didn't want to inadvertently break any of the perfume bottles and jewelry scattered around.

"More than I would've expected." Connor squatted next to the overturned nightstand. "Sure, in the front of the house, that's one thing, but back here? This should be her private retreat."

Danny glanced into the bathroom. The struggle hadn't gone that far. There were more perfume bottles there, along with the standard grooming products. A quick look over his shoulder showed Hillside still in the doorway to the hall. Going deeper into the bathroom, out of sight of the door, Danny pulled out a small Ziploc bag from his pocket and went to the hairbrush laying near the sink. As fast as he could, he yanked out a small handful of hair, and dropped it into the bag. When they got back to the Jeep, he'd let Connor see if he could get anything off it. Connor could normally get a vision off pictures and clothes. Hopefully the hair would work, even with his powers on the fritz.

"Anything back there?" Connor asked as he came into the bathroom.

With a soft smile, Danny held up the bag of hair before slipping it into his pocket. "Nothing that stands out," he replied loud enough for Hillside to hear. "Doesn't look like the struggle got this far."

"But he said there were signs around the pool area." Connor flashed Danny a warm smile. *"Thanks. That should help."*

"I hope so." Danny brushed past Connor on the way out of the bathroom. It felt good having Connor being more mellow and helpful rather than bullish and stubborn.

"Where's the back yard?" Danny asked as he approached Hillside. "Let's take a look at that area."

"Shortest way is through that door." Hillside pointed to a door on the same wall as the bed. "What makes no sense, is there're no windows in here to the outside. With that gorgeous yard, you'd think people would want to see it from their bedroom."

"Unless you're a closeted shifter and don't want every drone that flies through your yard seeing you rolling around in your bed as a jaguar," Connor muttered in Danny's head.

"Makes sense to me." Danny followed Hillside over to the door.

The backyard was several acres of well-manicured lawn that made the front look shabby by comparison. Like in the front yard, there were various topiaries that were shaped like a variety of predators and prey. There was a large pool near the house that had a privacy fence around it and a sunscreen over it.

"She does like her privacy, doesn't she," Hillside muttered as they walked down the steps toward the pool. "Can't say as I've seen any paparazzi shots of Ms. Lopez. At least not around her home. Most of the other stars in this neighborhood hit the tabloids every few weeks."

"Maybe her guards are better than most." Connor stopped at the gate that opened onto the pool. "Sorry, I meant 'were'."

"She might have more than just those two," Hillside said.

"But that would open the question: where were they?" Danny stepped into the pool area.

Lisa landed on the top of the fence and looked at them. *"I can say that seeing into this pool from above would be hard, even for the highest tech drone. I bet she loves water as much as Connor does."*

"Something jaguars are known for." Danny stopped as he took in the pool area. There was something odd, but he couldn't put his finger on it. It looked like someone had shredded pool toys. Floaties he couldn't identify bobbed deflated along the surface of the water. A metal table lay on its side next to two overturned chairs.

The odd smell, that Danny assumed was more magic, was there too. "What's the possibility Maria had a third guard and they were taken too?"

"She's important enough for that." Connor stopped next to him, looking over the scene and took another deep breath. "More magic. But why take one guard and Maria, and kill the other two guards? That doesn't make a lot of sense."

"A lot about this case hasn't made sense." Danny took time to look over the area as close as he could, but nothing stood out as a clue to what was going on.

"The water out here is going to block me," Connor said. "Let's do a look, and sniff around the grounds and see if we can find anything."

"Okay. Sounds good." Danny turned to Hillside. "We're going to do a quick sweep of the place in more sensitive forms. If we need to leave fur samples for the CSI team, we can."

"Really, Dawg?" Connor rolled his eyes.

"Yes, really. If they have samples of our fur, they can't claim we're contaminating a crime scene."

"Since they know the guards were shifters, they're going to be a little more thorough about things like fur," Lisa agreed with him as she took to wing again. *"I'll keep looking around, since neither one of you has taken the time to get my dress."*

"That sounds like a good idea. Hold on while I get a couple of evidence bags." Hillside turned and headed back into the house.

"Sorry, we've been busy." Danny stepped out of the pool enclosure and studied the yard more closely. The details in the topiaries were exquisite. Most looked like they'd been perfectly modeled after live specimens, right down to the spiral horns of a ram and the spots of the jaguar pouncing on it.

"You know, for someone still in the closet, she sure does have a lot of animal things around her house." Danny walked to the closest one.

"Yeah, almost like the Medusa of hedges," Connor agreed from his side. "I bet one of her prowl did these. Or maybe one of Montezuma's people came up from Mexico."

"But these aren't a cut and done," Danny countered. "From one of the documentaries I saw a while back, topiary has to be constantly maintained."

Hillside came back. "Okay, guys. I'm ready. Any areas you prefer not to have clipped?" He raised a pair of scissors in his right hand.

Danny shook his head. "It'll all be fine when we shift back, and we're not going to be like this long."

"I think this is silly," Connor muttered in Danny's mind.

"It might be, but we need to play by their rules, at least once in a while." Danny shifted and then held still

while Hillside clipped a small patch of fur from his back and put it in a bag.

"You guys have it easy," Lisa added as Connor got snipped. *"If they wanted a feather, I'd have a fit. Every feather is important to my ultimate aerial performance."*

"And you think I'm not aware of every one of my hairs." Connor slinked off across the lawn.

Danny started after him, then paused. *"I think we'll cover more ground quickly if we split up. Holler if you find anything."*

"You too," Connor replied, then looked over his shoulder and flashed Danny the cougar equivalent to a smile.

Not sure what they were going to find, Danny headed around front, hoping the killers might've gotten sloppy. So far, they hadn't, and with Connor not being up to his normal self, they were managing to stay a couple of steps ahead of them. He wasn't used to that.

Danny sniffed around the driveway and found a cigarette butt. *"Cat, are you near Hillside?"*

"Not at the moment, although the backyard is looking fairly clean, almost too clean." Connor huffed. *"Even though the jaguars were all over the place back here."*

"Same here." Danny glanced around. There were a couple of police cruisers in the driveway, and several uniforms on the steps heading into the house. A large black van was heading his way. Based on the large white BHCSI on the side of it, Danny presumed it was

the Beverly Hills CSIs finally arriving to properly catalogue the house. He trotted over to them, shifting as he got close.

The man who'd been riding in the passenger seat got out and came around the front of the van. "Since I don't know who you are, I'm going to guess that you're a member of Shifter Force."

Danny extended his hand to the man. "Agent Lupan."

"About time you guys had your own agency." The man returned Danny's handshake. "More and more shifter stuff coming across our desks and we don't always know what to make of it. I'm Lieutenant Zuckerman. I hope the scene is still intact."

Holding up his hands, trying to look innocent, Danny smiled. "We didn't move anything. I was just heading over to see about getting a flag, placard, or something to mark a cigarette butt I found out in the yard. From what I can tell it was tossed there a few hours ago. The scent hasn't totally dissipated from it."

The Lieutenant chuckled. "See, that's the type of thing I'm talking about. We need someone on our squad that can tell me a butt was still smoking a couple of hours ago. But there's more than that, isn't there? With the scents and everything." He looked at the two other men getting out of the van. "Start marking the scene. I'm going to go flag this butt, and I'll be in. Everything by the book guys. We screw this up and we'll never hear the end of it. Lopez is too big a name for mistakes."

The other two acknowledged and headed up the steps.

"Now, let's mark this filter and get on with things." Zuckerman gestured for Danny to take the lead.

Danny headed across the lawn toward the topiary of a lion that could've been the MGM lion roaring.

"How'd you guys know to be here?" Zuckerman asked as they stepped off the drive and onto the lush green grass.

"I got a call from one of the bodyguards," Danny said, knowing that a call could be used as evidence while Connor's visions couldn't.

"Why did they call you?"

"Here it is." Danny pointed to the brown and white end sticking slightly out of the grass. "I'd given Ms. Lopez my card a couple of days ago when we met with her about some of the other actors and actresses with her agent being blackmailed."

"And she gets kidnapped, so her bodyguards call you lot and not the locals." The lieutenant bent down and put a slender metal rod with a red plastic flag into the turf.

"Her guards were shifters, and so were some of the other actors being blackmailed." Danny hoped letting the CSI know important information to the case wouldn't be seen as outing Maria Lopez.

"Danny, while you've got the CSI's attention, I've got a shoe over here," Lisa said as she did an upward flight to draw his attention toward the other side of the driveway. *"And it looks like someone parked a van or truck here."*

"Lieutenant, we've got more over there." Danny pointed to where Lisa landed on a light pole.

Zuckerman looked in Lisa's direction. "Another one of yours? I bet she's handy."

"Agent Collins is great for recon and observation." Danny strolled beside the man as they headed for Lisa's find. "How did you know she's a 'she'?"

"Female kestrel. You can tell by the coloring. Unless you guys can change sex when you shift shape, she's a female." The lieutenant chuckled. "My wife's a big birder. I know things out of self-defense."

"She's lucky to have someone who cares enough to learn about things like that." Danny walked around the large marble fountain in the middle of the circle drive.

"Tell her that." Zukerman pulled out a couple more flags from the messenger bag over his shoulder. "Yeah, I'm going to say the vehicle needs to have the engine seals changed. Been a long time since I've seen a leak this big. The grass isn't totally ruined, so it didn't sit here long."

"That's what I thought," Lisa sounded a little smug. *"Just because I'm a girl doesn't mean I don't pick up on things like that."*

"I know," Danny replied.

"Nothing in the backyard," Connor announced. *"I'm heading around front. I think it's time for us to hit the road and see if I can get a reading off that hair you nabbed."*

"As soon as we're done with the CSIs," Danny replied. *"We've gotta play nice."*

"And hope it doesn't cost Maria Lopez too much." Connor came around the corner of the mansion in human form.

Danny glanced across the yard then back at Zuckerman. "That appears to be all my team has been able to find, at least things that your team can catalogue."

"But then there's the things we humans can't catalogue," the lieutenant said with a sigh. "Could you track the perps through the house by scent?"

"Only if we knew which scents belong in the house and which don't." Danny wasn't sure if it would do any good explaining something as complex as scent tracking to someone who couldn't experience it, but while they were playing nice with the locals, he decided to give it a shot. "From what we could tell, there was a large number of shifters and humans in and out of this place. And someone, probably the killers, left a new air freshener going that totally throws everything off. I made sure to point out the air freshener to Officer Hillside, so your team could include it in the cataloguing of the house."

Lieutenant Zuckerman nodded. "Interesting that something as simple as an air freshener can throw you guys off. These killers were ready for your team. Not sure I like that."

"I know I don't," Connor made it across the lawn to them. "But we've managed to-"

"Guys, I've got the warrant for Kelly and Associates' office," Moreau's mental voice interrupted Connor.

Danny nodded. "I hate to cut this short, Lieutenant, but we just got word that a warrant we've been waiting on has come through. We need to get to Hollywood. Hopefully we'll be able to find what we need to rescue Maria Lopez quickly."

"We're on our way, Thief," Connor said, then grinned. *"You know, I like the way that sounds."*

"I haven't agreed to it yet," Moreau complained. *"I've got the Hollywood PD ready to roll with us."*

"We should be there in thirty." Danny hoped he had the timing right. He wasn't sure if the fact he was getting more oriented in LA was a good thing or not.

"Good luck." Zuckerman started toward the mansion and stopped. "Do you have a card? If we find something you missed, I'll let you know."

Danny pulled out his wallet and handed him a card. "Thanks. We appreciate all the help we can get."

"Anymore, we all have to work together." Zuckerman put the card in his pocket.

Lisa flew over to the Jeep. *"If one of you could find my spare dress, that would be great."*

Danny dug out Lisa's spare dress while Connor got in the driver's seat and Lisa slipped in the door and into the back seat. Within minutes they were ready to head to Hollywood. As they got out of the driveway, news vans were beginning to line the street outside the estate's walls. Connor kept his speed slow enough to not hit any of the reporters swarming toward the gate, but fast enough they got out of his way. Danny was glad Connor was driving and not him. Reporters were just another complication to getting around in LA. With Maria Lopez kidnapped, he hoped reporters weren't going to be hounding their heels, slowing them down and potentially informing the perps of their every move.

Chapter 18

Connor pulled over in the parking lot of a small park and turned off the Jeep.

"Ah, what are we doing?" Danny asked softly from the passenger seat. "Don't we need to get to the talent agency and help Moreau issue the warrant?"

"In a few minutes. I want to see what I can get off that hair sample you grabbed." Connor held his hand out to Danny. "It might help us understand what we need to look for at the agency or let us bypass the place altogether."

Danny nodded as he reached into his pants pocket and pulled out the bag with a small wad of black hair. He handed it to Connor.

"I hope you get something," Lisa said from the back seat. "We need a break."

With a centering breath, Connor took the hair out of the bag. "Yes, we do."

He opened himself up to the energies of the sample, and the woman they were connected to. Something like hair should give him a firm link to the source of the material.

A soft humming filled Connor.

When he looked out of the person's eyes, Maria Lopez stood in a loose T-shirt brushing her hair. She smiled as she pulled her hair over her shoulder, letting it drape down her chest and carefully brushing it out until it shone with a healthy shine. She was in the same bathroom Danny had found the brush in.

Connor pushed the connection with the hair. He should be able to see Maria. With another deep breath, he felt Maria, still brushing her hair. *She was in the same T-shirt, sitting in front of the same mirror.*

"No." Connor shook his head. After another deep breath, he tried again.

The same scene replayed again.

Danny put his hand on Connor's shoulder. "What's wrong?"

"I don't know." Connor kept his eyes closed and took several deep breaths as he fought the urge to throw the hair clenched in his hand away. Instead, he handed it back to Danny. "I can't see anything beyond her brushing her hair. I don't know how old that image is. It could be this morning. It could be several days ago. Maria was happy sitting in front of her mirror."

"You can't get a connection with her?" Danny put the hair back in the bag he'd pulled it from.

"No. That shouldn't be possible. The hair should be a firm connection to her." He opened his eyes and glared at the tall buildings on the other side of the park. "I hate this city and what it's doing to my gifts. I hate the traffic. I hate the people. I hate everything about it." He hit the steering wheel several times. "I want to get this settled so we can go home."

Danny squeezed his shoulder. "I'm sorry this isn't working the way it should. Let's stop and look at this logically."

Connor chuckled. "When have you known my powers to work logically?" His powers just were. He got visions. They followed his visions. That's how it worked.

"Let's try." Danny seemed to avoid the question. "What can block your powers? Water, what else?"

"A magic protective shield…" Connor's mind snapped. "Water. She could be on an island, or boat, or oil rig."

With a soft smile, Danny patted Connor's shoulder. "That's what we need. Logical detective thinking." He glanced into the back seat. "Lisa, can you call Larea and ask her to check if Kelly or any of his people have access to those things?"

"Sure." Lisa pulled out her phone, and it started ringing before she could dial. She laughed. "Okay, that's weird." She swiped the screen to answer the call. "Hey Larea, are you trying to fill in for Connor?"

"What are you on about, Lisa?" Larea sounded confused, muffled, but confused.

"Connor's having trouble getting a reading on Maria Lopez," Lisa explained. "Do you have something for us?"

"I'm monitoring the Joe's List post for a jaguar. There's activity."

A faint spark of hope flared in Connor. "What do we have?"

"What kind?" Lisa asked, then put the phone on speaker, holding it between the seats. "I put you on speaker so you can hear Connor and Danny."

"Oh, okay. Well, someone is making arrangements for a hook up this afternoon. They keep changing email accounts, so I'm having trouble keeping ahead of them, but the john has agreed to pay five million for an hour."

Danny whistled. "Who has that kind of money?"

"There's plenty of pervs who do," Larea said. "But I'm trying to track his email down too. The john isn't being as tricky as the pimp is."

"Have they set up a location yet?" Connor asked, wondering if they'd have time to get there before something happened to Maria Lopez.

"Not according to the last email I saw. They said the john should head toward Long Beach, and more instructions will follow."

Pulling out his phone, Danny frowned. "It's going to take us a while to get to Long Beach. Looks like some major accidents on the highways."

"We don't have a time yet," Larea said.

"I'm betting we're not going to get much warning," Connor said, drumming on the steering wheel. Long Beach. Aren't there islands not far from there?"

"Yeah, several, with Catalina being the most common destination for people from the mainland," Larea said before anyone else had the chance.

"Then, see if Kelly has a house there. Also check and see if any of his known associates have one. I bet that's where they're heading." Connor let out a heavy breath. "That's going to mean more warrants and dealing with another local jurisdiction."

"I'll call Moreau and see if he can get on that warrant end of things." Danny stared tapping his phone, then stopped. "We're going to need an address before we can get a warrant."

"I'll get on that," Larea said. "I'll call when I get it." She ended the call.

"Okay. It's something." Connor started the Jeep. "Let's get to the agency and see if there's anything there that can help us. Dawg, see if Moreau can arrange for a helicopter for us. We're going to need to be at least in Long Beach quickly, and only one of us can fly."

"And I can't carry any of you." Lisa settled back in her seat.

"Exactly." Connor pulled into traffic and resumed their trip toward Kelly and Associates offices. They were running against a clock and he hoped they would find something. The bad guys were about to make five million dollars. It was enough money to change the way they were operating—he just hoped it wasn't enough for them to kill Maria Lopez after they and the john were done with her.

Danny stopped on the sidewalk and stared at the number of reporters gathered around. Not all of them were overly obvious, but there hadn't been a parking place closer than three blocks from the agency. Even the parking garage behind the building was packed with cars parked as tightly as possible.

"Is this all for Maria Lopez getting kidnapped?" Lisa asked from between Danny and Connor.

"I don't think there's any other major star news going on today," Connor muttered. "I wish she would've been more open to our help when we offered."

As much as Danny wanted to explain to Connor his strong-arm tactics were a major factor in Lopez not wanting to accept their help, he bit his lip. All the press around was going to make doing their job that much harder, but if they were lucky, they could escape unnoticed. After the condor case, Shifter Force was known to the press, but not well. That would play in their favor, at least he hoped it would.

In front of the agency, a number of Hollywood PD patrol cars lined up, keeping all but the most persistent reporters at bay. About half a block from them, Moreau stood talking with FBI director Mills. After flashing their badges, Danny led the way toward Moreau and Mills.

"This got out of hand fast," Danny said as Moreau and Mills turned toward them.

"That's an understatement," Mills grumbled. "I'm hoping you can be fast and get this resolved. Since humans are involved, we're going to be working together on this."

"We appreciate the help," Danny said. "Have you already been inside and handled the warrant?"

Moreau nodded. "Just came back out. We've got an FBI team ready to tear the place apart, but we knew Connor would want to go over things first. All the employees have been sequestered in one of the meeting rooms."

"How many people?" Connor asked, looking toward the doors that stood open.

"Only five of them on site when we arrived." Moreau started for the door. "We had one come back from lunch. I wasn't sure if you wanted to question them, or just go over the place."

Danny followed him and Connor and Lisa fell in behind them. Mills stayed on the sidewalk, looking like he wanted to say more, but staying strangely quiet.

"It might not help us find Maria Lopez, but we should check through the files down here," Danny said as they walked through the first-floor offices heading toward the elevator. "If we're right and they didn't let most of the shifters up on the second floor, then we might find something down here detailing others who've been blackmailed."

"Already on it." Moreau reached the elevator first and hit the button. "Figured that will help us build a stronger case, but knew we'd want to focus on anything that would help us find Lopez."

"Good man," Connor said as they entered the elevator. "She's our primary target right now. Once we save her, we can gather the evidence we need to lock Kelly and his thugs away."

"Sometimes it's best to get the evidence first." Moreau pushed the button for the second floor. "Jessie Alexander isn't being overly helpful at this point. She decided it might be a good idea to get a lawyer, especially after she heard Lopez was missing. Perkins and Black are still working with her, but they say she's a lot tighter lipped than she was earlier."

"Can't blame her," Lisa said as the elevator started moving. "If we're right about Kelly being our big bad, he's upped his game. Trying to kill her and kidnapping one of his rising stars shows us the man is getting desperate."

"He's probably planning on leaving the country as well." Connor crossed his arms and leaned against the back of the elevator. "We need to be ready for that."

"We are." Moreau stepped out first when the elevator stopped. "When the warrant was issued, we also contacted the FAA and put a notice out to stop him from boarding airplanes. We can't block all the ports around here."

"L.A. is like a big sieve as far as that goes," Connor followed him out into the waiting area.

The first thing that hit Danny was the quiet of the place. There weren't people talking. No receptionist sat behind the desk, but then Jessie Alexander was in protective custody. The absence of people gave Danny a chill; it made the gazes of the stars in the photos more piercing and harsh. For just a moment, it felt like over a hundred people were staring at him, demanding he do something.

"Let's start with Kelly's office." Connor strolled over to the heavy double doors like the pictures didn't impact him in the least. "Maybe we can figure out what he was trying to hide behind those god-awful cigars of his."

"Like what?" Danny was just a step behind Connor as he pushed opened the doors. "I mean those were some of the worst cigars I've ever smelled, but do you think they were on purpose?" He tried to think back on his one meeting with Kelly, the ill-fated one where Connor had so badly over-reacted.

On his way over to the desk, Connor shrugged. "Hard to say. I'd think that even a human's weak nose would find those things unpleasant."

Danny stopped in his tracks and stared at the back of Connor's head. "Did you ever shake his hand?"

Connor turned back to him, opened his mouth, and then closed it again. "No."

"So we don't know for sure that he's human. I mean, when we met him, that cigar was the only thing I could smell." Danny spun and looked at Moreau. "Can you call Perkins and have him or Black ask Jessie Alexander if she knows if Kelly's human or not?"

"Oh, my." Lisa sighed. "This just gets worse and worse." She headed for the other side of the desk from the one where Connor was working on going through the drawers.

"The way shifters in power are acting right now, we're no better than the humans," Connor muttered. "It's like we're letting our human sides override our animal sides." Shaking his head, Connor straightened. "This isn't helping. We need his computers. He's not putting anything on paper that I can tell, and the reek of those cigars is over everything." He stopped and got the faraway look that meant he was having a vision. In between blinks, he dropped into Kelly's desk chair.

Danny rushed around and knelt down by Connor's legs. "What are you seeing?"

Connor's eyes were closed. He opened his mouth. "So much anger. Hate is his powering emotion. He despises everyone and everything. He uses people for what he can get out of them and when they are used up, he makes them go away." The last words were but a whisper. Connor was going deeper into the vision.

"It's not like that." Kelly was on the phone, speaking to a studio executive.

"Rumors are bound to grow. They're like wildfire. There's nothing you can do to stop them."

"But they're just rumors." Kelly squeezed the arm of his chair so hard the wooden supports inside it shattered.

"We're not willing to take that risk. We know her last few movies have been blockbusters, but the audiences won't show up when they find out their latest obsession is a shifter. People don't dream of being with shifters, they dream of being with beautiful human women. You know this, Jerome. Plus, she's had three hits in a row. The odds are she won't have another one. We need new blood."

"I'll see what I can do." He forced the words out of lips that wanted to curl back and bare his teeth. "Send me a list of the specs you're looking for, and I'll find you someone."

"Thanks, Jerome." The man on the other end of the phone chuckled. "You understand the business. You know how things work. Maria Lopez has had her time in the spotlight. She's done now. Get rid of her before she brings down your agency."

"I'll handle it." Kelly threw the phone against the far wall so hard that it shattered on impact.

His fingers looked thicker than Connor remembered as he started typing on his computer. He pulled up John's List and began scrolling through the request pages. Stopping on one post, he read through it and smiled. "Seven figures, I can work with that, even if it's the last thing I get out of her."

He began composing an email.

The vision fled, leaving Connor staring at Danny. "The studios heard rumors that Lopez was a shifter; they were blacklisting her. One of them called Kelly to warn him. He's trying to get the last little bit he can out of her. He probably doesn't care if she lives or dies, as long as the john pays for her."

Lisa's phone rang. "It's Larea" She answered the phone. "Hi, Larea, what's up? Hold on, let me put you on speaker. We're all in a big room, they might not hear you otherwise."

"Okay." Larea's voice came through the phone. "I think I may have found them. Kelly owns a small island, less than an acre total, off Catalina. I can get you the coordinates."

"Thanks." Connor stood from the chair as Moreau walked in.

"Perkins is checking with Jessie Alexander," Moreau announced.

"Good. After my vision, I'm almost positive Kelly's a shifter, but we've got a location for his island getaway." Connor started out of the door. "Can you see about getting us a helicopter to get out there?"

"Sure." Moreau pulled his phone back out. "On the roof, or at the FBI building?"

"Ah, guys…" Larea was still on the phone. "Kelly, or whoever is talking to the john, says the boat to the island is leaving the pier in fifteen minutes."

Danny frowned. "Can we go for the roof? We'll need to see if Mills can get either some of the FBI, or the Long Beach PD, to the pier before the boat leaves to slow down the john."

"Then we all need to be moving." Connor was heading down the hall with the rest of them following behind him. There was no way they were going to be able to get to Long Beach and the pier in time.

"Thanks, Larea," Lisa said. "I think that'll be what we really need right now. I'll let you know when we catch the bad guys."

"Will do, stay safe." Larea ended the call.

Moreau was talking to Mills on the phone, laying out what they were going to need. Connor called the elevator. He hated the complexities of dealing with other people, but if they were going to rescue Maria Lopez, they had to rely on the FBI, and probably the Coast Guard, and more. There was no way they could get to the island without help.

Chapter 19

Danny stopped when they reached the top of the fire stairs and stepped out onto the roof. There was already a helicopter sitting there waiting for them. The scent of jaguar was strong, like it was blowing from the helicopter and being fanned toward them by the helicopter's still slowing blades.

"Well that was fast," Connor said as he started across the roof.

"Wait a minute." Danny put a hand on Connor's shoulders as he looked at the red machine with a logo for Wave Side Tours painted on it. "This isn't an official ride for us."

"What?" Connor frowned. A familiar scent rose up around him. "Jaguars. Why are there jaguars on the roof?"

"Please listen to us. We need your help." A powerful woman rose from behind one of the many vents around the building. She had a sleek elegance and looked Hispanic with long black hair, slightly brown skin, and dark eyes.

"Who are you?" Danny asked as he pulled his pistol.

The woman held up her hands. "I'm Pallas Ruiz. We need your help finding Maria Lopez. She's our queen."

"Queen?" Danny slowly relaxed, but he didn't put his gun away. There was too much going on. It was too likely a chance this was a trap, or worse. But her words did explain the scent of so many jaguars around Lopez's mansion. If Maria Lopez was the center of the LA jaguar pounce, the others would be looking for her.

"We don't have time for this," Connor grumbled at Danny's side.

"Relax, Cat. That helicopter might be able to get us going faster than waiting for the FBI to get one here. They might also provide us with some extra muscle." Danny glanced at the big man who sat in the helicopter's pilot's seat. He looked bigger than the two bodyguards who lay dead at the mansion put together.

"We're waiting on the roof," Moreau appeared out of the stair access door and stopped. Lisa bumped into him.

"Pallas, do you know where Maria Lopez is?" Danny asked.

The jaguar woman shook her head. "I can feel her anger, and her fear, but can't track it. Two of our other pounce members who are better at tracking our mental links within the pounce are following her while Ferdinand and I came for you. Mateo told us to find Shifter Force if anything happened to him, Phillip, or Maria. It wasn't hard to find you, it was just hard getting to you. So many people between us."

"So you used a helicopter to reach us," Danny pointed to the big red machine behind her.

"Yes. Ferdinand runs a tour company. I thought it would be easier. Can you help us find Maria?" Pallas wrung her hands. Her face was blotched as if she'd been crying.

"We're already working on it. Can you get us out to an island near Catalina?" Connor asked.

Pallas nodded and then brushed a strand of long black hair out of her face. "Give Ferdinand the coordinates, and he will fly us all there." She frowned. "There's only room for two more in the helicopter."

"Cat, are you picking up anything unusual in her mind?" Danny asked. He knew Connor well enough to know he'd already scanned her for any deceptions.

"She's telling the truth, and is distraught over Maria—although she's holding together really well." Connor smiled at Pallas. "I guess it's a good thing two of our members can get small when they shift. Moreau, call the FBI back and let them know we don't need their helicopter, we've got our own, then you and Lisa need to shift so we'll all fit."

Lisa chuckled. "Can't say as I've ridden in a helicopter while in bird form yet. This might be terrifying." She shifted and flew toward the helicopter's open door.

Connor picked up Lisa's dress.

Pallas made a twirling motion with her hand as they headed toward the whirlybird. Ferdinand gave her a thumbs up as everyone headed for the helicopter. Moreau was the last one in, as he finished his call to the FBI before shifting. The ring tailed cat hoped into the helicopter leaving a pile of clothes on the roof of the building.

Danny jumped back out and gathered up Moreau's clothes, gun, and phone. He wanted to start carrying packs to stow Moreau's and Lisa's essentials in to make their shifts to and from easier and keep everything together. They were still going to need to contact LAPD to get Lisa's phone and purse back from the CSI team, but they could handle that after they rescued Maria Lopez and had things wrapped up.

Connor suppressed a wave of fear as the small helicopter shot out from the shore and over the ocean. The water was all he could see. He reached over and took Danny's hand.

"You okay, Cat?" Danny squeezed his hand.

"I've never been on a boat or flown over the ocean. It's too quiet. Even after my abilities have all but been shut down, this is too much." He closed his eyes, thankful he could at least hear Danny's thoughts.

"We're all here for you." Lisa said as she clung to the back of Connor's seat, her talons sinking deep into the leather.

"At least I'm getting to see your fears," Moreau said, then rested his head on Danny and Connor's joined hands. *"It makes you much more relatable."*

"Thanks, I think." Connor mentally muttered, not sure how to take Moreau's words.

"Two more of our pounce will meet us on the island," Pallas announced through the headphones the ones in human form wore. "They will pay for taking our queen."

"We just want to make sure they don't get in the way," Connor said. "We have to get in there, save Maria, and stop Jerome Kelly."

Danny's phone rang. The sound was barely audible over the roar of the blades and the muffling headphones.

Pulling it out of his shirt pocket, Danny answered it. "Hey, Larea." He was shouting over the roar.

Connor strained, but couldn't make out her responses.

"Really? Okay. Tell the Long Beach PD we appreciate their efforts. Thanks for the info." He ended the call and put the phone back in his pocket. He glanced at Connor and brought the mic from the headphones around to be close to his mouth. "The Long Beach PD managed to apprehend the john at the pier. Turns out he's a US senator from Tennessee. Old white guy, filthy rich."

"I hope they're able to hold him on solicitation and accessory to kidnapping." Connor was tired of watching the old rich white men who manipulated the country get away with everything they did, like there were no repercussions from anything they did. He'd bought Maria like she was less than human, and in his mind, she probably was. He deserved to pay.

"She said the FBI is on their way to take custody of him." Danny smiled softly. "Maybe we can manage to make an example of him."

"I hope so."

"Mills will hold onto him," Moreau said through the link. *"He's not a fan of politicians who think they're above the law."*

Connor glanced down at Moreau who stood between the seat with his claws deep in the short carpet there, trying to maintain his balance. "How can you hear us?"

"Better ears in animal form." Moreau wrinkled his snout in a smile. *"We've all got our specialties. And I learned lip reading years ago, so the bits I miss, I can put together."*

"We're on approach to the island," Pallas announced. "Looks like a spot to set down on the beach."

Danny nodded and pulled out his pistol.

Connor stared at him then realized what he was doing. "Silver, just in case there's more shifters than just Maria Lopez."

"Right." Danny snapped the clip back into place. "They also take down humans, so we're going in prepared."

"Good." Connor got his own pistol ready, then checked Moreau's weapon in the roll of clothing.

Sand blew up as they came in on the beach. People were already running out of the house. The way they moved, they were armed and ready for a fight.

"Lisa, go high, you've got the best shot of finding Lopez," Danny said as soon as the helicopter touched down. "We'll have to fight our way into the house."

"On it." In a blur of reddish brown, she was gone.

"Pallas, Ferdinand, are either of you good in a fight?" Danny unbuckled his seat belt.

"We're going to rip them apart." Ferdinand set his headset on the dash and flung the door open, shifting as he went.

Moreau scampered out of the helicopter and shifted back to human. "Gun and shirt please." He pointed to the roll of clothes between the seats.

"With you." Danny grabbed the clothes and handed them to him.

"Claws first." Connor shifted in a smooth fluid wave that was one second human and the next, mountain lion.

"Be careful." Danny swung out of the helicopter, then stopped, using the door for a bit of cover. "Not much to hide behind out here."

"You too." Connor gave him a brief mental kiss, then dashed across the lawn, running an erratic zigzag pattern, alternating with Ferdinand and Pallas, heading toward the guards rushing them.

Danny wished it had been easier. He'd had a silly fantasy about being able to find Lopez, get into the house, rescue her, and get out. The fight was much closer to storming a castle, and they didn't have an army to do it with.

The men from the house opened fire. The bangs of automatic weapons fire filled the air with bullets. Danny didn't want to find out the hard way if they were silver or not.

"I'll stay low," Moreau said as he dropped to his knee next to Danny and got off his first couple of shots.

"High, I guess." Danny picked a target and squeezed his pistol's trigger. The shot caught the big man in the black T-shirt in the shoulder. He spun and dropped to the ground.

Glass exploded around them. One of the guards was firing at the helicopter.

"Guess we're going to have to find another ride back to the mainland." Moreau said as another guard went down.

"We should probably be glad they can't hit smaller targets." Danny took another guard out, then pointed up into the sky where Lisa was flying an erratic pattern toward the house while one guard tried to mow her down in a spray of bullets.

"Yeah, about him." Moreau got off a shot. The guard collapsed on the rocks that led toward the house. "Might as well provide her some cover."

"It's a good idea." Danny stopped shooting as Connor and the two jaguars took out the other guards.

Then three jaguars exploded from the ocean behind the helicopter. They charged up the beach in a spray of water, shaking off as they ran. They headed for the house, not pausing to check on Danny and Moreau.

"Pallas said there were more of their pounce on the way." Moreau stood. "We're not getting fired on from the house, we might as well head up there."

Danny kept his pistol in his hand, reloading as they rushed behind the cats. "Yeah, I can't believe it's being this easy."

"He's a Hollywood talent agent who got a little too big for his britches," Moreau replied from Danny's side. "Maybe he didn't plan on us reaching him in time. He's used to being in charge. People who are like that, manipulating everyone around them aren't going to think anyone can outmaneuver them."

It was beyond what Danny was used to dealing with. He nodded as they made it to the low rock wall that marked the edge of the beach and the start of the yard. The cats were already crashing through the bay windows into the house.

Images flooded into Connor. He pushed them back. After weeks of his gift not working the way he was used to, he suddenly saw too much.

Bullets flew around him, he ran, leapt, dodged just in time to miss all of them as he knew where they were going to be and how to avoid them.

"Ferdinand, go right." With every dodge, the future changed. He knew Danny and Moreau were going to be fine. Danny was going to save the day, like he often did.

"Pallas, the one on the left is about to have to reload, take them down." He was alive again. Every second, he could see it all, had to see it to keep his team alive.

The jaguars were used to taking orders, and instantly obeyed when he told them what to do. *"Lady Bird, keep going, Moreau's about to take out that moron. You're in the clear."*

"Thanks, Cat." Lisa flipped her tail as the man shooting into the sky went down. *"Guess you're working on all cylinders."*

"Yeah, not too many people around." Connor dodged left and then roared as he came up under the machine gun the guard was shooting at him. He headbutted the man, knowing the action was going to force him backwards, topple him over and that he'd knock himself out on the stones of the retaining wall.

By the time he woke up, the coast guard would have arrived and be able to take the man into custody.

As more jaguars came out of the ocean, the number of futures swirling around him increased. But he'd already seen them coming.

Beside him, Ferdinand took out a guard, ripping his throat out with a vicious slash of his plate-sized paw. The big jaguar barely slowed down as he raced toward the house.

Pallas screamed as a bullet caught her in the flank. *"It's not silver,"* she said. *"Let everyone know."* She killed the guard who'd shot her and kept running.

Connor relayed her information and followed her. The last of the guards was down, but they still had to get into the house. There were seven more guards there; most were going to die.

Kelly ran out the front door of the mansion, shifting to some kind of dog, or coyote. He didn't leave a pile of clothes as he went. He ran as fast as he could toward a dock on that side of the house where a speedboat was docked.

Danny, Moreau, and Pallas took out after him.

Connor blinked back the vision, not letting it slow his run across the patio toward the plate glass window that shattered under Ferdinand's leap.

"Danny, Kelly's a shifter too. Some kind of canine. He's going to head out the front door very soon. Pallas, go with them."

"We're on it." Danny replied.

"He will die *for taking our queen."* Pallas broke off following Ferdinand into the house and ran around the outside, limping slightly from her gunshot wound.

Visions of Stars

The glass from the window bit into Connor's paws as he landed in the elegant living room that looked out onto the coast. The pain was enough to break his visions. For a moment, he had no idea where everyone was and what was about to happen to them. Limping slightly, he made it past the glass, which was scattered nearly to the entrance of the gourmet kitchen. With a quick shift to human, the pain eased, and Maria Lopez's fear hit him.

A guard in the hall took aim at Lisa, trying to focus enough to hit the small flying target. She managed to get off a shot. Lisa whirled around as the bullet bit into her wing. She went down, and more shots were fired.

"Lisa, don't go down that hall," Connor shouted as he shifted and ran toward the hallway.

The future shifted again.

Gunfire erupted from upstairs.

"Thanks, Cat." Lisa sounded like she was still in one piece.

"Glad it came in time." Connor bounded up the stairs, following Ferdinand who didn't seem bothered by the bloody footprints he was leaving as he ran across the hardwood floor. *"Ferdinand, we've got a guard in the hallway."*

A red wall of rage was all that was coming from the big jaguar. He had one goal in mind. Another jaguar rushed past Connor, clearing him in a single leap as the hall turned.

More shots were fired.

Ferdinand roared in pain as the gunfire stopped. The wet sound of a throat being torn out rolled down the hallway.

On the stairs, a jaguar roared seconds after shots rang out.

The light of that jaguar's life faded from Connor's awareness as another jaguar killed the guard who shot him.

Jerome Kelly ran from the office on the first floor. Danny and the others had him, Connor didn't care where his future went. He was focused on getting people down the hall and through the door to reached Maria Lopez.

Two guards stood just beyond the door at the end of the hall.

Maria Lopez knelt on a big queen sized, four-poster bed. She was naked, with a glowing collar marring the smooth curves of her neck. Beside her a little girl wearing a similar collar was curled up in a tight ball, crying as Lopez stroked her hair.

One of the guards turned. "Keep her quiet. We have orders to kill you if we have to."

"Everyone stop!" Connor ran around the corner and stopped.

"What's wrong, Cat?" Lisa landed on his head.

Connor took a deep breath and shifted to human. "They're going to kill her if we go charging in."

He frowned at the carnage in the hall. Ferdinand lay dead, a silver bullet between his big, brown, jaguar eyes. The guard who killed him, had been torn to shreds by the other jaguar, who stood on the corpse looking back at Connor.

"Do you have a plan?" The jaguar's mental voice was deep and dangerous. He sounded like he was planning on trying to bust down the door and hope they could avoid the guards killing Lopez and the girl.

Two fight scenes at the mansion. Two spots where magic had been used. It made sense. Connor also knew that if anything happened to Montezuma's granddaughter and great granddaughter, there was going to be hell to pay.

"I've never done this before, so let's see how it works." Connor pulled out his pistol and closed his eyes, letting his gift tell him where to fire. Before anyone could object, he shot twice, then changed targets and shot twice again, hoping he was right about where the guards were on the other side of the door.

A hyena ran out the front door of the mansion as Danny and Moreau came around the corner. Pallas was closer to it and even though she was limping, she was closing.

Without much of a thought, Danny shifted. He'd be faster on four legs than two. The front yard had more grass than the back had, and it was softer under his paws as he charged after them.

"Pallas, we need him alive," Moreau shouted as he ran full out after the three of them.

The female jaguar didn't pause as she leapt at the hyena. At the last second, Kelly turned and rolled, easily avoiding her. He got back on his legs and kept running toward the pier.

Danny ran so fast the grass under his paws was just a green blur. He had no doubt that if Pallas got Kelly in her jaws, she'd kill him. Even as she recovered from her missed jump, she was off and charging after him.

Gunfire came from the boat. An oriental woman stood there with an automatic weapon aimed their direction.

Pallas kept going, taking two shots in the shoulder. Moreau skidded to a halt and returned fire.

The woman on the boat ducked down.

Even wounded, Pallas only slowed a little, but it was enough for Danny to pass her and close in on Kelly, whose breathing sounded like he wasn't used to making long runs to safety.

Danny jumped on Kelly's back, bringing the hyena down hard.

As his jaws closed on Kelly's neck, Pallas slammed into him. He bit down harder than he intended. Releasing Kelly, Danny rolled away from him.

Pallas straddled him in her human form. Blood ran across her naked form, dripping from her breast like red milk. Her hands were more claws than fingers. "You offended the jaguar god." She drove her hand into his chest and ripped out his still-beating heart. Holding it up to the sky, she roared before collapsing on top of Kelly's corpse.

When his shots through the door weren't answered with more shots, Connor rushed to the door and opened it. The two guards lay dead.

Maria Lopez was still on the bed, and quickly snatched the pristine white spread and wrapped it around her daughter and herself. She looked at Connor. "I should've listened to you, puma."

"I'm used to people telling me that." Connor walked over to her and looked at the collar on her neck. "This is keeping you human, isn't it?"

The jaguar queen nodded. "Yes. Where he got them, I have no idea."

Somewhere outside a jaguar roared.

Lopez turned her head and smiled. "He's dead. Good."

"Connor, Kelly's down. So's Pallas." Danny sounded tired. *"Moreau's got the boat secured, and we've got more boats coming in fast."*

"Thanks. We've got Maria Lopez. We lost Ferdinand too." With another mental kiss, Connor kept his attention on the situation in front of him.

"Let me try to get these off you." Connor gripped the collar, his fingers brushed Lopez's skin.

A woman at a podium with tall masculine statues standing behind her was opening an envelope. "For best actress in an action move, the award goes to Maria Lopez for Amazon Queen."

People in the audience cheered. Jaguars roared.

Connor tugged on the collar, even though it was leather, it wouldn't snap.

"There's a lock, silly." Lisa hopped back onto his shoulder. *"Let me."*

"How?" Connor let go of the collar, opting not to tell Lopez about the vision. He didn't want to spoil her surprise when she won.

"I've been practicing being more useful in this form." Lisa flexed her talons. *"Tell her not to freak out. I'll need to stand on her neck for this."*

"Ma..." Connor started to speak to her mind, then realized he couldn't hear her in his. The magical collar must be blocking her in more ways than she realized. "Ms. Lopez, my associate is going to pick the lock, but she'll need to stand on you to do it."

"Whatever it takes," she sounded as snarky as ever, then her voice softened. "Thank you."

Lisa hopped onto Maria, and started working on the lock with her needle-like talons. After a couple of minutes, the lock popped open.

"Good job, Lady Bird." Connor pulled the lock off, then removed the collar.

"Me next?" The little girl stuck her head out from under the covers and tugged at her collar.

"Yes, my love." Maria Lopez picked her up and sat her in her lap. "You'll need to hold still."

Lisa hopped over onto the child's back and quickly had the lock opened.

The sound of a helicopter landing in the front yard drew Connor's attention away from the quiet tears that were suddenly rolling down Lopez's face as she hugged her daughter. He walked over to the window, to give the jaguars some privacy as the other three that had swum out to the island came up and snuffled their queen and princess.

"We saved the day again." Lisa perched on Connor's shoulder. *"I bet my clothes are full of glass, aren't they?"*

Connor shrugged, doing his best not to dislodge her. "Don't know for sure, but probably." In the distance, more boats, with the emblems of several agencies were pulling up to the pier. Danny stood over two bodies. Pallas' hand was still outstretched with something large and deep red clutched in it. Moreau held a woman at gunpoint. There was going to be a lot of paperwork, but they'd stopped Kelly and the shifters of Hollywood weren't going to have to worry about him manipulating them anymore.

Chapter 20

Danny took Lisa's bag and put it behind the rear seat of the Jeep. "Come on, Bird. You don't want to miss your flight." It felt good to finally be heading out of LA, even if they weren't all leaving the same way.

It had taken longer than he thought it would to wrap everything up. Kelly had criminal runners going all over the city and deep into Mexico. After Maria Lopez made a couple of phone calls, Montezuma deployed jaguars and other shifters south of the border to shut down anyone who had connections with Kelly. Other than the hate Connor had felt from the office, they still had no sure reasoning why Kelly had been exploiting other shifters, but many times, hate was motive enough.

It turned out that Jessie Alexander had the keys to Kelly's kingdom and was doing everything she could to close it down. The amount of knowledge she had made Danny never want to get to the point where he needed a secretary; she had too much intel on Kelly's day-to-day life, even if she hadn't known what it meant until everything came crashing down.

Reggie Winters was going to be spending time in jail since the law said that even though he was being manipulated into breaking the law, trying to kill Jessie

Alexander, and assaulting Officer Black were conscious decisions on his part. Danny wasn't looking forward to explaining it all to Trina. Jime had refused to get further involved, after he heard Danny and Connor were heading back to New Mexico. The thing was, with Winters being a shifter, and he'd been manipulated by a shifter into doing crime, the human authorities were confused about what to actually do with him, beyond locking him up.

Lisa climbed into the back seat next to Moreau and patted his thigh. "Don't worry. You're going to love Santa Fe. My mother will be happy to see both of us."

"Moreau's going home with you?" Connor asked as he started the Jeep and headed for the airport.

"Yeah." Lisa leaned against him, leaving Moreau looking slightly uncomfortable. "He has no family and no home. Since he's one of us, we thought he could find a place in Santa Fe. I still want to talk to you about renting your house."

"You may have to wait until Danny and I have a place in Jemez set up." Connor glanced over at Danny and smiled.

Danny smiled back. It was good to have things back on an even keel again. Connor had left most of dealing with the locals and feds to Danny and Moreau, which had made everyone happier about things.

"I thought he had a cabin there." Lisa frowned and looked like she was having to work out what was going to happen since her plan wouldn't do.

"I do, but right now Jime's using it." Danny gripped the bar in front of him as Connor accelerated onto the highway. "And the cabin Connor had was a rental. We plan to see if we can build somewhere around there."

"But we have to find the right piece of property first. We're going to need plenty of space, but also have the mountains in just the right place to get satellite signals for phone and internet." Connor changed lanes to go around a pickup truck that was packed full of people, front and back.

"So this could take a while." Lisa shrugged and glanced at Moreau. "I have a couple of days to find us a rental, since you're following the guys home."

Moreau turned and shot her a worried look. "And can I trust your judgement on accommodations, even temporary ones?"

Lisa laughed. "Of course you can. I have great taste when it comes to things like that. I'll find somewhere you'll love. Do you want in the city, or out?"

"For now, let's go in. That way I can get to know the place before we head out into the country with the guys."

"Okay." Lisa pulled out her phone. "I'll let Mom know and she can get started on the search while I'm in the air."

Danny hoped Moreau knew what he was getting himself into. He hadn't met Lisa's mother, but Connor had told him tales about family parties and she sounded like a force to be reckoned with.

Connor pulled out of the hotel where Moreau had been staying. "Let's roll, Dawg. We have a couple of options. It's about twelve hours to Santa Fe. We could drive straight through and get there about midnight, or we could stop in Flagstaff for the night. We'd get there about dinner time, get a few hours' sleep, and continue to Santa Fe tomorrow morning." He glanced in the rearview mirror to make sure Moreau was following in his Explorer.

"I vote for Flagstaff." Danny closed his eyes. "You know you don't like for me to drive the Jeep, and I don't feel right about you driving twelve hours without a rest. Plus, I might need to relieve Moreau if he gets tired."

"Flagstaff it is." Connor turned east onto Interstate 40; he hoped the traffic wouldn't last all the way out of California, as that would take forever. "Why don't you see if you can find us a motel?"

"How fancy do you want?" Danny sighed and opened his eyes. "Free breakfast, wi-fi, and a pool?"

"Not sure about the pool. Breakfast and wi-fi would be good." Connor was tired of water playing havoc with his psychic ability. Although he'd kicked into high gear on Kelly's island, as soon as they got off it, things went back to the way they'd been for weeks and he was tired of it.

Danny fiddled with his phone for several minutes as Connor wove them in and out of traffic. "Okay. Got it. Two queen-sized beds, breakfast, wi-fi, and there is a pool, but we don't have to use it."

"How far off the highway?" Connor slowed for the traffic.

"Not." Danny looked up from the screen. "Right on I-40."

"Any place for dinner?"

"I'll check." Danny played with his phone some more. "Looks like there are several places not far. We can decide when we get there. Might even let Moreau decide for once."

Connor shook his head. "Not sure about that. He needs to remember he's the junior member of the team."

"And here I was thinking we were starting to relax on some of these things." Danny put his phone in his pocket.

"We are." Connor patted Danny's leg. "We're going to work more as a team and less as the Connor McGriffin show." They'd had several long talks about his behavior and need to be in control. His grandmother had even called in the middle of one of them and told him how proud she was that they'd worked things out.

Connor belched as he entered the motel room. "I think I had too many breadsticks." He picked up the remote that was lying on the dresser and turned on the TV. "I'm going to check the news and weather. You get the first shower."

Danny shook his head. "Come on, Cat, we're good here. We don't have to act all stupid about things." He walked over and hugged Connor. "We're out of L.A. and you should be getting back to normal. Let's get us back to normal too."

Connor kissed him. "Good. I just didn't want to assume too much."

"Thank you for that. It's good for you to not assume things."

A feeling of rightness filled Connor as Danny pushed his shirt from his shoulders and returned his kisses.

"I can't say you won't get mad at me again or that we'll never fight again." Connor stroked Danny's hair as Danny fiddled with Connor's belt. "All couples fight. Any who say they don't are lying. You can't live with someone for any length of time and not argue. But please promise to always come back to me."

Danny ran his fingers through Connor's hair, leaving tingles in their wake. "I know you don't mean to come off the way you do sometimes. It's just you. You get frustrated that people don't always understand your ways. But you need to remember we're all on the same team."

"I'm doing my best." Connor kissed Danny again. "I let Moreau pick dinner."

Danny laughed. It was a sound Connor had missed hearing. "Yes, you did."

Connor's heart swelled as he pulled into the drive of the small adobe house in Santa Fe. It was good to be home. Having to take time to drop Moreau by Lisa's mother's place had delayed them half an hour, but he suffered through it.

A sidewalk went from the drive to the front door passing between plots of red lava stones. On the side next to the house were several yucca and century plants.

Although the yucca had bloomed a couple of times since Connor planted it, the century plant had yet to bloom. He'd been told it could be up to twenty years before it bloomed, and then it would die and he'd have to re-plant. Being away from home so much, Connor liked the succulents since they took so little care.

He was looking forward to some time off with Danny. They had been on the run so much since they met, that they hadn't had time to really talk about the future. Their fight had proven to him that he wanted Danny in his life. A few days in Santa Fe, and then maybe drive over to Jemez Springs and relax in their favorite spot on the banks of the river.

Reaching into the back of the Jeep for his bags, he walked to the front door.

Danny followed close behind.

Connor unlocked the door, stepped inside, and stood on the Aztec sun inlaid in the tiles of the floor. He took a deep breath and coughed at the smell of stale air. "Wow! I think we need to open some windows and air this place out." Setting his bags at the start of the hall to the bedrooms, he walked over and opened the sliding doors to the back patio. "Welcome home, Dawg. Why don't you see if there's anything to drink in the fridge?"

Danny walked into the kitchen area, took a couple cans of cola from the fridge, and two ice-filled glasses. "What now?"

Connor took one of the glasses and cans and plopped down on the couch. "Come over here and sit by me. Let's just relax."

"I have a better idea." Danny filled his glass, then gestured toward the hall.

With a shrug, not totally sure what Danny had in mind, Connor filled his own glass, took a sip and stood. "Lead on, Dawg."

Danny went down the hallway to the enormous bathroom with its four-foot square tub and turned on the taps.

Connor came to the door of the bathroom. "What are you doing?"

Taking a bottle from the shelf, Danny poured some liquid into the tub, and musk-scented bubbles foamed on top of the water. He turned and put his arms around Connor's waist. "Getting ready to relax with you."

"Dawg." Connor pushed Danny back. "I don't want to ever get into a bathtub again. You know what happens."

Danny pulled in closer again and nuzzled along Connor's chin. "Let's make a deal, Cat. As long as we aren't on a case, we'll relax together in the tub. If we're on a case, no bathtubs, or pools."

Bolstered by Danny's calming presence, Connor turned his head and covered Danny's mouth with his own. It was good having a partner in all parts of his life.

If you'd like to stay on top of new releases and upcoming work by A.M. Burns, please join our mailing list.
And if you enjoyed this latest adventure, please leave a review. It's easy and won't take you very long.

Visions of Stars

A.M. Burns Bio

A.M. Burns lives in the Colorado Rockies with his partner, several dogs, cats, horses, and birds. When he's not writing, he's often fixing fences, splitting wood, hiking in the mountains, or flying his hawks. He's enjoyed writing since he was in high school, but it wasn't until the past few years that he's begun truly honing his craft. He is a previous president of the Colorado Springs Fiction Writers Group: www.csfwg.org. Having lived both in Colorado and Texas, rugged frontier types and independent attitudes often show up in his work.

Stay in touch with A.M. Burns through his website
www.amburns.com

and Facebook pages
www.facebook.com/authoramburns/

Feel free to drop me an email
andy@amburns.com

A.M. Burns & A.T. Weaver

A.T. Weaver Bio

A.T. is a great-grandmother in her 70s who lives with her cat, Kiyah, in downtown Kansas City. She didn't start writing until she was 60. When a friend said he'd like to read a book where, 'the boy gets the boy and they ride off into the sunset', her response was, 'I can do that.' She's never liked to be told what she can or can't do. Even with her bad knees and age, she says, "Don't tell me what I can't do. Let me tell you what I can do."

Keep up with A.T at:
Blogsite: https://alixtheweaver.wordpress.com/
Email: alixtheweaver@yahoo.com
Facebook: https://www.facebook.com/alix.t.weaver
https://www.facebook.com/pages/A-T-Weaver-writer/149528070288

Other Books by A.M. Burns and A.T. Weaver:

For several months, Detective Greg Williams and his partner have been trying to catch the Black Fin gang. Their latest intelligence is good, so they go on their most risky raid yet. But things go horribly wrong. While recuperating from the wounds he received during the botched raid, Detective Williams and his captain realize there might be a leak in the Portland police department. When they begin digging, things get worse for Williams.

At the urging of his captain, Detective Williams heads into the mountains, hoping a little distance from the department will give the Black Fins and their police informants the opportunity to slip up. His working vacation soon takes turns he could never have imagined when he meets the reclusive writer, Ken Draiag, next door, who turns out to be more than Greg ever imagined. But the Black Fins aren't about to let Detective Williams rest, they soon track him down, but with Ken's help, Greg manages to stay alive and fight back as forces he never knew existed reveal themselves to be working against him. Will Greg survive the Black Fins' ultimate plot?

Available wherever you buy books!

When Sunny Nelson walks into the house built by an ancestor, strange things start happening. First, he senses an attraction to April Davis. He hasn't been attracted to a woman since he discovered the difference between boys and girls. Of course as soon as he sees her brother, Jeff, he forgets April. Later, as he turns the old house into a B&B, he starts having dreams and visions about people who lived in the house. Together April, Jeff and Sunny discover the secret of Catriona's Curse.

Available on Amazon

A.M. Burns & A.T. Weaver

Tal O'Duirwood, druid dragon, enjoys his quiet life of solitude in the Colorado mountains. When the need arises, Tal is the one the Coalition of Magical Creatures calls on to handle problems no one else can. For years he's worked on his reputation as the thing of nightmares for those who step out of the shadows. He never realized what was missing from his life until his gets an assignment to travel to Yellow Sky, Texas and help a witch and her students there stop a vampire invasion. Once there, he finds things were not as he was told. The witch is actually a werecoyote, and one of her students has eyes for Tal. Can Tal help stop the vampires in time to save his blossoming love? Will his heart, so long closed off from the world, be able to open to the touch of the handsome young mage?

Available at your favorite bookseller.

www.ingramcontent.com/pod-product-compliance
Lightning Source LLC
Chambersburg PA
CBHW071232190726
48292CB00007B/2249